CLANDESTINED

T. M. Brenner

CLANDESTINED

For all my cousins.

You've been there for me, grown with me,

lived with me, laughed with me. I can never

begin to repay the love that you've shown me.

1

I can't believe she killed me. The girl that I love; the one person in the whole world I chose to give my heart to. She took my life away from me. I can't feel anything. I can't use my arms or my legs. My head won't even move.

My body twitches as the last few pulses of electricity run through me. The world starts to go dark, but before it does I see her: the girl who I thought was an angel. But instead of being an angel of mercy, she's an angel of death, come to reap my soul.

Her cold eyes stare down at me, but the shadow she casts hides her face. I can't read her expression. Does she feel bad for what she's done? Betraying me like this? Does she even love me? Did she ever love me?

Those are the thoughts that float through my head as the world slips away, sending me to a place of forever darkness.

'How did this happen?' you might ask.

It started two days before my senior year of High School. I was at the grocery store by myself, trying to choose between Frosted Flakes and Apple Jacks. Life was so easy back then that the toughest challenge I faced was picking which cereal to buy.

My parents were out of town, so I had to fend for myself with the cash they'd left me. As I made my decision, and reached out for a box of Apple Jacks, I saw motion at the end of the aisle. I thought I was the only person in the store, because it was so early, so I looked up to see who it was.

My heart stopped. I'm pretty sure I was legally dead for a few minutes before I could feel the familiar thumping in my chest return. She was the hottest girl I'd seen in my entire life;

long blonde hair, amazing green eyes, and lips that were made for kissing.

I quickly looked away as I felt my face turn pink. I think she noticed, because when I looked back out of the corner of my eye I could see she was smiling. She was also walking straight toward me!

I froze. I didn't know what to do or what to say. This goddess was now standing so close to me that we were almost touching. The feeling of her next to me was warm and electric and alive. My jaw dropped, and her smile got brighter. She reached her arm out, inching closer... toward a box of Mini-Wheats.

My brain shut off. My body wouldn't move. There was nothing I could do and nothing I could say. She just turned away from me. I watched as she slowly walked down the aisle, out of my life, maybe forever.

Taylor, you effing idiot!!! Why didn't you say something? Saying anything would have been better than nothing. Even if it was just 'hi' to see if she'd acknowledge your existence. At that point I was so angry at myself for not saying something that I grabbed a box of Lucky Charms off the shelf, crushing some of the deliciously sugary dehydrated marshmallows inside.

It took me so long to recover from the hormonal implosion she'd caused me, that by the time I finally realized I might still catch up to her, it was too late. I caught a final glimpse of her leaving the store, but I couldn't chase after her with groceries in my arms. The last thing I needed was jail time for shoplifting.

Once I paid for everything and pocketed the loose change, I hurried back out to my Challenger. I couldn't help but look at the few remaining cars in the parking lot, hoping that she might be in one of them. No luck; she was gone.

Still filled with adrenaline, I drove a little too fast out of the parking lot. As I squealed my tires, I nearly sent the back end of my car into the side of a flower delivery truck. Pulling out of the skid, I fought the steering wheel and finally made the car go where I wanted it to. It's not always easy controlling my '70 Challenger.

I spent the rest of the drive home trying to calm down. The near accident, mixed with seeing the girl of my dreams, had kind of messed with me. I took some deep breaths, rolled down the window and let the cool breeze relax me.

Before I knew it, I was home. My house isn't the biggest on the block, and it isn't the smallest. If you were to pick the most obvious and interesting home out on the block, and then kept doing that, you wouldn't pick my house until the very end. It sticks out like a very normal sized, uninjured thumb.

I grabbed my two small sacks of groceries, locked my car and headed inside. Once I was done putting the rest of the groceries away, I fixed myself a bowl of cereal. Lucky Charms is a good friend to have when you're watching a Harry Potter marathon on a lazy Saturday afternoon, which is what I did.

A few more bowls of cereal, and a hot shower later, and I was ready for bed. As my eyes closed, I tried to remember every detail of my mystery girl. The white button-up top that wasn't quite buttoned all the way to the top, the blue skirt that hugged her butt and waved goodbye to me as she walked away. Her golden hair that flowed down her shoulders like a waterfall. And that smile. I will never forget that smile. Drifting off to sleep, the last thing I remember thinking about was her eyes.

2

The next day, I was outside washing my car in the driveway, rinsing off the wheels with the garden hose. My Dad had spent the last two years helping me restore it from a rusting pile of crap, and even then it took me forever to save up for it.

Anyway, that's when I looked up and saw her again. My mystery girl was sitting in the back seat of her parent's silver SUV. Next to her was a girl that I guessed was her younger sister. Her parents seemed to be arguing in the front, but I couldn't tell over what, other than they were both really unhappy.

They pulled up to a house across the street from mine that had been vacant for a few years, thanks to the awesomely bad economy. I hadn't noticed that we had new neighbors yet, but I was kinda distracted when I came home the day before from the store.

I watched as the mystery girl stepped out of the SUV, along with the rest of her family. While she was standing sideways to me, I saw that her beautiful lips were frowning. I'd give anything to put a smile on that face. That's when she turned and looked at me.

We locked eyes. I froze, unable to do anything but stare. And she stared right back at me. It took me a few seconds to realize that the hose I'd been using to wash the car was now soaking my socks and basketball shoes. Seeing this breath-stealing girl again caused me temporary numbness of the brain and feet, probably because all of my blood was rushing somewhere else. That's when she smiled.

I realized at least part of her smile was over me drowning my shoes with a garden hose. I looked down and re-aimed the hose, and when I looked up again she was already out of view.

Hurrying back inside, I took my shoes and socks off at the door then raced down the hall into the bathroom to towel my feet and legs dry. After I'd done a decent job of cleaning myself up, I heard the doorbell ring.

Not expecting anyone, I wasn't going to answer the door. I figured it was probably someone trying to sell something, but I had to see who it was. I went up to the entryway, slid back the privacy curtain that covered the glass on each side of the door, and there she was: the girl of my dreams. My first thought was 'crap' because she saw me peeking out at her. I took a deep breath and opened the door.

She was even more beautiful, staring up at me, than when I saw her in the SUV. A white tank top and jeans showed off the perfect curves of her body. Not skinny. Just... perfect. She was nearly my height. I think the word 'amazon' popped into my head.

"Hi," she said. "I just moved in across the street. I noticed you staring at me while we drove past. Thought I'd come over to see why."

"Oh, uh, just wondering who was moving in next door," I said sheepishly.

She looked me up and down, trying to figure out if I was telling the truth. After a moment's pause, she finally spoke.

"I guess you look harmless enough. Are you still in school?"

"Me? Oh, yeah, I'm going to be a senior, starting tomorrow."

"Interesting; so am I. I'm Madison," she said, offering me her hand.

"Taylor," I said, shaking her hand a little too firmly. It took a few seconds to realize I hadn't let go of it, but once I did, I quickly snatched it away. "Sorry."

She giggled. "It's okay. So what were you doing?"

"Just some chores. My parents will be back tonight, and I'm trying to do all the stuff I was supposed to be doing while they were gone the last few weeks."

"Think you'll finish in time?"

"Probably not," I replied, smiling.

"I wish I had something as normal and boring as chores to do."

"What do you mean?" I asked.

"Oh, nothing," she said quickly. I could tell she was hiding something, but I wasn't going to ask. "Anyway, I should probably go help my folks out. Glad I'll know at least one person tomorrow when school starts. It was nice meeting you, Taylor."

"Yeah, you too," I said, still feeling a bit shy.

She smiled at me, which made my face turn red, then she turned and walked away. I watched her cross the street, and just before she was out of sight, she looked back. I put my hand up, thinking I was going to wave, but didn't. Instead, I just awkwardly kept my hand up. She gave me one last smile then went inside her house.

I closed the door, took a few deep breaths then smacked myself on the forehead. I could have done a lot worse, but things didn't go as smoothly as I wanted. She called me 'harmless', which is definitely what girls find attractive, said no one ever.

As I worked to get my chores done, I replayed the entire conversation over and over in my head. Vacuuming, dusting, laundry and cleaning didn't do much to distract me from thinking about my epic fail with the goddess next door.

Anyway, as I finished the last of the chores, my parents came home. I helped them bring their things inside. My Mom asked how things went, and I didn't want to tell her about my embarrassing conversation with the girl next door, so I just said 'okay' and left it at that.

Falling asleep that night was hard. It's always hard the day before school starts, but it was especially hard now that I knew I'd be seeing her again.

Only, I didn't end up seeing her Senior year as much as I would have liked. It turned out that we only had one class together: English. It was the one class I always looked forward to, and always dreaded. We had assigned seats, and we sat clear across the room from each other. I tried looking over at her without being obvious, which was helped by the fact that I was in the back of the room, and she was toward the front.

I kept hoping she'd turn to look at me, but she never did. It was kind of strange, actually; most days she'd come in looking dead tired, like she'd been up all night. I didn't feel too bad that she didn't pay attention to me, because she never talked to anyone much. She kept her distance from people. I couldn't figure out why, because she seemed so friendly when I met her.

A few weeks into the school year, I found out from a friend that she had a boyfriend, but it sounded like he was a jerk and didn't treat her well. Maybe there was still hope for me. But I wasn't going to try to steal her from someone else. That just isn't my style.

Despite torturing myself with constant thoughts of her, senior year was pretty good. I took all the fun electives I hadn't yet taken. Drama class was my favorite. My teacher was awesome, and treated us like adults. He trusted us to build the sets, do the lighting, and no one ever got hurt. He was a great guy; wore Hawaiian shirts and flip-flops, and loved what he did. One of my favorite people ever. Wish that there were more people like him in the world.

Time went by too quickly, like real life was rushing at me. Besides going to school, I spent time trying to plan out the rest of my life. What college I wanted to attend, what job I wanted to have once I graduated... it was all kind of a blur.

I did try to have some fun outside of school, but I didn't go to any dances until Prom. I had a date, but it was my friend Amy who I was just friends with. We'd dated when we were in eighth grade, but realized quickly we made better friends than boyfriend and girlfriend. I had a fun time with her, but I'd wished I could have taken Madison. I couldn't though, because she was still seeing 'the jerk'.

As the dance went on, I noticed that Madison never showed. It distracted me, and I felt bad for Amy, who could tell I wasn't doing a good job of paying attention to her. She knew I had a thing for Madison, and guessed that I'd been hoping to see her there.

As we left the dance, I heard sobbing coming from the alley next to the ballroom our school had rented. I gave Amy a small kiss on the cheek and told her I'd catch up to her, that I just wanted to make sure whoever was crying was okay. She told me to go be the hero I was destined to be, and that she'd meet me at my car. I gave her the keys and thanked her.

As I approached the alley, my feet made just enough noise that it alerted the crying girl to my presence. The sobbing stopped. I peeked around the corner, and saw Madison sitting on a set of stairs, her hair in a mess and her eyes filled with tears. I pulled my pocket square out of my rented tux and held it out to her. More tears came out as she reached for it. She covered her face, trying to hide what she was feeling from me. Giving her a few seconds, I finally spoke.

"Can I sit down next to you?" I asked.

She just nodded her head, but wouldn't look at me. I asked the obvious and stupid question, but I didn't know what else to say. "Are you okay?"

After a long moment she was able to get her tears under control. A few sniffles later and she was ready to talk.

"I'm sorry," she started. "I just broke up with my boyfriend. I wanted him to come, but I didn't want him to be here. I know that doesn't make any sense."

"How come you didn't want him to be here?" I asked.

"Because he's a monster. He's the most evil person I've ever known. I just wanted him to come so I wouldn't be alone."

I had a hard time getting the next few words out.

"He... he didn't hurt you, did he?"

"No, not physically. He knows I'd kill him if he did. But he plays mind games. Manipulates people. Makes them think they're the bad guy, when he's the evil one. Tried to make me think I was crazy, so that I'd be dependent on him."

"Yeah, I've heard of that. I think they call that 'gaslighting.'"

"It's more than that, but yes, it's like he was controlling me. I'm just glad it's all over." She took a long breath. "I'm sorry, I hope I'm not ruining Prom for you."

"Madison, you aren't ruining anything."

A look of surprise came over her face. "You remembered my name?"

"Of course I did," I said, maybe a little too eagerly.

"You're Taylor. You're the guy who lives across the street," she responded.

"And we're in English class together," I mentioned.

"Oh. I'm sorry I didn't notice. It's the first class of the day, and I don't sleep most nights. I feel lucky just to survive them."

"Survive them?" I asked, unsure of what she meant.

"I... I can't... can you please pretend you didn't hear me say that?"

I thought about if for a moment. I was practically a stranger to her, so I decided to let it go. "Sure, I can forget that you said that. Just promise me that nothing bad is going on at home."

"No, everything is fine at home. My parents are wonderful. My life's just... complicated."

"With a boyfriend like that, I can understand why."

"Yeah, well, he isn't my boyfriend anymore. I hope he goes back to the pit of hell that he crawled out of."

"Me too," I replied.

She glanced at me with a funny look on her face, trying to figure out what I meant by it.

"I just mean that he sounds like an idiot if he treats you that way. You deserve better," I said.

"How do you know that? You don't really know me."

"I can tell. I'm pretty good at reading people. You seem bright, sweet, and you obviously have a good heart. If you didn't, you wouldn't be crying right now."

"Maybe I'm just weak," she replied.

"Nah, you seem tougher than you look."

That made her smile. There was still sadness in her smile, but I could tell it made her feel a little better.

"You should probably catch up to your date," said Madison.

"I just came with a friend. I'm not seeing anyone," I blurted. "But I probably should make sure she's okay."

"Thanks, Taylor, for talking with me," she said.

"Any time, day or night," I replied.

Before I got up, a thought popped into my head.

"Do you need a ride home?" I asked.

She paused for a moment. "If you have room, I'd really appreciate that. My parents dropped me off, but I'd rather they don't see me like this."

"It's no problem," I said.

We both stood up and walked to my car. When Amy saw us walking toward the Challenger, she recognized Madison, got out of the front seat and moved to the back. Madison noticed and said something.

"You don't need to get in the back seat."

"It's no biggie. You look like you could use a comfortable place to sit. My name's Amy."

"I'm Madison, and thank you."

I helped Madison into the car, trying my best to be a gentleman. After closing her door, I went around to the driver's side and got in.

"Amy, I'm sorry, but I'll need to take you home first. Madison lives across the street from me," I said, as I turned on the car and started to drive away.

"No worries," she replied, winking at me in the rear view mirror. I mouthed 'thank you' to her, hoping that Madison wouldn't see. Looking out of the corner of my eye, I noticed that Madison was actually staring through her window, watching the world pass by her.

The drive to Amy's was a quiet one. Madison was still dealing with her emotions, and Amy didn't want to say anything that might hurt my chances with Madison. Amy is an amazing friend, and the best wingman I've had the pleasure of flying with.

After fifteen minutes, we finally arrived at Amy's. I helped Madison out of the car, so that Amy could climb out of the back seat. I admit, it was another excuse to hold Madison's hand, but I was trying to be as nice of a guy as I could. Amy got out, and I walked her to her front door. She gave me a small kiss on the cheek, whispered 'good luck', then went inside.

The walk back to my car was hard, because my heart was beating out of my chest. Madison was standing there, politely waiting for me. Helping her back in, I closed the door, made my way around the car, got in and started the engine. Before I could pull away, Madison spoke.

"I don't think I'm ready to go home yet."

"That's okay. Was there somewhere you did want to go?" I asked.

"Just... not home."

"Are you hungry?"

"I don't really want food," replied Madison.

"What about coffee?"

"Sure. Can we just go through the drive-thru? I don't really feel up to being around people right now."

"Yeah, we can do that."

I knew a place nearby that had pretty good coffee and snacks, named "C' is for Coffee Which is Good Enough for Me.' Their mascot was the 'Coffee Monster', a puppet with brown fur and crazy eyes that spun around.

Madison got a latte with caramel flavoring, and I just got mine black. The coffee is good enough that I don't think it needs all of the extra stuff, but understand why other people like it sweet.

We parked at the far end of 'C' is for Coffee, away from any other cars or people. After a few sips, Madison decided to speak.

"How come you and Amy aren't a thing?"

The question kind of surprised me. I did my best to recover and give her a reasonable answer.

"We make great friends, but we just don't feel that way about each other."

"Oh," she replied. "Is there anyone you are interested in?"

That question was even harder to answer. I took my time and chose my words carefully, without giving myself away.

"As an international man of mystery, there are some secrets I never reveal."

Madison laughed. It was nice seeing her smile. I decided to change the subject to something less dangerous.

"So what do you think of our city?" I asked.

"City?"

"Town? Okay, I admit, it's kinda small."

"You think?" said Madison.

"Well, what are you used to? Did you live somewhere big, like New York?"

"I've been, but didn't live there. I've been all over the world."

"Really? I've never been outside of the state. Do your parents like to travel, or are you an Army brat?" I asked.

"Something like that," she replied. "As an international woman of mystery, I too have secrets I never reveal."

That made me laugh. Madison seemed quite proud of herself.

We talked a little while longer, mostly about school, until both of our cups were empty. I wanted to keep the conversation going, but I could tell Madison was ready to go home. I backed up and pulled out of the parking lot then drove us back to her place.

The drive was quiet, but that was okay. We both seemed to be in a better mood, and I didn't want to ruin it by saying the wrong thing. I think Madison was preparing herself for the conversation she was going to have with her parents, so I let her focus on her thoughts.

I parked outside my house, but let her out of the car and walked her to her door. The outside light was on, and the lights were on inside, but I couldn't see anyone through the windows, so we were alone.

"Taylor, thank you for listening to me, and for the ride."

"You're welcome," I said, not knowing what else to say.

She leaned in and gave me a small kiss on the cheek, but as she pulled away I accidentally turned a little, and our lips brushed. My face went immediately pink, as did hers. I couldn't help but smile, and embarrassed, she smiled too.

"Well, uh, goodnight," was all I could manage.

"Goodnight," said Madison, smirking at me.

I did my best to turn slowly and walk back to my house. When I reached the door, I looked back, and there was Madison, still standing there, with her hand up in the air like she was waving, but not actually waving. I smiled a big stupid grin as I went inside.

3

The rest of the school year went by quickly. I looked forward to English class even more now, because each morning Madison would look toward me and smile. Every day I planned to ask her out on a date, but every day I reminded myself she'd just broken up with her boyfriend, and I didn't want to be a rebound for her.

The last few weeks of senior year were crazy, and I tried to spend time with my friends as much as I could. I might see some of them over the summer, but most of us were going away to college, and it would be a long time until we saw each other again.

Then graduation day came. It was a blur of seeing some friends for maybe the last time. Amy was going away to Europe for the summer, traveling abroad, living in hostels and tasting exotic foods.

I wished I could have done something like that: travel the world, see things, learn things, experience things. But my summer was going to be pretty boring. My parents were going out of town again, so I'd be alone for most of it.

The graduation ceremony was long and a bit boring. The valedictorians tried their best to tell us that the real world will be alright, and inspire us to follow our dreams and all that, but I spent most of the ceremony thinking about Madison. She was in the very back of the seats in the gym, while I was a little further up. I turned back to look at her and smiled, and thankfully she smiled back.

After the ceremony, I tried searching for her, but couldn't find her. I said goodbye to friends, but had hoped to speak to Madison last; maybe finally ask her on a date. No such luck. When I went home with my folks, I was sad, when I probably should have been happy, and excited to finally be out in the real world.

My folks left for my uncle's the next day, and I'd never felt more alone. It went on a few days like that, until unbelievably, Madison came over to say hi. I was cleaning up the house, had the windows open so the sun could come in. I looked across to Madison's house, and outside in the garden her parents were arguing. I hadn't seen them do it often, but it worried me.

Not long after they went back in, Madison came outside. When I saw her crossing the street toward my house, I ran as fast as I could back to the bathroom, checked my hair and teeth, then ran back to the front.

Before Madison could knock, I opened the door.

"Hey, Taylor," she said.

"Hi," was all I could manage. I stood there waiting, not knowing what to say. Thankfully she did the talking for me.

"I didn't get to say goodbye to you at graduation," said Madison. "I meant to, but I had to leave early. Something… important came up."

"Oh, I'd wondered. I tried to find you," I admitted.

"Really?" she said, smirking. "So, are your parents home?"

"Nope, I'm home alone for the next month. They're in Chicago, visiting my uncle."

"Interesting," she said, thinking to herself. "So when is the party?"

"What party?"

"Isn't it tradition to throw a party when your parents are away?" questioned Madison.

"I guess, but I've never thrown one before."

"Seriously?"

"Yup. Just never have," I reply. I realized that a party might be a good excuse to see her again. "You sound pretty interested; you wanna help?"

She smiled the brightest smile I've ever seen.

"Sure, I can help," offered Madison. "It'll give me a chance to say goodbye to people I missed at graduation."

"By the way, what were your parents fighting about?"

"My parents? They were fighting about me, actually. I can be a bit of a wild child sometimes. My Dad says I'm capricious, but I prefer the term mercurial. Sounds cooler."

"Wow, you seem really book smart. That's amazing!"

"What, just because I'm a girl?" Her eyes narrowed.

"No, it's because you're a girl *and* you're beautiful."

"So beautiful girls are dumb?" She had a look that could slice a man in half.

"Yes. Beautiful girls are dumb," I said, laying on the sarcasm really thick. I hoped she knew I totally didn't mean it.

I've always found if you're cornered in a conversation, the best thing you can do is admit to whatever it is you're being accused of. Then they have nowhere to go with it. Thankfully for me, Madison has the best sense of humor. She giggled and rolled her eyes at me.

"Did you want to come in?" I asked.

"Yeah, that'd be great."

"Be careful, the floor is a little slippery. I was mopping."

"Yeah, I noticed you were cleaning... " And then she slipped on the wet floor, right into my arms. I caught her before she hit the ground, and pulled her upright, our eyes just inches from each other. I swear my heart stopped working. I think for a second her heart skipped a beat too, although she'd never admit it. Maybe it was just wishful thinking on my part.

That's when I absentmindedly looked down at her breasts, then quickly looked up, realizing my mistake.

"Enjoying the show?" asked Madison through squinted, sparkly, fake-angry eyes.

"Yeah. I mean, I, uh... " There was no way I was digging myself out of this one. "Did you want something to drink?"

Madison leaned her head back, standing more fully upright, so that her breasts moved forward toward me. Her movement caught my eye again. I couldn't help but look, and she of course noticed me looking, again.

"Sure. Do you have lemonade?"

"I'll go check," I replied. I stood there, unmoving.

She cocked her head slightly to the side, waiting for me to leave the room. I could see a grin form at the corner of her mouth. Once I recovered, I went to the kitchen.

I grabbed a glass from one of the cupboards and nearly dropped it in the process. I closed my eyes and tried really hard to calm myself down. With numb hands I set the glass down on the counter, opened the fridge, pulled out the lemonade and managed to pour a glass without spilling. No girl had ever had this strong of an effect on me.

I came back out to the living room. She took the glass from my hands then took a sip. I watched the way her lips parted, allowing the golden sweetness to flow into her mouth then trickle down her throat. I've never wanted to be a cold beverage more in my entire life.

"Thank you," she said.

"No worries."

"I should probably get back to the house. My parents are no doubt wondering why I came over here."

"Oh. Okay," I said, disappointment written on my face like a pair of testicles in Sharpie.

"Well, thanks for the drink, Taylor," she said, hesitating.

"You too." I blushed, silently torturing myself on the inside for my response that didn't make any sense. Doing my best to recover, I finally spoke. "Will you come back soon?"

"Signs point to 'yes'," she said with a cute little smile.

And with that, Madison left.

4

The next day I did some cleaning around the house, put in the movie 'Big Trouble in Little China' and laughed as Kurt Russel did his best impression of John Wayne.

Just as the movie ended, and I was singing at the top of my lungs to the theme song, I heard a knock at the door. I really hoped whoever it was hadn't heard me.

I turned off the TV in a panic and jumped off the couch. In two big steps I made it to the door. It was her, and the look on her face let me know she'd probably heard me. It figures. So I did the only thing I could think to do in a situation like that: I opened the door.

"Oh, Madison, hey," I said.

She giggled. I could feel my heart race and my skin turn bright pink.

"Hey yourself," replied Madison, smiling from ear-to-ear.

"Wanna come in?" I asked.

"Yeah, that'd be why I'm here."

She stepped inside, brushing past me. I almost passed out, lightheaded from being so close to her.

"So do you have a pen and paper?" she asked.

"For what?" I said, my brain no longer working right.

"For planning the party we were talking about."

"Oh, yeah. Party. Sure, let me get those and I'll be right back."

I went into the kitchen, grabbed a small notepad and pen, and came back into the living room. She'd moved to the couch, one leg folded underneath her. Madison had taken her shoes off, some kind of open-toed sandals or something. She'd also moved a few of the pillows that my Mom loved to decorate with off of the couch and onto the floor, leaving me room to sit next to her. I wandered over to the couch and sat down.

"So, do you come here often?" I asked, jokingly.

"List," she said.

"Right."

"Okay, so what kinds of things will we need for the party?"

"Drinks?" I said.

"That's a good start. What were you thinking?"

"Well, I don't think that alcohol is a good idea."

"Why not?"

"I don't want people to trash my house, and I don't like the idea of my friends driving home drunk."

She smiled at me. Just sat there for a moment and looked at me.

"You know, Taylor, you're a good guy. I haven't met too many of those."

"I'm sorry to hear that."

"Don't be. Just be happy that you stand out a little."

"Thanks," I said.

"So what kind of drinks then if we're not doing beer?" asked Madison.

"Well, we could get a bunch of sodas. Probably get some food too. How about pizza?"

"Don't know. My guess is that people don't want garlic breath when they're kissing."

"Kissing?" I said, smiling.

"Or, you know, whatever," said Madison.

"I like the sound of 'whatever'. How about we do sandwiches? We could get a twenty foot sub."

"That sounds better. Just don't get onions or peppers."

"But that's like the best part!" I said.

"I love them too. But still, you don't want your guests to have bad breath. Or fart."

I couldn't help but laugh. Here is this extremely hot girl just talking about gross stuff like it was no big deal. It made me even more attracted to her. She seemed like a kind of a no-holds-barred type of girl; just saying whatever was on her mind.

"Okay, so we've got drinks and food covered," said Madison. "What about music?"

"I've got a kick-ass sound system. My Dad and I built some speakers, and they shake the house."

"Seriously? You built speakers? That's so cool!"

"Wanna see them?"

"Yeah, you can show me yours."

I did my best not to blush, but I think my mouth hanging open gave me away.

"Follow me," I said, trying hard not to stutter.

I lead her back to my room, but made her stop just shy of the door.

"Wait, give me a minute to clean up," I said.

"Yeah, go ahead."

I opened the door just enough to sneak in then closed it right behind me. I opened up my closet, threw all my dirty clothes inside, threw away the Hungry Man Dinner trays I'd piled up, and made my bed. I could hear her giggling on the other side of the door as I ran around the room, knocking stuff over in my hurricane of cleaning. Once I was pretty sure the room was good, I opened the door.

"You can come in now," I said.

"Are you sure it's safe?" asked Madison.

"No, not really."

"I guess I'll just have to take my chances."

Madison came inside my room and sat down on the bed, spending some time looking at a few of the drawings I had up on the walls.

"Did you draw those?" she asked, pointing to a picture of Marilyn Monroe, and another of Alfred Hitchcock. I just smiled.

"OMG, those are amazing! Is that what you're planning on studying in college?"

"No, I'm probably going to go into computers or something like that."

"Why computers?"

"Eh, my Dad kind of wants me to get into it. He's a big time computer nerd, and he has my whole life planned out for me, down to which college I'm going to."

"I hope I get to go to college."

"Why wouldn't you go to college?" I asked.

Madison kind of stared off into space for a moment, and she never did respond.

"You wanna hear my speakers then?" I said, trying to change the subject.

"Yeah, please; something old-school. Maybe some Led Zeppelin."

"Wait, you like Led Zeppelin?"

"Hell yeah!"

There are moments in life when you know that fate's done you a solid. I don't know why, but someone up there is looking down on me and smiling.

I already had Zeppelin on my phone, so I turned on my stereo and thumbed my way to Kashmir. Madison laid back on my bed, put her hands behind her head and closed her eyes. I stood there, staring at her, tracing the outline of her face with my eyes. Following the curve of her cheeks, down to her sculpted yet feminine jawline. I couldn't stop looking at her.

Once the song had finished, I paused my phone. She looked up at me and smiled. That smile would be the death of me.

5

"So who are you going to invite?" asked Madison.

"I guess everybody," I replied.

"Wait, how many people is that?"

"I'm not sure. There's maybe two hundred people at Marion High, and I figure if we're lucky a quarter of that will show."

"This really is a small town."

"Yeah, Marion is pretty tiny, but we still have some cool things. We've got cable TV, mini-golf and El Camino: a restaurant that serves the best hot dogs, hamburgers and chili cheese fries in the world. No joke."

"I LOVE chili cheese fries!" exclaimed Madison.

"Even if they make you fart?" I asked.

"Even if," she replied. "So you'd be kind enough to invite freshmen to the party?"

"Sure, why not?"

"I don't think most seniors would do that. It's decent of you."

"I've never really worried about that sort of stuff. I figure everyone is a friend until they turn out to be a d-bag. Generally, you have to work pretty hard at it for me to think you're an asshole. Oh, sorry: language."

"It doesn't bother me. Asshole," she said, smiling like the Cheshire Cat.

"Oh, hey now!" I said, pulling the pillow out from under her head and throwing it on top of her. She giggled then threw the pillow in my face. I grabbed onto it, and moved it down my chest. Looking down, I could see her slightly messy hair. I can't believe how incredible it looked. In fact, it made me think of what it would be like to wake up next to her; how amazing it would be to see what she looked like in the morning.

"Taylor?"

"Yeah?"

"What if I told you I wanted you to sit next to me, here on the bed?"

Act cool, Taylor. Don't let her know how much you like her. Don't let her notice how hard you're breathing right now.

"Only one way to find out," I said, trying my hardest to contain myself.

"I want you to sit next to me, here on the bed."

I could feel my heart beating hard in my chest. While some parts of me stopped working, other parts of me were working overtime.

Madison propped herself up on the bed and shook her head a little to let her hair flow back out of her face. She leaned forward, ever closer to me. I just closed my eyes, hoping that this wasn't a dream. I started leaning forward too. That's when I felt a gentle hand on my chest, stopping me.

"Oh, I'm sorry!" I said, pulling away from her.

Madison just smiled at me.

"It's okay. I just don't want things to get out of hand," she said, "I should probably get going. I'm sure my parents are wondering why I'm taking so long."

I felt so bad about what I'd done. I hoped I hadn't taken things too far and scared her off.

"Hey, you want to hang out tonight? They're having a 'Supernatural' marathon on TV."

At the sound of the word 'Supernatural' her eyes grew big. "You watch Supernatural?" she asked.

"Yeah, doesn't everybody?"

"No, not everybody. Some of us live it."

"What do you mean?" I asked.

"Oh, um, nothing. Seriously; nothing. I just think that Dean's hot."

I've never wanted to kill a fictional character more in my life.

"Yeah, that sounds like fun," she said. "What time?"

"How about six? I'll even make dinner," I said.

"Wait, you cook? That's amazing!"

"What, just because I'm a guy?"

"No, it's because you're a guy and you're beautiful. I mean handsome."

"So handsome guys can't cook?" I tried my best to make the same face she'd made at me.

"Yes, handsome guys can't cook."

I just smiled at her.

"Okay, I'm leaving now," she said, smiling back at me. I got out of the way so she could stand up then I followed her down the hallway, watching her glide across the floor like she was on roller skates.

Halfway down the hallway she looked over her shoulder at me. She noticed me staring at her butt. I thought I might be a dead man, but she just grinned and turned her head back in the direction she was walking.

Madison stopped just shy of the door, turned around and gave me a very sweet kiss on the cheek.

"I'll see you at six," she said.

I stood there helplessly as she closed the door behind her. I peeled back the privacy curtain and watched her bounce as she walked across the street.

6

Fixing dinner was a nightmare. I wrote down a list of all the ingredients I'd need, or thought I needed, then went to the store. It took me about an hour to make my way through the aisles of the new mega-grocery that had just opened in town. Cooking was even more of a pain, and I made a huge mess in the kitchen. I even got some spaghetti sauce on the wall.

Madison was there at exactly six. I guess when you live across the street, being on time isn't that difficult. She'd changed into a sundress that showed off her long legs, and a few inches of cleavage. I can't explain how I had the self-control to keep my hands to myself, but if I had a super power, that would be it. My super power sucks.

"So what's for dinner?" she asked as I let her inside.

"Spaghetti, meatballs, Italian bread and salad," I replied.

"So you made something with garlic?"

"Yeah, why?"

"In case people want to, I don't know, kiss! Or whatever!"

I just smiled.

"Or whatever?" I pushed.

"Yeah... whatever!"

"I guess I'll just have to brush and floss my teeth afterward."

"And chew gum?"

"And chew gum. I already have the table set. You can help yourself; everything's in the kitchen."

Madison walked through the dining room and into the kitchen. Following her, I grabbed a plate, loaded it up half with pasta and half with salad then coated the lettuce in Italian dressing. After I'd added cheese to the top of my spaghetti, I grabbed a slice of Italian garlic bread and set it on top of my mound of noodles.

Following Madison back into the dining room, I set my plate down.

"Want something to drink?" I asked.

"Sure, do you have Coke?"

"Yeah, absolutely." I went and grabbed two.

It was honestly one of the best meals I'd ever had. The best part of it wasn't the food, as much as watching Madison eat the food. Watching her suck the long lengths of noodle between her lips, getting a little sauce in the corners of her mouth, which her tongue would dart out to clean up. Even watching her put whole meatballs into her mouth was amazing.

"So what's the story about the locket you're wearing?" I asked.

"Just something my Dad gave me. It's got pictures of me and Angela in it," she replied.

"Angela's your... sister?"

"Yeah. Oh, I forgot, I hadn't mentioned her yet."

"I saw her when you first moved in, but I had no clue what her name was. What year is she?"

"She'll be a junior next year."

"You want to invite her to the party?"

"I think we kinda have to. If I ever get invited to a party without her, she gets upset and tries to sabotage it for me."

"Well I'm totally cool with it. No one's probably going to show up anyway. A lot of people are on vacation with their folks, or have better things to do," I said.

"Better things than a party? Do such things exists?" asked Madison, jokingly.

"Well, I think I'm doing one of them right now."

"Which is?"

"Getting to watch you eat."

"Definitely a spectator sport."

I just stared at her, smiling.

I wolfed down the rest of my plate while Madison ate her smaller meal.

"That was really good, Taylor," said Madison.

"I'm glad you liked it," I replied.

"What brand of sauce was that?"

"I made it from scratch."

"Wow. Not bad for a handsome guy who can't cook."

That's when it happened. Madison let out a really super loud burp. It was both gross and awesome at the same time.

"I didn't think girls could belch like that!" I said.

"I used to be able to burp the alphabet. Pretty impressive, huh?"

"Very. Do you have any other secret abilities you're hiding from me?"

She looked at me for a few seconds, unmoving.

"Maybe," she said.

"Like what?" I asked.

Nothing. She wouldn't say a thing.

7

"Hey, we should turn on the TV; the next episode should be starting," said Madison, trying her best to distract me from the question I just asked.

"Sure, we can do that."

The episode we watched was the very first one, with the girl who was on Smallville once. I think I read somewhere she was going to play Wonder Woman on TV but it fell through. It actually really bothered me, what they did to her character in Supernatural. But I guess it's just fiction.

We sat on the couch together. About halfway through the show she rested her head on my shoulder. When the show was almost done, she'd innocently placed a hand on my thigh. Or at least I'd guessed it was innocently. The physical reaction I had to it wasn't so innocent. Anyway, I placed my hand on hers.

Even though she was tall for a girl, her hands were still tiny compared to mine. They were soft and smooth. I could imagine what they'd feel like touching me. Once the show was done, I got up and made my way to the bathroom. About halfway down the hall she spoke.

"I'm going to run across the street to brush my teeth. Where are you headed?" she said.

"Doing the same. In case there's kissing, or whatever," I responded, smiling.

I heard her giggle, and then the sound of the front door closing behind her.

I brushed and flossed, and found a package of Mint Chocolate Chip Extra Gum in the kitchen. I don't normally like mint and chocolate, except for Andes Mints; those are awesome. But that gum is pretty amazing. I saved a couple of pieces for her.

I walked back out into the living room and sat down. A few minutes later she knocked on the door and let herself in. She'd changed into a pair of very short shorts and a tight-fitting shirt that showed off her breasts.

"Are you chewing gum?" she asked.

"Yes ma'am, I just might be chewing some gum," I responded in my best fake southern accent.

"Why, you did that for little 'ole me? How very gentlemanly of you," she said in a much more convincing southern belle accent. "What kind is it?"

"Mint chocolate chip."

"Seriously?"

"Yeah, why?"

"That's the same kind I'm chewing."

"Seriously?" I asked.

"No, not seriously. I couldn't find any gum."

"Well, I saved you a few sticks."

"My hero!" she said, launching herself next to me on the couch. She snatched up the sticks and chewed them like she'd never chewed gum before.

"Wow, I don't normally like mint chocolate chip, but this gum is pretty good," she said.

"Yeah, I was thinking the same thing."

"Oh, look, the show started back up again."

"Right, the show."

We snuggled up on the couch again. I laced my fingers through hers, and I still couldn't get over how tiny and perfect her hands seemed. I could smell her shampoo, which smelled like a mix of flowers and vanilla. I imagine it's what a love potion would smell like.

The next episode had something to do with a cursed lucky rabbit's foot, but I was too busy thinking about all the things I wanted to do to Madison to notice, or even care that I was watching TV. I wasn't sure if she was enjoying the show or not. I did notice her chest seem to rise and fall rather heavily, and every once in a while she licked her lips.

During a commercial, she reached across me for the remote, and then muted the TV. She looked at me, a little frustrated.

"Am I going to have to make the first move?" she asked.

I laughed.

"Before we get any more serious," I started, "I need to find out some important things about you," I said.

"Oh really?" she questioned.

"Really."

Her smile turned into a look of concern.

"First, what's your favorite muscle car?" I asked. I could tell that the question made her less worried.

"Dodge Challenger," she said.

"Classic or current?"

"Both."

"Is that why you like me, because I have a cool car?"

"It helps," she said, fighting back a smile.

"Okay, I'm gonna let that one slide. Favorite fast food place?"

"I've only been there once, when I went to Disneyland when I was thirteen, but I've always remembered it. In-N-Out Burger."

"Wow, very nice. Finally, favorite TV show?"

"Vampire Diaries."

"No, I'm sorry, the correct answer was 'Psych'. Too bad, you almost won a trip for two to Tahiti," I said.

"Do I get a consolation prize?" asked Madison.

"Absolutely. Me."

"And that's supposed to console me?"

"I didn't say it was a good prize," I replied.

"But I can do anything I want with my prize?"

"Anything you want."

She moved in close to me, and I moved in closer, until our lips touched. I couldn't believe I was kissing this amazing girl. We touched the tips of our tongues together, probing each other's mouths, falling into a perfect rhythm, feeling the strong attraction we had for each other. I kept my eyes closed, enjoying the sensation of it.

I ran a hand behind her neck, up into her hair, and held it firmly, pulled on it a little. She really seemed to enjoy it, because she started breathing even heavier, and started making deeper and longer 'Mmmmmmm' sounds. Madison pulled back for a second and smiled at me a smile that was both innocent and evil at the same time.

"Um, more kissing please?" I pleaded.

"Oh, you'd like more kissing? Well, it'll cost you."

"What will it cost me?"

"Your shirt."

"You want me to take my shirt off?"

"Yeah, I do."

I tore my t-shirt off, throwing it behind me.

She looked at me like she was a tiger that wanted to eat me. She put her right hand on my left shoulder, then moved her hand down and across my pecs, until she was touching my six-pack.

"You're beautiful," she said.

"Not as beautiful as you," I replied.

She closed her eyes and tilted her head back. After a short time, Madison grabbed the backs of my hands and rubbed her still covered breasts with the palms, first up and down, and then in small circles. She pulled my hands and wrapped them around her, leaning forward into me, pushing me onto my back, resting her chest against mine.

Her body was so warm. I kissed her more deeply than I'd ever kissed anyone. I grabbed her hips and slid her upward, moving her shirt-covered breasts directly in my face. She squealed, making the sexiest noise I'd ever heard.

I kissed the skin between her ample breasts, feeling the warmth radiate from her chest, where inside her heart beat fiercely. I turned my head, continuing to kiss the soft, pale skin that surrounded me.

I grabbed her hips again and slid her down my body until our mouths were perfectly aligned. We kissed; I have no idea how long for. Probably hours. All I know is that I didn't want it to end, but unfortunately, eventually, it did. Madison sat up, smiling at me. I put my shirt back on as I watched her straighten her hair and button up her top.

"Thank you so much for this perfect evening. Dinner was good; your kissing was better," she said.

I just smiled.

"Goodnight, Taylor."

"Goodnight."

And then she kissed me again. I opened the door for her, and walked out behind her onto the front porch to make sure she got into her house okay. Once she'd crossed the street and reached the door, she turned and blew me a kiss. After I saw her slip inside her front door, I turned around and went back into the house.

8

The next day, Madison stopped by as I was mowing the lawn. I was nearly finished, so I ran the mower along the final edge of the front lawn then shut it off.

"How's it goin'?" she asked.

"Good. No more mowing today, thankfully. I'm gonna go put the mower away. Feel free to help yourself to whatever's in the fridge," I replied.

I watched her turn and go inside as I hurried to wrap up the lawnmower cord. I stuffed it on top of the mower then pushed the mower into the open garage. Shutting the garage door behind me, I made my way into the connected dining room. I found Madison sitting on the couch, sipping a glass of iced tea. She turned to me and smiled as I sat down next to her.

"Here, try this," she said.

I took a drink.

"Wow, that's really sweet," I said.

"Yeah, it's called sweet tea. I lived in the south for a while, and it's sort of a thing there."

"A thing?"

"Yeah, you know, a thing."

"Oh, a thing... "

Then, just to throw me off guard, she pulled up her shirt and bra and flashed me. She could tell that her trick had worked, because I couldn't find the will to force my jaw closed.

"That's not fair, I'm all sweaty," I said.

"Oh, I don't care," she responded.

"Well I do. I'm gonna go take a quick shower. Can you entertain yourself for a while?"

"I can entertain myself for a long while," she said, winking at me.

Wow. All I can say is 'wow'. Just the thought of her... was driving me absolutely insane. Anyway, I went to the front bathroom, stripped down and hopped in the shower. It was a tub that also worked as a shower, and had a simple white curtain to keep the water in.

As I was rinsing the soap off my face and the shampoo from my hair, Madison snuck inside the bathroom. I didn't realize it until it was too late, because my back was turned to her as she came in.

"Hey," was all she said as she peeled back the curtain, looking at my naked ass.

Startled, I turned around. She saw everything, and she grinned, a very, very broad grin.

"What do you think you're doing?" I said, covering myself.

"Just making sure you're okay. Figured you might need a lifeguard," she joked.

"I'm not drowning, but I could definitely use some mouth-to-mouth. Just wait until I'm out."

"Okay."

"That means go away."

"Okay."

She just stood there.

"Now."

She sighed. "Okay, I'm going."

I waited until I heard the door close before I stepped out of the shower and toweled off. I was both surprised and a little disappointed she'd actually followed my directions. Although now that she'd seen me naked, it was only fair that I got to see her naked. I just had to figure a way to make it happen.

I kept the towel around my waist and made my way to my bedroom. The door was ajar, but I didn't think anything of it. I walked inside and Madison was sitting on the bed, admiring my drawings again.

"Come here, Taylor," she said, motioning me to stand next to her. So I walked over to her. Once I was within striking distance, she grabbed my towel and yanked. Again, she saw everything. Again, she had a very, very big grin.

I let her stare at me. Take all of me in with her eyes. Then, when I thought she'd had enough, I turned around, walked over to my closet and started putting on some clothes. I put on a black t-shirt with a big yellow Batman logo on it that showed off my biceps, and pulled on a pair of shorts.

"You go commando?" she asked.

"Sometimes. Tighty-whities are dorky, and boxers are a waste since I'm already wearing shorts," I explained.

"My goodness, you're going to cause a scandal!" she joked.

"Yeah, a regular international incident. I'm sure my bulge will show up on the eleven o'clock news, having scared innocent bystanders who say I always seemed nice but a little dangerous. Then the next clip will be about someone with the last name 'Johnson'. Newscasters love irony."

Madison laughed.

"So why'd you come over?" I asked.

"To see you, and to finish planning the party."

"Oh, right, the party. I'd nearly forgotten, what with the tits and everything."

She squinted her eyes at me, pretending to be upset and trying to hold in her smile.

"Okay, so we know the 'who', which is everybody, and we know the what, which is sandwiches and drinks..." she said.

I interrupted, "Sandwich. One big-ass sandwich."

"Right, sandwich and drinks. We also know the where, which is your house. The big question left is when."

"How about Friday night?" I said.

"Sure, that sounds good. What time?" asked Madison.

"You think six? Too early?"

"Six is good. Just expect people not to show 'til seven."

"How come?" I asked.

"No one wants to be 'that guy.' The one that shows up too early to the party, being too eager."

"I guess we better start calling," I said.

"Do you have everyone's phone number?"

"I have a lot of phone numbers. What we can do is call people, and then ask them to call people they know. Then we don't have to do as much calling."

"That sounds pretty smart. Not bad for a dumb guy who can't cook," joked Madison.

"I make up for my lack of intelligence and cooking skills with exceptional kissing and a large penis."

"Yes, yes you do," she said with a knowing smile on her face.

"You're beautiful."

"Thank you," she said, blushing a little.

We spent the next hour calling the thirty people I figured would have phone numbers for all the people we were trying to invite. Everyone sounded excited about the party. A lot of them admitted they'd never even been invited to a party before and asked what they should wear, what they should bring, if they could bring a friend; that kind of thing. It was kind of cool making people happy like that.

"You know what we should do?" asked Madison.

"Make out."

"Yeah, that too. But what we should really do is go on a date."

I was kind of surprised I hadn't thought of that. I was kind of surprised we hadn't already gone on a date, since we'd already kissed, and she'd seen me naked.

"What would you want to do?" I asked her.

"We could do traditional: dinner and a movie," she suggested.

"Is there anything out that you wanted to see?"

"Not really."

"How about bowling?"

"Ick, rental shoes? No thanks. How about ice skating?"

"Yeah, cause rental skates are so much better," I replied.

"I actually own my own skates."

"Then you must be pretty good with them. Pass."

"Why?"

"You'll destroy my fragile male ego with your double toe loops."

"Oh, yes, we wouldn't want to hurt the ego of a well hung, good kissing dumb guy who can't cook."

"Yeah, we're sensitive like that."

"How about Laser Tag?" she suggested.

"That would be epic!"

"Would you believe that with an AR-15 I can shoot an entire magazine in a grouping the size of a grapefruit at a distance of fifty feet?" she asked.

"Sure, if I knew what an AR-15 was," I responded.

"Boy, do you have a lot to learn."

"You don't know the half of it. But that definitely sounded cool! I'm guessing it's a gun?"

"A gun? A GUN? It's only one of the best semi-automatic rifles in the world! It's the civilian version of the M16!"

"Madison, I seriously didn't think you could possibly be any hotter, but I was wrong!" I said, pausing. "The M16 I've heard of. I use it a lot in the Call of Duty games. So how do you know so much about guns?" I asked.

Her eyes got big and innocent looking, like a deer in the headlights.

"My Dad, he likes to hunt," she said.

"The guy with the fake tan and sweater tied around his neck? He's into guns?"

"Uh, sure, why not?"

"No offense, but he just doesn't seem the type."

"He gets that a lot."

I still wasn't buying it, but I didn't think it would be a good idea to press things, so I let it drop.

"So, Laser Tag," I said. "There's a place one town over that has Laser Tag. Should only take us forty-five minutes to get there."

"ROAD TRIP!" squealed Madison, bouncing up and down. "We have to get snacks, and music, and more snacks!"

"Madison, it's not really a road trip; it's only a forty-five minute drive!"

"Nope, anything over half-an-hour that's driven in an attempt to seek out fun is considered a road trip. That's according to Triple-A."

"Really? Let me go get one of their manuals and we'll see what it says."

I ran to the kitchen, opened a catch-all drawer and pulled out a Triple-A guide. I pretended to skim through it.

"Ha! No mention of any time ranges for road trips," I said.

"Here, I'll find it for you," she said, grabbing the guide from my hands. She flipped to a random page and said "See? It's right here." She'd placed her middle finger in the crease of the book as a bookmark, making sure I got the idea. I laughed pretty hard.

"Fine, it's a road trip then. Do you know what we absolutely have to have for a road trip?" I asked.

"Jalapeno Beef Jerky," Madison and I said in unison.

We both stared at each other in shocked disbelief. In that moment the moon and the stars aligned. The sky split open and cast a beam of white light down on us. I swear I could hear a choir of angels singing in the background. Okay, so maybe I'm making some of it up, but it was a defining moment. That's when I absolutely knew she was 'The One.' The one girl in all the world who had my heart, and always would.

9

A little later that day I drove us in the freshly cleaned Challenger to Hyattburg, the next town over. Before we got very far, I stopped at a gas station and topped off the tank. I figured we had plenty of gas, but it gave Madison a chance to go inside and get us some snacks. I used the debit card my folks had given me. They were pretty cool about those sorts of things. They figured it'd be a good idea to help me build up my credit score. Instead of giving me a cash allowance they just put money in the account.

Before they left they gave me five hundred bucks; a mix of fun money and just-in-case money. They were hoping I wouldn't spend it all, but trusted my judgment. Unfortunately, they hadn't factored in the possibility that I might find a super-hot girlfriend in the meantime. The nice thing though about Madison is she's pretty down-to-earth. She doesn't expect me to buy her expensive things. But she is super appreciative of it when I do.

Once I'd finished pumping gas, I got back in the car and waited. I'd only been sitting in the car for a few minutes when Madison emerged, carrying a large paper sack.

"Did you buy the whole store?" I asked.

"Almost. I just wanted to make sure if we crashed in a ditch somewhere that we wouldn't starve to death."

"Good thinkin'. So what all did you get?"

"I got Jalapeno Beef Jerky of course, some pepperoni sticks, an assortment of sodas, a bag of chocolate chip cookies, Hot Tamales, red licorice, a bag of Jalapeño flavored chips, some Boston Baked Beans, the candy, not actual beans, some Snickers bars and some condoms."

"Wait, what did you just say?" I asked.

"Snickers bars," she quickly responded.

"I thought you just said 'condoms'."

"You did?"

"Yeah, I did."

"That's interesting," she said, trying her best to keep a serious face.

I couldn't tell if she was just joking about the condom thing.

My parents were kind of reserved when it came to things like sex, so we didn't really talk about it much. It was kind of a taboo topic, something neither I nor my parents were comfortable talking about together. They did give me some good advice though, and that's to make sure when I do have sex for the first time that it's with someone I love, and not just because I want to lose my virginity. That it's a completely different experience when you have a connection with someone. I knew I had that kind of connection with Madison. I already had feelings for her, and we'd only been together for a few days. It was crazy, but it was true.

I went ahead and pulled out of the gas station once Madison got her seat belt on. She opened up the jalapeno jerky and put a piece in my mouth then chewed a piece of her own.

"What do you want to listen to?" she asked.

"What did you bring?"

"I've got my phone, so we can listen to pretty much anything."

"Sounds good. You can connect it to the cable sticking out of the stereo. Do you have any Scorpions?" I asked.

"Will 'Rock You Like a Hurricane' work?"

"Abso-luckin-fruitly!"

We totally rocked out for a while, singing along at the top of our lungs. It was pretty awesome. I'd like to say that Madison sings like an angel too, but unfortunately she's just as bad as I am. It made singing with her a lot more fun, but I figure she isn't destined for the big stage.

Eventually we reached our destination: Battle Stations 2010. Apparently when the place opened in the 80's, 2010 seemed like a long way off; very futuristic, where we'd all have flying cars, and self-tying shoes and hoverboards. For whatever reason the owners never changed it. Now it's just kind of a funny name.

We went in and paid for a few rounds in advance. The first game I'm pretty sure Madison was just getting used to the rules and how the light guns worked. We were pretty even, ending up on opposite teams. I tried my best to avoid shooting her, as I thought it was bad form to shoot one's... girlfriend? Friend that's a girl? Whatever she was at the time, she had boobs and she was interested in me, which meant she was off limits. When we finished the round our scores were tallied. I just barely came in first for my team, and Madison came in first on hers. I edged out the overall victory by a narrow ninety points.

The next round was different. Madison was running around like a crazy person, tucking and rolling around corners, shooting high value overhead targets from long range behind cover, sneaking behind people all stealthy-like and shooting them in the back. She was a ruthless killer and showed no mercy. After we finished the round, everyone in the room went up and congratulated her. She'd come in first out of all of us by 1,100 points. I think it was also an excuse for some of the guys to get to talk to a girl that beautiful and sexy.

The third round was even more unbelievable. Madison wasn't hit once. She was so athletic, and moved so fast, that she kept every member of the opposite team, my team, effectively 'frozen' and unable to score. It was truly a massacre. It wasn't humiliating, just... humbling. That was the general feeling I got from everyone else. No one knew how to react. Because when the point totals were shown, her score was 12,470, while the next highest score, a teammate of hers, was 1,030. My team's combined score wasn't that high. She'd broken the highest recorded score at Battle Stations 2010 by 4,000 points.

It was kind of cool that she did, because the high score hadn't been broken in twelve years, and was set when some kid named Connor McKinley had a really, really good day. The owner happened to be working and came up and congratulated her, giving her a free one-year membership to B.S. 2010. They also took her picture and put it up on their wall of victors.

I gave her a big wet kiss as we were leaving. She was extremely excited, I could see it in her eyes and her smile, but she held all of that excitement in so that it didn't seem like she was rubbing in her victory.

Thankfully, once we got out to the car, she released some of that happiness in a flurry of kisses all over my lips, face and neck. It was as if she'd become a hungry wolf, trying to eat my face, and I loved it! I matched her pace, kissing her all over too, and her skin flushed red. Because we were in public, and because we were in the front seat, we didn't go too far.

The drive home was fun too. We went over some of what had transpired during our battles.

"It took me a little while to figure out how far the sights were off on the light gun they gave me, but once I did, I think I shot pretty well," said Madison.

"That's a major understatement! You were so amazing!" I said. "In fact, there's a prize at home that goes along with your win."

"Really? What is it?"

"Me."

"But I've already got one of you. Maybe I could sell the other you and buy a new car."

"You'd whore me out?" I asked.

"No, I'd just sell you. I'm sure there's a market for strong boys that are well hung."

"But you wouldn't keep two? Isn't two better than one?"

"It'd just be confusing. Besides, I'd have to number each of you, and I don't think you'd like being referred to all the time as 'Number Two'."

I honestly can't remember the last time I'd laughed that hard.

"So what was your favorite part of laser tag?" she asked.

"Probably just watching you move around like a cat. Do you secretly work as a ninja for the CIA?"

"I don't technically work for them; I'm an independent contractor brought in to take care of issues that no one else can," she said, too matter-of-factly for it to seem like a joke.

"Seriously?" I asked, half joking, and half wondering where she actually had learned all the shooting and running and moving and tactics stuff.

"No, of course not! DOY!!!" she said, laughing. "Why would the CIA hire a teenage girl?"

"Because you're hot! Maybe it's like 21 Jump Street. Maybe you're actually in your forties and pretending to be a teenager."

"Do I look like I'm in my forties?" she asked.

"Hell no!" I responded quickly.

"Damn straight," she said.

The rest of the trip home was fun, but I still thought something was going on that I didn't know about; that I was missing something important.

10

I dropped Madison off in front of her house. She'd mentioned that she had some stuff to do, and should probably spend some time with her parents. In the meantime, I worked on getting the house ready for the party.

I collected up all of the easily breakable things I could find and put them inside an old steamer trunk my parents kept at the foot of their bed. It normally just contained blankets, but I pulled those out and stuffed them under the bed. The coolest feature of the trunk is that it had a place for a padlock, so I used a spare lock we kept in a kitchen drawer, and stuck the key on my keyring.

After I'd hidden pretty much everything breakable or valuable, I thought about how I might decorate the place. Then I realized: why would I decorate? It's not like it's a costume party, or a birthday party or something. It's just a bunch of people hanging out. There was no way I was going to make the place look like the 'Enchantment Under the Sea Dance.'

I reference 80's movies sometimes, and it's all my parent's fault. My Dad is a huge John Hughes fan, and he's kind of got me hooked too. I also loved movies like Back to the Future, Real Genius and a Nightmare on Elm Street. It was cool seeing Captain Jack Sparrow when he was my age in that one.

It was still a day away, but the house was pretty much ready to go. Now I just had to keep it that way. I'd vacuumed, scrubbed, dusted, sanitized and swept every last inch of the house, which is funny, considering I was about to have hundreds of teenagers partying in it.

I took a shower to wash all the dirt off me, which felt a lot better than normal. I don't know why, but it seems like after doing a lot of physical work like cleaning, that showers feel better, food tastes better; everything seems better. Even my clothes were more comfortable than they normally were. Part of it could have been that I was in love, and I felt like I'd already conquered the world.

I gave the local sandwich shop a call and placed an order for the Mega-sandwich, which I'd hoped would be enough food for everyone. I figured I could just put the different sections on the dining room table and stack it up some if I needed to. I also went to the store and got a bunch of different sodas, which I filled both the fridge in the kitchen and the one in the basement with.

Dinner was good. I had some leftover spaghetti and meatballs from the night before. I watched a couple of movies, one of which my parents probably would have killed me if they'd caught me watching. I also lifted weights, did some stomach exercises, and went out and ran two miles.

By the end of the night I was starting to worry about Madison. I figured she'd probably show up in the evening to spend time with me, or at least kiss me goodnight. I was actually hoping for a little more than just a kiss, but right then I just wanted to make sure she was safe. I grabbed my keys and headed over to her place.

Her house was pretty nice, a bit bigger than my house, with a knee high white picket fence that was just for decoration. The only thing it would have kept in or out would have been Smurfs, and even then, Brainy probably would have come up with a smart way to get over it. The house was a light gray/green color, and came with a two car garage.

I went up to the door and knocked. It took a moment for the porch light to finally come on. Her Mom came to the door, looking kinda pissed off.

"Hi ma'am, is Madison home?"

"Ah, you must be the next door neighbor boy that Madison's told us nothing about."

"I'm Taylor, it's nice to meet you," I said, offering my hand for a shake. She kind of sneered at me and kept her arms crossed.

"She's not home right now," she said.

"Oh, okay. Is she alright?" I asked.

"She's fine."

"Can you tell her I stopped by, please?"

"Sure."

I could tell that I hadn't made a good first impression, but it didn't seem like it was my fault. I hadn't said or done anything wrong, and it didn't sound like Madison had said anything good or bad about me to her folks. I wondered if maybe something else was up. There was nothing I could really do right then. I kind of peeked around Madison's Mom to see if maybe Madison was hiding around a corner, deliberately avoiding me. I don't know why she would. When I had dropped her off, everything seemed good. But either way, I didn't see her hiding out in her house.

So I walked back home. I stayed up a while, putting together a song list for the party that was less than twenty-four hours away. I was throwing a house party, and it was all because of Madison. I really hoped that she was alright. Not knowing was really starting to bother me, and not having her cell number yet kept me from being able to call her. That was something I'd need to fix, quickly.

I stayed up a few hours past when I normally went to bed, and eventually I just couldn't keep my eyes open. I got the list done, but that didn't mean anything. I don't really pray that often, but I said a small prayer that she was okay.

11

The next morning, after I'd fixed myself some Lucky Charms for breakfast, Madison came over. I could tell something was wrong immediately, since her normally bright smile wasn't all that bright. It seemed like she was forcing it for my benefit.

"Madison, are you okay?" I asked as she came in the door.

"Yeah, I'm fine, why?" she questioned.

"You just don't seem, well, like you right now."

"I'm really sorry, Taylor. I have a lot on my mind."

"Like what? I hope you know you can tell me anything."

"That's so very sweet of you, and you are, you're an incredible listener. It's just something I can't talk about."

I could tell something worse than what I'd imagined must have happened. I tried to ask her more questions, but she wouldn't give me any answers.

"Can we just watch some TV together for a little while?" she asked.

"Sure, we can do that."

Trying to be a good boyfriend type guy, I didn't push it any further. In some ways I kind of wished I had, just so I'd know what was going on, and not just jump to the worst case-scenarios.

A re-run of Psych was on, and it was the episode where Shawn refers to Gus as 'Guy Buttersnaps.' It was kind of hard to laugh at the episode since I'd been so worried about Madison. She wrapped her arms around one of mine and rested her head on my shoulder. I glanced at her a couple of times out of the corner of my eye, and it looked like tears may be forming in them. It was killing me to not know what was going on.

In between episodes the news came on. It was a short teaser for a later news broadcast. I kind of got the idea of what they were saying without really listening. Apparently four armed men had broken into a vault looking for some sort of rare Egyptian necklace. There weren't many details other than an unnamed person had stopped them, and one of the robbers had fired his gun, which ricocheted off the vault wall, killing one of the other robbers.

I glanced over at Madison, and I could tell something in the newscast had affected her. She looked up at me and couldn't hold in her emotions any more. She started crying, harder than I think I've ever seen someone cry. I just held her there on the couch, letting her get my shoulder wet with tears. Her entire body shook when she sobbed, and it broke my heart to see her this way. I kissed her on top of her head as I gently rocked her. I'm not sure why I rocked her, it just felt like the right thing to do. It seemed to help, as her sobbing died down. Maybe it was just enough for her to know that I was there for her, regardless of what happened.

Once it seemed like she'd been able to let all of her emotions out, I went and grabbed a box of tissues and handed them to her. She blew her nose loudly, which made us both laugh. She smiled at me, and more tears ran down her cheek. Madison used more tissues to dry her eyes, and she seemed to be doing a lot better now that she'd been able to let out whatever she had inside of her.

She stood up and went to the bathroom down the hallway. I could hear her blowing her nose some more, and then I heard the water run for a little while. When she came back out, her face was a little pink, probably from washing it. She sat next to me on the couch and kissed me. The kiss was sweet and felt like a kiss of love and thanks. It didn't have the burning passion behind it that normally fueled her kisses.

It was nice to feel and see this other side of her though. Where she didn't seem fully in control, where her heart was soft, where she was just... human. I didn't know what was causing her tears, but I imagined it was something serious. I was just glad I could be there for her.

After her kiss of gratitude, she kissed me again. This time it was longer, slower, and filled with an even mix of passion and caring. I kissed her back, trying to show her how strongly

I felt about her, and that I would never judge her. A few moments into kissing, she stood up from the couch, took off her shirt, and walked toward my bedroom. I watched as she took off her bra and dropped it on the ground in the hallway. She stopped when she was at my bedroom door, looked back at me and smiled. Madison turned the knob, walked in, and laid down on my bed.

It took a moment for me to realize I was supposed to follow her. I got off the couch, walked down the hallway, and tried my best to not step on her clothes. I walked into the bedroom and shut the door. I'm not sure why I shut the door behind me, since no one would be coming into the house.

I took off my shirt and threw it on a chair in the corner of the room. Madison was lying back on the bed, looking at me expectantly, partially covering her breasts with her hands. As I got closer to her, she reached out to me, urging me to hold her. I laid on top of her, wrapping my arms underneath and around her. Her breasts felt so warm against my chest.

I kissed her, putting more of myself in my kiss than I ever had before, hoping that she could feel what I felt for her. Feel that I was also sharing some of me with her. Her sadness quickly changed into passion, her kisses became hungrier.

Working my way down her neck, I kissed her smooth skin, eventually moving to her breasts. I spent time nibbling on her nipples, kissing the underside of each breast, gently cupping them in my hands and squeezing them.

I wanted to do something special for her, something that would hopefully make the pain go away, so I unbuttoned the top button on her jeans and slowly pulled her zipper down. I looked up at her to make sure I wasn't going too far. She smiled at me, which I took as a 'thank you' for respecting her enough to make sure it was okay to do what I was doing.

Grabbing her jeans at the top, I peeled them downward. She arched her back, allowing me to pull them down to her thighs. They bunched up, so I tugged at the place where her jeans touched her bare feet and slid them off. Madison spread her legs a little bit. I wasn't sure exactly how far she'd let me go with this, so I started small. I kissed her ankle, working my way up her calf to her thigh. I spent time kissing both thighs, then slowly made my way to her blue cotton panties.

What I did for her next was amazing, but I'm not going to talk about it here. I love her too much to share something that secret and special with you. I'm sorry; just know that what I did made her happy. Very, very happy.

Once I was done satisfying her, she looked down at me, smiling her beautiful, bright smile. I looked back at her. She leaned down and kissed me, touching the tip of her tongue to mine. After a few seconds, we broke the embrace.

"Madison, you're glowing," I said.

"You are too," she replied, smiling sweetly.

"No, Madison, I don't think you understand. You're actually GLOWING."

We both looked at her skin. Somehow, it had become paler, almost white. A soft light seemed to pour out of her body. I looked up into her eyes, shocked, not knowing what to say or think. And that's when she finally said something.

"Oh, shit."

12

"How are you doing that?" I asked, not believing what I was seeing.

Madison kind of freaked out, jumped off the bed, picked up her panties and jeans and tried frantically to put them on.

"Wait, Madison, hold on," I said.

She just kept fighting to get her jeans pulled all the way back up. So I stood up and gently wrapped my arms around her. She immediately stopped struggling, and after a second or two she relaxed.

"You weren't supposed to find out," she said.

"Find out what?"

"That I'm a freak."

"You're not a freak. What do you mean?" I asked.

She broke our embrace and went down the hallway to retrieve her bra. Thankfully, as she was putting it back on, she came back to my bedroom. I was worried she might leave before I got any answers. Madison sat down on my bed and motioned me to sit next to her, but she wouldn't meet my eyes.

"Taylor, I know this is going to be very, very hard to believe. And I have to ask that you try not to freak out. That you don't do anything stupid. And that you don't hate me."

"I could never hate you. Why would you even say that?"

"Because what I'm about to tell you is really difficult. It's unbelievable. I didn't even believe it at first. But I need you to believe me."

"I will, I promise; I'll believe you."

"Okay. About six years ago, about the time that things were starting to really... develop, weird things started happening to me," she said.

"Like, what kind of weird things?" I asked.

"Well, it started small. First, my sister fell off her bike and skinned up her knee when we were out riding one day. She had me take a look at it, and when I touched her, my hands started to glow. After holding her leg for just a few seconds, the wound closed up, and her knee was as good as new."

"So you're saying that you have healing powers? That's so cool!" I said

"Really?" she asked.

"Hell yeah, I'd kill to have that power! I'd go around, running through hospitals, giving everyone a high-five until they all got better."

"I don't know that I could heal that many people like that. I only have so much energy I can draw from at a time. But there's more than just the healing. I'm also pretty much indestructible," she said.

"Like Superman indestructible? Like, bullets can bounce off of you?"

"No, they just hit me and fall down. It's more like I have an invisible force field for skin instead of steel."

"That's pretty unreal, Madison."

"There's... more."

"Seriously?" I asked.

"Yeah. By the way, you seem to be taking this really well."

"Maybe I've seen too many movies. I've always wondered what it would be like to be a superhero."

"It's not all that great, trust me," she said. "Anyway, I can also shoot beams of white energy from my eyes."

"Like heat vision?"

"No, more like a lighthouse shooting rays of light. They don't affect normal people, or objects."

"Wait, what do you mean 'normal people or objects'? What else is there?" I asked.

"I'll try to get to that. But there's still more," said Madison.

"Um, how much more?"

"Two more."

"Holy crap, this is crazy!" I said, sort of smiling.

"If you only knew. Anyway, I'm also super strong."

"Like, could you lift a table?"

"Easily."

"How about a cow?"

"Yup."

"A car?"

"I've done it a few times."

"How about a tank?"

"I've never tried, but I suppose that would probably be my limit," said Madison.

I sat and thought about what she'd already told me. I was having the hardest time absorbing everything she'd said. It just didn't make any sense. This kind of stuff didn't happen in real life. Honestly, at that point, the only thing I knew she could do was glow, and I remembered from biology class that there were some fish that could do that. Maybe she'd just eaten some weird fish and it made her skin glow. Maybe Madison was just... mad.

I shook that idea out of my head about as fast as it popped into it. I'd only known her for a little while, but the things that she was telling me, although crazy, might make some sense when I thought about other things I knew about her. That and she had no reason to lie about it, and she didn't strike me as the lying type, let alone someone who would make up such huge, potentially relationship ending lies. So I did my best to believe her.

"Okay, so what's the last one?" I asked.

"It's my favorite," she said. "The best way to tell you is to show you." Madison stood in front of me, facing me, in the center of the room. Then she took her bra off.

"So far I agree; it's your best power," I said, looking at her perky breasts.

"You hush," she said, blushing. Madison closed her eyes, smiled, and two wings popped out behind her. They glowed, just like her skin was glowing. It was the coolest thing I'd ever seen. I was completely dumbstruck. I didn't know what to say, so I just said the stupidest thing that came into my mind.

"Whoa."

Keanu Reeves would have been proud.

After a few seconds of staring, I stood up and looked over her shoulder to see where the wings had come from. They were firmly attached to her back, as if they'd been there the entire time; just a simple extension of her body. I finally collected my thoughts a little and started asking more questions.

"So can you fly?" I asked.

"My wings would be pretty useless if I couldn't," she responded.

"Well, you could always use them to knock over bad guys, or if you were running really fast and needed to stop suddenly. Air brakes; that'd be a good use for them. Or just gliding. Maybe you could jump off rooftops and swoop down."

"But thankfully my wings do work. I'm actually getting pretty good at flying. The hardest part is the landings."

"Yeah, my Dad made me watch some DVDs of an old show called 'The Greatest American Hero'. He had problems landing too. Supposedly he got a super suit and lost the manual for it," I said.

"I only WISH that my powers came with a manual. Do you have any idea how tough it is to develop breasts AND wings at the same time?" she asked.

"Nope, no clue," I said, laughing.

"Thank you for laughing at my suffering."

"Any time," I said, kissing her on her tasty lips. After giving her a long, reassuring kiss, I pulled back.

"So are your parents or sister like this?" I asked.

"No, I'm the only one in my family with superpowers," she said.

"I hate to ask, but what exactly are you?"

"I'm a girl, asshole!"

"No, I'm sorry, I mean, are you an angel?"

"I guess you could call me that. I certainly have a lot of angel-like traits, don't I?"

"Not the least of which is your smile," I said. That made her smile at me, a thoughtful, somewhat sad smile.

"Are you the only person in the world like this?" I asked.

"No. There are... others. Not all of them are good people. In fact, some are pure evil. That's one nice thing about my eye trick. I can sometimes fry the evil out of people. Or at least fry people that are evil. There's some sort of frying going on, and I'm pretty sure it includes evil people," she said. I couldn't help but laugh a little.

"So do your parents know? Does your sister?" I asked.

"Yes, they do. That's why they're against you being my boyfriend. They're just worried about your safety, since you're... normal," she said.

"Wait, am I your boyfriend then?"

"Of course. What else would I call you?"

"Yeah, but I never like, asked you, officially or anything. And don't I have a say in this?"

"Nope," she said, smiling.

"Well, it's good that you have two perfect breasts to help cushion the blow."

"Gee, thanks."

"You're welcome," I said, smiling. Madison contracted her wings, which magically disappeared into her back.

"So how did you get your powers? Were you bitten by some radioactive insect, or dropped into a vat of chemicals, or better yet, were you injected with some super-serum, and if so, can I buy some on eBay?" I asked.

"They just started developing along with everything else. They've never been able to figure out why," she said.

"Wait, who is 'they'?"

13

"I work for an independent group called White Ops. They lend me out to the FBI, CIA, NSA... If it has initials, I fight for it," she explained.

"So truth, justice and the American way?" I said.

"Something like that. Anyway, all those different groups have copies of my DNA. I was nice enough to lend it to them."

"Why would you do that?"

"It was kind of a compromise. They wanted to test me, and I didn't want to live in some secret underground lair, hanging out with Dr. Evil for the rest of my life."

"Really? Not even for 'one meeelyon dollarrrss'?" I joked.

"No, not even for that," she said, giggling.

"So why is it named White Ops?"

"Well, you've heard of Black Ops?"

"Sure, it's where you do spy stuff off the books. Remember, I play Call of Duty."

"Well, since I'm basically an angel, they thought it'd be a clever name."

"Ah, so they kind of named it after you? Or are there more angels out there?"

"As far as I know, I'm the only one. Other people have different abilities. So far there's only a handful of us that I'm aware of, and we're as unique as snowflakes."

"Well that's good, I guess. If there were a lot of you, I would imagine the battles would end up on TV. Not a good thing when you're trying to be a super-spy," I said.

"No, not good at all," she replied.

I started thinking more seriously about what she was telling me. I tried to put together the pieces of all the things that had happened. It explained why Laser Tag was so easy for her, how she could seem, and actually be, perfect, and it made me think about one other thing: why had she come over to my place, crying.

"Madison, were you the one who stopped last night's robbery?"

She looked away from me then took in a sharp breath and composed herself.

"Yes. But it went wrong. They were after a very old Egyptian necklace that held magical properties. Oh, I forgot to mention: magic also exists. In items. Some people seem to be able to cast it. Anyway, I was trying my best to subdue the robbers, but one fired his gun at me. It missed, but the ricochet... killed one of them. It's the first mission I've been on with a... fatality. Bullet entered the man's brain... I couldn't do anything to save him. My healing powers only work on living things. I can't bring things back from the dead," she said, tears streaming down her face.

I didn't know what to say to make things better, so I just held her for a while. She sobbed some, but not as much as when we were watching TV. I think Madison felt relieved that she finally had someone she could talk to about it. I think the way her parents are, that she doesn't feel comfortable sharing that kind of stuff with them. Her parents aren't bad people, they just don't know what to do to protect their daughters, so they worry about every last thing. It's understandable. I mean, how many parents have a superhero for a kid?

"So you don't think I'm a freak?" she whispered.

"Of course not, Madison. I think you're beautiful, and brilliant, and sweet, and sexy, and amazing."

"You really think I'm amazing?"

"More amazing than anyone I've ever known."

"Taylor?"

"Yeah?"

"I think I'm falling in love with you."

My heart beat so hard that I had difficulty breathing. I thought about it really hard to make sure that what I was about to say was true. I'd never said those words to anyone before. I guess it helped that she'd said it first. But I was sure I felt the same way.

"I think I'm falling in love with you too, Madison."

She looked up at me and kissed me. A soft, gentle kiss. This one was only filled with love. And I kissed her back, sharing my feelings for her. I love her so much that I would walk into hell for her. I didn't realize that at some point, I might actually have to.

14

After we kissed for a while, and laid on my bed, holding each other, we decided we needed to start getting ready for the party, which was only a few hours away. Madison picked up her clothing and went back to her place to clean up and get dressed in her party outfit. I have no idea what a party outfit is, but my guess is it's meant to attract members of the opposite sex, and make members of the same sex jealous. The closest thing I had to that was my 'Save Ferris' t-shirt with a picture of Cameron Fry on the front. I actually had a girl once offer to switch me t-shirts.

Anyway, I grabbed a quick shower, messed with my hair, brushed my teeth, flossed, shaved; all that good stuff. I did a quick spot-check to make sure I hadn't missed hiding anything breakable, made sure the house was clean, and then I set to getting everything ready for the party.

The sandwich guys came, and it took them about ten minutes to unload the massive sandwich in sections. I looked at it and thought that the dining room table would collapse under the weight. I'd asked for a number of different ingredients, and they made rows of the same type so people could easily choose what they wanted.

I got out the sodas and put them on the counter in the kitchen. I figured they would stay cold enough on their own, plus I didn't want to have to hassle with ice. Then I realized I didn't have any plates, napkins or cups. I grabbed my keys and hauled ass to the grocery store. I bought a whole bunch of the cheapest supplies I could find, which were all red thankfully. It would have sucked having a party where everyone was drinking out of cups with cute little kittens or butterflies on them.

Six o'clock came. Madison showed up on time to be supportive, but no one else did until about six-twenty. Then it became a steady stream of people coming in. It was kind of cool greeting people, saying 'hi' to people I'd seen in school but hadn't really met. Madison was awesome helping out while I welcomed people and got the music started. Most of the surrounding neighbors were on vacation, so I didn't have to worry about the noise too much.

One thing I quickly learned was that it doesn't matter so much what snacks or drinks or music you have at a party; what matters is the people. Just let them feel welcome and they'll have a blast. Also, generally people are good at keeping themselves busy. So you don't need to worry so much about keeping them entertained. But I guess that's what life is all about in the end: people.

Once I relaxed, the party was a blast. There were twin brothers who were really into dancing and wanted to show everyone what they could do. So people made kind of a circle around the living room and outside, looking in through the windows. They'd brought their own iPod, which I hooked up to my stereo, and they danced to some dubstep, doing some effing incredible popping and strobing moves. I'd seriously never seen anyone dance like that before in real life.

Almost everyone from school came, and some of them brought friends from other nearby schools. Nearby meaning forty miles away. Madison's sister Angela came, and she looked a lot like Madison, only younger. She seemed pretty cool, and was excited to finally meet "The Mysterious Taylor". That kinda sounds like either a bad name for a magician, or a good name for a book.

"So Taylor, do you have a younger brother?" asked Angela.

"Ha, no, sorry. It's just me and my folks," I said.

"That's too bad, you're cute!" said Angela. I turned and smiled at Madison.

"Okay Angela, quit making eyes at my boyfriend," said Madison.

"What, afraid of the competition?" said Angela.

"No, just afraid what might happen to your face if you try," said Madison, jokingly. I hoped.

"Ladies, ladies. There's plenty of T-man to go around," I said. This made Angela shake her head, and Madison give me a very dirty look.

"Never mind, you can have him," said Angela.

"I was just thinking the same thing," said Madison, still giving me a dirty look, but smiling slightly. I was completely in love with Madison and had zero interest in anyone else. I love her, and she's perfect, so why would I wreck that?

Anyway, I got to hang out with some of my closest friends, Erik, Collin and Original Recipe. Original Recipe isn't his real name; it used to be Kevin. He's kind of into rap and hip-hop a little too much. Instead of just being a person he's trying to become a 'brand', and sometimes he refers to himself in the third-person. I just hope he studies marketing if and when he goes to college. The guy is good at creating an image and a lasting impression.

"Original, what's up?" I asked.

"Not much, man. Your house kicks all kinds of ass, son!" said Original Recipe.

"Thanks, glad you could make it. Did you check out my new girlfriend?"

"Yeah, you must be hung like a horse to get a girl like that."

"I do okay, but I think she likes me for me," I said.

"Wow, then you really are lucky!" he said. I tried my best not to take it as an insult.

Original Recipe told me he was going to try and get a few girl's numbers and I suggested he might be better off just going after one; one really good one. That quality might be better than quantity. He told me he'd think about it and I didn't see him the rest of the night.

Erik and Collin had come without dates, so I did my best to suggest a few girls that might not have dates either, and who I knew were pretty cool.

"Taylor, you have got to hook me up with a redhead," said Erik.

"Why a redhead?" I asked.

"They're supposed to be really freaky," he said.

"I think I see where this is going. I do know a redhead, but she's a nice girl with a sweet heart," I said, smirking.

"That sounds like secret code for 'she's ugly as sin'," said Erik.

"Fine. If you don't want to meet her, you can find a girl on your own," I said.

"Nah, go ahead and introduce me. What's the worst that could happen?"

So I had Erik follow me over to Tanya, the redhead. I wish I'd had a yardstick right then to measure just how far Erik's jaw dropped. Tanya was absolutely beautiful, but she was very sweet and didn't know the affect she had on the majority of the male population. That's what I always thought true beauty was: when you were beautiful and didn't wield it as a weapon. Tanya went to another school, and I'd met her a year ago through her friend Janice, who went to my school. We hung out together once, and although she was amazing, we both agreed we just weren't 'The One' for each other.

Erik had some problems speaking when I introduced them, but I assured Tanya that he didn't normally have a speaking condition, and it was just her beauty that made him tongue-tied. This seemed to relieve some of the pressure for both of them, and Erik was finally able to talk like a human being. After playing matchmaker for Erik, I concentrated my efforts on Collin.

Collin was a little harder to work with. Erik had just graduated, like me. Collin was going to be a junior the next year, and not a lot of girls seemed interested in dating a younger guy. I think part of that was maturity level, as girls seemed to be a little wiser than boys at the same age.

"Collin, it just so happens that I know a girl who's about your age, beautiful, blonde, and unimpressed by the average guy. You want I should introduce?" I asked.

"Uh, sure. Do you think I can handle it?" he asked.

"Absolutely. Just be yourself. You're a cool guy; you got this."

"Okay."

So I had him follow me over to Madison's sister, Angela.

"Angela, this is Collin. He's kind of a hot item right now and needs protecting from all the other ladies in here. Do you think you can do that for me?" I asked.

She looked at him and smiled. He smiled back. I don't know if it was love at first sight, but they were definitely cute as a pair. They both got a little shy for a moment, but eventually Angela broke the ice. I left them alone so I could find Madison and tell her the news.

Madison wasn't as happy about me playing matchmaker with her sister as I thought she might be.

"Madison, you don't have to worry, Collin is a perfect gentleman. I wouldn't have introduced him to your sister if he didn't have a heart of gold and a brain that knows it's okay to look but not touch," I said. "Plus, he knows I'd kick his ass if he tried anything."

"You can't blame me for being protective of my sister," said Madison.

"I totally don't, and I do get it. But I'd trust Collin with my life. I'm giving you my personal guarantee no harm will befall your sister."

"You do realize you're saying this to someone who can probably rip you in half with her bare hands, right?"

"Yes miss, I do."

"Alright then," she said.

"Wanna dance?" I asked.

"Sure. Promise you won't crush my toes?"

"I'm pretty sure that since you're indestructible, that even on my worst day I couldn't crush your toes."

"I'm only indestructible when I glow."

"Good to know. I have to say, I'm glad I was able to make you glow," I said, smiling. She blushed and gave me a little smile that let me know she was happy I'd made her glow, too.

We danced to a few fast songs, which I'm pretty good at.

Then came a slow song. I don't even remember what song it was because I was too busy looking into Madison's beautiful green eyes. As I was holding her, we kissed. It was the perfect mix of love, sexiness and happiness. Once the song was done, Madison grabbed my hand and pulled me back to my bedroom.

15

Madison had me enter first then locked the door behind her. Her evil smile made my pulse quicken. Closing the blinds in my room, she took her shirt and bra off as she slowly walked toward me. I could feel blood rushing through my body. Once she reached me she kissed me, immediately probing my mouth with her tongue. I started to reach for her shorts, but she held onto my hands for a second, letting me know she had something else planned.

Madison got down on her knees and unbuttoned the button on my jeans. She looked up at me, making sure I was okay with what she was doing. I smiled and nodded at her and she smiled back, an extremely excited smile.

I won't go into detail about what she did, but I'll just say that she returned the favor from before the party. I couldn't believe how amazing it felt. I lost feeling in my hands and toes, and it took me several minutes to recover enough that I could uncurl my fingers.

"That was so incredible, baby. No one's ever done that for me," I said.

"I've never done that for anyone before, either," she said, smiling sweetly. "I wanted to do that for you. You made me feel the same way."

I smiled at her. We stood there, staring into each other's eyes, smiling. Unable to stop smiling. Madison kissed me one more time then put her bra and shirt back on. I pulled my jeans back up and straightened my shirt. After one last kiss, and holding her hand for a second, we left my room.

Madison and I went back the party, talked to friends, made new ones, and generally enjoyed ourselves. For the most part, everything was going smoothly. The music was still blaring, people were still dancing and talking. The only real problem was when a girl accidentally dropped her sandwich in the kitchen. It took a few seconds to clean up, so no big deal at all.

I was in the living room, just having a look around at all the people, when this six-foot-four asshole walks into my house wearing a long black leather coat, leather pants, and sunglasses. He had a black mane of hair that I wanted to cut off with a lawn mower, and two days' worth of stubble. If you couldn't tell, I hated the guy instantly. I mean, who the hell wears a long black leather coat in the summer?

Anyway, he came inside, obviously looking for someone or something. He was a man on a mission, and I was worried what that mission might be. If we were in a movie, I would have guessed he was a Terminator, because he moved like a robot, seemed emotionless, and looked like he could sustain a few hundred rounds to the chest. Unfortunately, my parents didn't have any guns in the house. Although knowing what I know now, it wasn't that bad of an idea at the time.

Mr. Tall-dark-and-douchey walked through the crowd, bumping into people but not paying attention to them, not caring about their existence at all. He apparently didn't find what he was looking for in the living room, so he passed through the dining room and made his way into the kitchen. That's where Madison was. Oh how I wished he wasn't there for her. I couldn't see any other reason why a guy like that would have come to a party full of high school kids. I figured he'd rather be carving tattoos into his arms with a bowie knife, or drinking motor oil mixed with gin. This guy was greasy.

I followed behind him, doing my best to be subtle. Once I rounded the corner into the kitchen, I found him talking to Madison. My blood boiled. It looked like she was really angry to see him, which I took as a good sign. Then she opened the door to the backyard and walked outside with him. That I wasn't cool with.

The privacy curtain on the kitchen window prevented anyone but me seeing them, since I was peeking around it. The discussion became heated, and my heart raced. Madison started glowing, which caused the guy to back off a step. I grabbed a knife from the butcher's block, and put the butt of it in my palm, cupping it, doing my best to conceal it. Then I went outside.

"Madison, there you are. Are you okay?" I said.

Panic filled her eyes.

"I'm okay, Taylor. Dantalion and I were just talking," she said, not taking her eyes off of him.

He looked over at me and just smirked. I tightened my grip on the knife.

"Boyfriend?" he asked in a gravelly smoker's voice, looking me up and down.

"No, just my neighbor," said Madison.

The words stung, hurting me more than anything this d-bag could do to me.

"Leave," said Madison, looking at Dantalion.

He chuckled to himself once, turned back to look at Madison then looked at me one last time before leaving the way he came. Madison stopped glowing and I closed the door after Dantalion, leaving me and her outside.

"Who the hell was that?" I asked.

"Dantalion," she replied.

"Yeah, I'd figured that out already. I mean who is he to you?"

"It's a really long story."

"One that you aren't willing to tell your 'neighbor'?"

"Taylor, he's dangerous. He has powers too. I was trying to keep you safe. If he knew how I felt about you, he'd come after you too. He's evil, through-and-through, and you're one of the most important people in my life. I'll do everything I can to protect you, even if that means lying for your safety. I hope you can understand that."

I thought for a moment and let the information sink in. I had a hard time letting go of the feelings of anger and betrayal; struggling to realize the truth of what she was telling me.

"I'm sorry I doubted you," I said.

"It's okay. I can understand why you felt the way you did. And I'm sorry, too."

"So how do you know this guy?"

"Well, before there was White Ops, there was Gray Ops."

I rolled my eyes.

"Let me guess," I started to say, "Dantalion was the black part of Gray Ops that made things darker."

"Yes. I know it sounds stupid looking back at it, but the intelligence community isn't always that intelligent. He would deal with the missions that I wouldn't. Handle situations that were immoral at best, and highly illegal at worst. Assassinations, conspiracies, blackmail; you name it. He was useful to the government, and they paid him for it. They also figured it was better to have him as an ally than an enemy. People worried that he might work for another government if we didn't hire him," explained Madison.

"Okay, I can understand all that. I can see that he must have 'gone rogue' or whatever, and now he's after you. But why would he bother with you specifically? It doesn't make sense to me. Why doesn't he just go and work for another country?"

Madison paused for a second, closed her eyes and cringed.

"He's my ex."

It felt like someone had punched me in the gut. I didn't really know what to feel or say about it. My emotions were a mix of a lot of unpleasant feelings, some of which were now aimed at Madison.

"You dated THAT guy?" I said, more of a statement than a question.

"Yes."

"For how long?"

"Not long. It really doesn't matter. What matters right now is you," she said.

"What about later? Will I still matter to you later?"

"Of course you will, Taylor! I love you."

That woke me up a little. I loved her too. Even after finding out she dated this a-hole, I still loved her completely.

She really was an angel to me, even without her powers, and I didn't want to let her go. I don't think I could if I tried. When you find that one person in the entire world that fills in all the missing pieces of your soul, you fight for them. You forgive them. You do whatever it takes to be with them.

"I love you too, Madison. I just can't understand what you would see in a guy like that."

"I think a lot of it had to do with him being the only person I knew around my age that was male. I saw him all the time because of the job. And he has a motorcycle. I don't know, sometimes bad boys are kinda hot. Look, Taylor, I'm not the same naive person I was then, I promise you. You have no idea how much I value you. I love everything about you, and I hope you can forgive me for the mistakes I've made in my past."

I thought about what she was asking. I didn't have too many skeletons in my closet, but I do know what it's like to make mistakes. I decided to forgive her, and love her for the person she is, not the person she was.

"I'm not going to have to fight your seven evil exes, am I?" I asked.

"No, there's just the one," she said. "And you're not going to fight him. It was really sweet, really brave, and really stupid of you to bring that knife with you."

"What knife?"

"The one you've been holding in your right hand the whole time."

"How did you know?" I asked.

"I work for a half-dozen government agencies. They trained us to notice things," she said.

"Do you know any cool secrets? Are the aliens in Area 51 real?"

"I'm really sorry Taylor, but I can neither confirm nor deny that," she said out loud, but nodded her head 'yes'.

My jaw dropped.

I whispered, "Seriously?"

She giggled. "No, not seriously. Or at least not that I've heard about. But it's not like they tell me everything."

I leaned in and kissed her, letting her know I still loved her and forgave her.

"We should probably go check on the party," I said.

"Probably a good idea," said Madison.

16

The party lasted for another hour or so before guests started leaving. A lot of people came up and thanked me, saying it was the best thing to happen all year. A few people stayed behind and offered to help clean up: Collin, Angela, Erik and Tanya. I think part of it was that Collin and Erik felt they owed me for hooking them up, and it was an excuse for the two couples to spend more time together.

Collin and Angela took care of picking up dirty cups and plates, and throwing them into some large plastic lawn bags I had. Erik and Tanya straightened up furniture and vacuumed. I tried to salvage as much untouched food and soda as I could from what was left on the table. It looked like there was enough food left for the six of us to have a few days' worth of meals, so I separated out the food in plastic bags and stuffed them in the fridge until people were ready to leave.

Madison took care of the debris out on the lawn. Thankfully for her, picking up the garbage outside wasn't too bad, all things considered. The grass though was pretty heavily trampled on. I figured I should be able to fix it before my parents got back. As the gang was finishing the clean-up, I opened the trunk storing all the breakables and put them back where I found them. I did a quick spot check, and the house pretty much looked exactly the same as before. I thanked all five of them by offering to take them out to get ice cream.

Unfortunately, my Challenger isn't the world's roomiest car. It seats four comfortably, five uncomfortably, and six... let's just say that's not exactly legal. Erik and Tanya volunteered to stay behind and watch the house, and I asked them what they wanted from Cold Stone.

"Cake batter, Heath Bar, and cherries," said Erik.

"I'd love chocolate with chocolate chips and almonds," said Tanya.

"No worries. Are you two going to be okay?" I asked.

"Yeah, we'll be fine," said Erik, winking.

"Just do me a favor you two, don't go in any of the bedrooms while we're gone," I said.

"Wouldn't dream of it, buddy," replied Erik.

Tanya actually looked a little bummed by my comment. So I leaned forward and whispered in Tanya's ear. She brightened up and winked at me.

Madison, Angela, Collin and I made our way to the Challenger. I was very happy to see it still parked in the driveway, and that nothing had happened to it during the party. My guess is the reason all the bad things happen to kids at parties is because of alcohol. I'm really not trying to be preachy or anything, I'm no saint. It's just that not everyone is responsible enough to handle that sort of thing.

Madison sat shotgun, and Collin and Angela sat in back. It was kind of sweet; I saw in the rear-view mirror Angela reach over and hold Collin's hand. After a few minutes, Madison couldn't hold it in any longer. She leaned over and whispered to me.

"What did you say to Tanya that made her so happy?" she asked.

"Just four little words," I whispered back.

"Which were...?"

I paused a few seconds for dramatic effect.

"There's always the couch."

"Oh. Ohhhhhhh," she said to me, smiling.

"Yeah."

"What are you guys talking about?" asked Angela.

"Grown up stuff," said Madison.

"It's about sex then, isn't it?" said Angela.

Poor Collin's face went bright red. He didn't know what to say, and thankfully he was smart enough to keep his mouth shut.

The Challenger's A/C didn't work, so we had to roll the windows down to stay cool. We went inside and placed our orders. I made sure to leave a decent tip, and we laughed as they sang a song for us.

I always get their 'everybody's' size of cheesecake ice cream with chocolate chips, coconut, walnuts and strawberries. It's the perfect blend of rich and creamy, tropical, smokey-sweet awesomeness. If you haven't tried it, you haven't lived. Regardless of who I have serving it to me, the employees always make up a little bit extra so that they can sample my concoction. I've never had a dissatisfied customer. Er, employee.

As we left Cold Stone, I looked across the parking lot. Sitting on his motorcycle, trying extremely hard to look cool and failing, was Dantalion.

"Guys, we need to get in the car. Quick," I said.

"How come?" asked Angela.

"We just need to hurry back... before the ice cream melts. We don't want to give Erik and Tanya soup, do we?"

Madison looked over at me and nodded that I'd done well. I wonder if I'd be any good at the spy business. Probably not. I'm not the best at keeping secrets, especially important ones. Anyway, everyone hurried and got in the car. Dantalion fired up his motorcycle and pulled in right behind us. As I turned out of the parking lot, he followed. I really hate that guy.

Anyway, I went up the street and took a right hand turn. He turned right. So I sped up and he sped up. I got so sick of him following us that I got us up to eighty then slammed on the brakes. I actually scared the crap out of him, to the point that he swerved around the car to avoid hitting us and lost control of his bike. It hit a curb and sent him flying onto the sidewalk, tumbling end-over-end.

"Did you guys see that?" asked Angela. "Shouldn't we go back and help him out?"

"No, definitely not. He's dangerous," said Madison.

"How can you tell? Do you know him?" asked Angela.

"Um... no, I don't know him. I can just tell by the clothes he's wearing, and his motorcycle. And the fact he was tailgating us the last few miles," replied Madison.

The rest of the drive home was normal. Madison had put the ice cream on the floor in the car which kept it safe when I hit the brakes so hard. We pulled up into the driveway and I gave the horn a quick 'accidental' honk to let them know we'd arrived. I went first, just in case, and I found Erik smiling sheepishly, and Tanya straightening her hair. One of the buttons on the middle of her shirt was unbuttoned, and I'd remembered it being buttoned before we left. Hmmmm, how odd. And yes, I'm being sarcastic.

Anyway, we sat around the now clean dining room table and enjoyed our ice cream. Madison and I spent most of the time watching each other eat. It's incredible how sexy it was to watch her eat her ice cream. I think she may have been making a production of it; licking it first before putting it in her mouth. I couldn't help but think back a few hours to what happened in my bedroom. It was so mind-blowingly amazing I couldn't wait to spend more time alone with her.

I finished eating what I could comfortably fit in my belly then put the rest in the freezer. Madison asked me to put her ice cream in as well. Once they were finished, Collin walked Angela home, and Erik walked Tanya home too. I don't know how long it took Erik and Tanya to get home, but I'm guessing they probably detoured somewhere. It was nice seeing Erik happy with the girl I'd suggested, especially after his initial reluctance.

That left Madison and me alone in the house.

Yes: alone.

Bow-chicka-bow-bow.

We walked back to my bedroom. Before we spent any 'alone time' together, I had to ask her more about Douche-talion.

"So what did he want from you?" I asked her.

"He wants me back in his life, as his girlfriend," she admitted.

"And you said...?"

"No. How could you even think I'd consider being with him again?"

"Because he wears leather pants and has better hair than most women."

"I told you, I love you Taylor. I never said that to him. I've never said that to anybody before. I don't know how I know, I just feel it. Like we're two halves of the same person," she said.

"And I love you too, Madison. I'm sorry, I'm just worried. Not of him. I'm worried about losing you. Especially since your life's so dangerous."

"I can protect myself. You know I'm pretty much invincible."

"Only when you glow. What happens if you aren't able to protect yourself in time?"

"I've been trained by the best to make sure that I can react to situations quickly. To see things before they happen, and stop them. The person I'm most worried about right now is you, Taylor. Dantalion has a wicked temper, and after you ran him off the road you've become a target. Maybe more so than even me. He loves that bike more than anything," she said.

"More than even you?" I asked.

"Way more."

"Then he really is a stupid D-bag."

"Yeah, he is."

"Is there anything else that Dorktalion wanted from you?"

"Yeah, there was one other thing: he wanted me to start working with him again. He's been hired by a private firm, but he wouldn't say which one. Unfortunately, it'd be impossible to guess who he's working for since there are so many bad guys to choose from."

"You refer to them as bad guys?"

"Sure. You got a better name for them?"

"Nope."

"Anyway, I told him to leave, only with much worse words," she said.

"Like what?" I asked.

"I dropped an f-bomb on him."
I couldn't help but laugh.

17

Sitting on my bed, we continued talking about Captain Asshole.

"So what are you going to do about Mr. Wrong?" I asked.

"Kick his ass," replied Madison.

"I like the way you think."

"You should, I'm pretty smart."

"And beautiful."

"And sweet."

"And sexy."

"You think I'm sexy?" she asked.

"I think you're the hottest, sexiest girl in the entire world," I admitted.

"Really, so if I was to do, let's say... this... would you think that was sexy?" she said, as she licked her lips then ran a hand seductively down the side of her face, down her beautiful neck to the warm place between her breasts, down to her stomach and then down even lower...

I sat there with my mouth wide open. I seriously could not believe just how sexy it was to see her do that. I steadied myself and tried to think of a way to get her back. I wondered if I could turn her on the way she was turning me on.

"Two can play at that game," I said.

I locked eyes with her then slowly took my shirt off, revealing my muscles. I flexed them in the hopes that it would excite her.

Unbelievably, we watched each other from across the bed, undressing, touching, feeling, wanting, and breathing until we both lost ourselves.

Madison put her hands on my shoulders, and gently pushed me back onto the bed, so that I was fully stretched out.

She laid on her side, next to me, her head on my chest just below my chin, and I wrapped my arms around her, holding her. It was so warm, and perfect, and I wished our bodies would simply melt together, reforming something new, something incredible, something 'us'.

I held her for a long time. Too long. She'd fallen asleep in my arms, and I'd fallen asleep not long after that. By the time we woke up it was four in the morning.

"Dammit!" said Madison, when she woke up and looked over at my clock.

It startled me awake. She rolled off of my body and frantically put her clothes back on.

"Madison, are you okay?" I asked.

"My parents will kill me!" she said.

"Wait, you're eighteen, right?" I said.

"Yeah."

"Then what can they do to you?"

"Kill me."

"Aren't you indestructible?" I said.

"Okay, well they can't literally kill me I guess. Unless I'm asleep. But still, I love my folks, and I don't want them to worry about me. This is the first time I've ever slept over at a boy's house, or even stayed out this late, other than for work. So I imagine they're not too happy with me right now," she replied.

"Do you want me to walk you back?" I asked.

"No, probably better you don't. You they could kill."

"Seriously?"

"Let's not risk it. Besides, I can sneak in and go to bed, and make it seem like I was there the whole time. Or I might tell a fib and say that I was on an important assignment nearby or something. I just don't want my folks upset at you before they even know you."

"I'm pretty sure your Mom already hates me."

"She doesn't; she's just afraid for your safety is all. Speaking of which, make sure to be careful. Dantalion knows where you live now. That's definitely not a good thing," she said.

"Don't worry, if he shows up I'll just scream like a little girl and wait for you to come rescue me," I said, smiling.

"So you'll be my damsel in distress?" she asked.

"Do I look like a damsel?"

"No. Especially with a perfect... like that!"

I smiled the biggest smile I'd ever smiled.

"Thanks, baby. Just so you know, you have the most incredible body I've ever seen," I said.

"And just how many bodies *have* you seen?" she asked, looking a little pissed.

"All of them."

"All of them?"

"All of them."

"Well, then I guess I should take it as a compliment that you think mine's the best," she said.

"That's what I was hoping," I said.

She came over to the bed, gave me a long, passionate goodbye kiss then left, closing the front door behind her. I just laid in bed, thinking about her, until I drifted off to sleep.

18

I woke up, still completely naked and uncovered. My feet were cold, but other than that it hadn't hurt my sleeping any. In fact, it was one of the best nights of sleep I'd ever had. I think it's because for the first time in my life I was happy. Truly happy. Content I think would be a good way to describe it.

I worked out for a bit, doing some bench, some bicep curls, and a few other things then took a shower. I turned the nozzle onto this really cool mist setting that made you feel kind of like you were in a tropical rainforest, only without the bugs. I'm not a big fan of bugs. Demons, ninjas, scurvy pirates and zombies don't seem to bother me, but eight legged things the size of my fingernail kinda freak me out.

I had a leftover sandwich for breakfast. I could have had Wheaties, I could have had a V-8, but instead I chose to have a leftover sandwich. Hey, I'm still growing! Anyway, that day was one of the longest days of my life. I didn't hear from Madison at all. I looked across the street to her house and their SUV was gone. In the late afternoon I finally decided to go over there, knocked on the door but there was no answer. It was kind of bothering me. Not a lot, but enough that I wanted to know where she was.

I went back home and did my best to keep myself distracted. I still had no way to contact her, because like the dumbass I am, I forgot to ask for her phone number. Or even her email address. Anyway, I thought it might help if I got my thoughts out on paper, kind of like writing a journal or something, since there was absolutely nothing I could do. What you're reading right now is based a lot on what I wrote then. I just turned it into a book. I have to say, I really do love writing. I'm not as good at it as Madison is, though. She's a natural. I really wish I had her heart and her mind. She'd probably tell you I did have her heart, which is mostly true. I just wish I could take that talent and passion that runs through her veins and use it in my own writing.

That night, after having sandwiches for both breakfast and lunch, I caved and ordered a pizza. Combination, add jalapenos and pickles. It was awesome. The pickles totally add a new dimension to pizza. I saw them on a list of ingredients and just had to try them. If you get the chance, I highly recommend them.

I watched the Dark Knight on Blu-Ray, which is one of my favorite movies. But it just didn't hold my attention. Nothing really held my attention, other than writing about Madison. I wondered if her parents were pissed about last night, and were keeping her from seeing me. I think I was just mildly obsessed with her.

It was really hard to sleep that night. I couldn't find a comfortable position to sleep in. I kept getting up out of bed, hoping to see Madison's parent's SUV parked outside their house, but no such luck. For the next three days it went on like that. I wrote, and I missed her. Nothing seemed to matter much to me at the end of three days. I pushed myself to carry on my normal routine of working out, running, taking care of the yard. I thought about calling some friends, but I figured I'd end up bothering them. So I just kept busy. I lost a little weight since I wasn't eating as much. Thankfully, in the evening on the fourth day, Madison's parent's SUV reappeared in their driveway.

19

I decided to wait a half an hour after seeing the SUV back in the driveway before I made my way over to Madison's house. But after fifteen minutes of waiting, Madison came over. Her hair was a tangled mess and it was obvious she'd been crying. Her nose was red, and her eyes were still wet with tears. I let her inside and motioned her to the couch.

"Can I have a drink of water?" she asked, her voice sounding hoarse.

"Sure, no problem," I said, getting up and grabbing her a glass of water. She sat there, holding the glass between her hands, staring at it, not taking a single sip. I was getting really concerned. Something obviously had her distracted and extremely worried.

"What's wrong Madison? You know you can tell me anything."

She started crying again. It took her a few minutes to calm down to where she could talk.

"It's Angela. She didn't come home the other night. At first, we thought maybe she was with Collin and had been out doing something she probably shouldn't be doing. But we called Collin's parents and they said he'd been home all day long and he hadn't seen her since he walked her home. We've been searching, but haven't been able to find her. My guess is that Dantalion took her."

"Have you called the police?" I asked.

"In a way. White Ops knows about the situation. They also understand that I won't be helping them until I get my sister back. So they're willing to help some. But since my sister is neither an asset nor a high profile person in need of rescue, there's only so much they can do. I have some friends and contacts who have offered to help on their time off. Getting her back will have to be a clandestine operation."

"I've heard that word, but what the hell does it mean?"

"Clandestine?" she asked. I nodded 'yes'. "It means secret. That's all."

"Oh. So how can I help?" I asked.

"That's really sweet, Taylor, but you don't have any superpowers," she said. "No offense, but I think the only thing you'd be good at is getting yourself killed."

"Not if I train to be a soldier. I play a lot of video games and I understand a lot of the basics of combat tactics, and what different types of guns do, how to reload them, stuff like that. And although I'm not as skilled as you are, or super-fast or anything, I'm still a good shot. You know I did well at Laser Tag."

"Laser Tag and video games aren't the same thing at all, Taylor. We're talking life and death here. You would be shooting at people. Really, really bad people, but still, people. I've never purposely tried to kill anyone, mostly because I don't use guns. They're only a last resort for me, and thankfully I've always been able to use my powers. Knowing how to use guns was just in case I was ever powerless."

"I know it's different," I said. "But I'm an adult. I'm old enough to be drafted. To die for my country. I can take care of myself. I swear I won't get in the way. I'm pretty good with computers; maybe I could help track her down. Or I could do communications, like talk to White Ops for you while you're busy, and relay messages. I could even be your personal chef. I just want to help."

Madison thought long and hard about including me in her self-appointed mission. I could see the gears turning inside that beautiful brain of hers, weighing the problems, the consequences against need and desire. She wanted more than anything for me to help. For me to be by her side through the most difficult thing she would probably ever have to face. Then she asked a very important question, one that helped her decision.

"Would I be able to stop you from trying to help?" she asked.

"No," I admitted.

"Then it'd be better if you were trained how to protect yourself; at least some basics. Things that will help you survive if we run into problems. And it'll be easier in some ways to protect you if you're with me. I have a feeling that if Dantalion is bold enough to take Angela, you'd be next. And he probably wouldn't just kidnap you."

"That makes me feel a whole lot less better."

"You need to know what you're facing. He has no morals. He can't be reasoned with. The only things he cares about are himself and money. And unfortunately, right now, the other side is paying better," she said.

"So how do I get trained?" I asked.

"I'll have to take you in."

"To White Ops?"

"No, I was thinking the Salvation Army could train you."

I gave her a bit of a fake dirty look, then thought about it.

"Actually, that would be a good name for a legion of angels," I said.

Madison laughed, a raspy laugh that made her choke. Thank goodness that under the seriousness of what we were facing she could still laugh a little.

"So how do we get there?" I asked.

"We can drive. The nearest base of operations is about an hour north of here," she said. "I'll take you there first thing tomorrow morning. Get some sleep. The training will kick your butt. You think you're in good shape now? Wait until you get through a couple of days of training there. Your muscles will be in so much pain you'll ask them to shoot you to put you out of your misery."

"Gee, that sounds like fun. Can I change my mind?" I asked jokingly.

"No," said Madison, reaching in and giving me a kiss.

"What was that for?"

"It was a kiss of gratitude, dumbass," she said.

"Can I get a B.J. of gratitude instead?" I asked, hoping I wasn't about to get punched.

"We'll see," she said, squinting her eyes at me playfully. "Taylor?"

"Yeah, Madison?"

"I love you. And thank you."

"I love you too."

"Okay, I'm going home to talk to my parents, and then hopefully I'll get some sleep. Goodnight, Taylor."

"Goodnight," I said as she got up and left, closing the front door behind her.

20

I had a hard time falling asleep, but once I did I slept okay.
When I woke up the next morning, I felt like I'd had about four cups of coffee. It was the first time I'd ever been invited to hang out at a secret spy headquarters and I was really excited about it. I also liked the idea of learning how to fight, and possibly kill people like I was some sort of assassin-slash-ninja-slash-pirate. That's a lot of slashing.

We took the Challenger, but Madison drove. She actually blindfolded me when we first set out, so it's a good thing she drove. Otherwise, I'd likely be stuck in some ditch somewhere. After a half hour of being blindfolded, she told me I could take it off.

"Which should I take off first, my shirt or my shorts?" I asked.

"The blindfold, silly-pants," said Madison.

"Ah, I knew that. So are we close?"

"Getting there, but we're only about halfway. Do you recognize any of these roads?" she asked.

"Not really," I said.

I actually did recognize the roads, since I'd done a lot of driving once I got my car. I knew just about every street, sidewalk and turn within a hundred miles of my house. I don't know why I didn't tell her the truth. It wasn't that I didn't trust her, it's that I didn't trust 'Them'. White Ops. I didn't know them, but up until recently they'd employed the psycho Dantalion. In my book, that makes them not worth trusting.

As long as Madison thought I didn't know their location of operations, she'd honestly say to them she believed it and all would be okay. And I could still find the base if I had to come rescue her. It was the first and only lie I've told her. I don't want to ever lie to her, but this was too important. *She* is too important.

After a few dozen Red Vines and some Dubstep music later, we reached a large farm. The field looked recently tilled, as thousands of lines of dirt ran parallel to each other. There was a gravel driveway, and an old, very large house at the far end of it. As we pulled closer, I could see that a lot of the windows were knocked out. The porch swing only had one chain connected. It looked like it'd been abandoned for the last forty years. Apparently White Ops wasn't all that brilliant, because it was obvious to me that a farmer wouldn't till land that he didn't live on. It just didn't make sense. I doubt anyone would notice unless they were looking for it, but it just struck me as weird.

The house at one point had been painted forest green, but in its current condition it was hard to tell. An old beat up tractor was parked next to the house, as was the rusted out shell of a '54 Dodge.

Madison pulled the Challenger to the back of the house. Right behind it was an old barn that looked like it could collapse at any moment. Madison inched the car inside between some bales of hay and rust covered tools. That was another thing that struck me as odd. Why the hell did they have hay when they didn't have any animals? Madison rolled down the window and spoke in a loud, clear voice.

"Madison Wheatfield, code Alfa November Golf Echo Lima," she said. All of a sudden the floor started lowering. The car rattled a little from the vibration of the machinery moving us underground.

"Wait a minute, that code you just gave... doesn't that spell out the word 'angel'?" I asked.

"Um, yeah, why?" she questioned. I just rolled my eyes. I might be able to learn some stuff from White Ops, but it seemed like they could learn a lot from me, too.

"So how far underground is it?" I asked, just before the sound of the machinery stopped.

"We're here," she said.

"Wait, we only went underground about twenty feet."

"Well how far down do you have to be underground? Underground is underground, right?"

"I guess. It was just disappointing is all," I admitted.

There were no lights on in the room yet. The ceiling slid closed over the top of us and we were plunged into darkness. After waiting a few seconds, a door finally opened, which was only big enough for people to fit through. I turned to Madison.

"Hey, what should we do with the car then?" I asked.

"Just leave the keys in the ignition. Someone will park it for us," she explained.

"Where?"

"Where what?"

"Where will they park it?"

"They'll take it back up and outside, and park it around back," she said.

"Wait, so they bring cars down so that they can take them back up? Why not just build a lift that can only carry people?" I asked.

Madison stared at me blankly.

"Oh, right, they probably need a way to bring large equipment down here," I said.

"Not really. Most of the stuff they have is portable. In fact, I'm pretty sure a regular elevator would have worked just fine," she admitted.

"Your tax dollars at work," I said, laughing.

A man, about fifty years old, came through the door. He looked kind of like an evil scientist, or at least a scientist who shouldn't be around people. He wore a white lab coat and kept several pens and pencils in a protector in his left breast pocket. Another thing I noticed was his hair was slicked back with some kind of slimy substance. This guy gave me the creeps.

"Madison, is this the young man you were telling us about?"

"Yes. Dr. Zumwaldt, I'd like you to meet Taylor... wait, I don't even know your last name."

I mumbled my last name to her.

"Wait, what was that? I couldn't hear you very well," she said.

"Swift."

"Um, I'm sorry, I thought you just said your name was Taylor Swift."

"It is," I admitted.

Madison couldn't stop laughing.

"Hey, it's not like I picked it! I tell you what, when we get married, I'll change my last name to yours," I said.

"You want to marry me?" she asked, beaming.

"Not so much anymore," I said.

She thought for a moment.

"Taylor Wheatfield isn't much better," she said.

"Yeah, not really," I admitted.

We both looked back at Dr. Zumwaldt, who appeared slightly unhappy with us.

"Are you two ready?" he asked.

"Yes, sorry about that," said Madison.

"Follow me," he said.

21

We followed Dr. Zumwaldt down a short corridor, turned left and ended up in a large room, if you consider my bedroom a large room. There were four desks that had been wedged into the room as tightly as possible. On each desk was a laptop, notepad, pens, and a small sign with their name on it. There were also two vents, one to let air in, and the other to let air out. A mini-fridge, microwave and water cooler rounded out the look of the place. Biggest disappointment in history. It's kind of like when you find out that Superman isn't real. Some people might say Santa Claus, but he's real alright. That fat, cookie-thieving bastard!

A man who looked like he was also in his fifties saw us enter, stood up, and reached out a hand to me. He looked like a quarterback: square jaw, big shoulders and salt and pepper hair. I reached my hand out and shook his.

"I'm Director Scott. Good to finally meet you, Mr. Swift," he said.

His voice sounded a lot like the guy on that old show 'Unsolved Mysteries'. I've watched reruns on Spike.

"You too. So how did you know my last name?" I asked.

"Well, we are a clandestine intelligence agency. It's kind of our job to know things. That, and it's written on your parent's mailbox," he pointed out. "Google street view."

"Right."

"Anyway, Madison filled us in on bringing you into the fold. She'd like you trained to be a, how did she put it? Ah, yes: a ninja. Her words, not mine. Basically, we'll teach you some hand-to-hand combat, shooting, tactics; maybe even a little espionage. Your trainer's going to be Mike over there," said Director Scott, pointing to the rather scary looking man sitting at a desk opposite him.

Mike stood up. Sitting down he looked pretty dangerous. Standing up, he was slightly less than whelming. He stood about five-foot-two, but he was built like a brick. Even his muscles had muscles. Numerous holsters were attached to his outfit, holding all sorts of guns and knives and grenades. I just couldn't get over the fact that I was looking down at him. Like literally.

"Good to meet you, Taylor," said Mike, shaking and crushing my hand.

"You too," I said as I squeezed back as hard as I could.

Finally he let go of my hand. I could see it throbbing, and eventually the feeling in my fingers came back. Something seemed a little odd, so I went ahead and asked the big question.

"So why are you guys letting me in on the mission? I figured you'd be pissed about having an untrained civilian along," I said.

"You're not completely useless. You're bright, athletic, clever, or at least that's what our intel indicates. You know the names of a number of different weapons and in general how to use them. You're also good with computers. Honestly, we could do a lot worse. Plus, Madison said she won't work for us anymore if we don't at least try to get you up to speed," he said.

"Any other reason?" I asked.

"Yes. I honestly don't care if you die. You're completely expendable. It's Madison's fault if you get shot and killed, so she only has herself to blame."

That really didn't sit well with Madison, but he kind of had a point. She turned to me.

"Taylor, if you're not sure about this I can always take you home," said Madison.

I thought about it for a moment.

"I'm still in. Sorry, I'm in love," was my response.

Madison just looked at me and smiled. A happy, but worried smile.

"So first things first," said the Director, "we'll get you trained. Mike here will spend the next few days turning you into a living weapon. The rest of us will work on putting a plan together, and hopefully figure out where they might be hiding Angela. Do you need to contact your family, Mr. Swift? Because once you start your training, you won't be able to communicate with the outside world for the next three days."

"I should probably call my Mom, just to let her know I'm okay. They're out of town, but they check up on me every so often," I said.

"Good enough. Go ahead and make your call, and then you and Mike can leave," said the Director.

Madison took my hand and guided me out of the tiny room, down the hallway, and back up the lift. It was nice to get out of there, since I'm not a fan of small spaces to begin with. I walked a few dozen yards away. Thankfully, even out in the middle of nowhere, I was still getting a signal. I had to have my Mom repeat herself a couple of times while we were on the phone, but otherwise it wasn't that bad.

"Hello?" she said.

"Hey Mom, how's Chicago?" I asked.

"It's a very nice place. We watched a Cubs game, ate hot dogs at the stadium, and went to a few museums. How are you getting along?"

"Pretty good. I found a girlfriend, we threw a huge party for two-hundred people, and now her sister's been kidnapped by an evil ex-boyfriend with superpowers. Also, a secret government agency is training me how to kill people so that I can help my new girlfriend, who's actually an angel, get her sister back."

"Wow, that certainly sounds exciting!" said my Mom, not believing a word of it. My Mom and I sometimes like to kid around about stuff, telling big tales to each other. If I really thought she'd believe me, I wouldn't have told her a word of it. The nice thing was that I told her the truth. I was completely up front about the whole thing. So if I ended up dead, they'd know why. They would have a hard time actually believing it, but they'd know why.

"So did you really meet a girl then?" asked my Mom.

"Yup."

"Do you think you love her?" she asked sweetly.

"Yeah Mom, I think I do."

"Then make sure to use protection. If you're anything like your Father, you won't be able to keep your hands off of her."

"Oh, good lord Mom, I did NOT need to know that!" I said, throwing up in my mouth a little. Okay, not really, but I thought about it. "I'm gonna let you go now. If you try and call and I don't pick up, it's because I might stay at a friend's place for a couple of days and play some Call of Duty."

"As long as you aren't staying at her place."

"No Mom. For starters, her parents are home."

"Well that makes me feel a little better. Can I have their phone number?"

"No Mom. I love you. Goodbye."

I could hear my Mother sigh on the other end of the phone. She said she loved me and 'goodbye' then reluctantly hung up.

Madison noticed I was done and walked over to me.

"So how did it go?" she asked.

"I told her everything."

"Whoa, are you crazy?"

"Nope. My Mom doesn't believe half the stuff I say, even when it's true. The truth is so impossibly ridiculous that I knew she wouldn't believe me," I said.

"So what did she say?"

"She asked if I was in love with you."

"And what did you say?" she asked.

"I said that I am."

"And then what did she say."

"She said to use protection."

That got Madison to laugh.

"And then she told me my Dad couldn't keep his hands off her when they were dating," I said.

"EWWWWW!!!" said Madison.

"Yeah. They're not even *your* parents and you think it's gross. Does White Ops have any gadgets I could use to erase that from my memory? Like in 'Men in Black'?" I asked.

"Not that I know of," said Madison.

"Damn."

22

"Y ou ready, kid?" asked Mike, who had come outside and walked up to us.

"Yeah, I'm ready," I responded.

Madison gave me a long, very sweet and very wet goodbye kiss. I reached around her and squeezed her butt, pulling her a little closer to me. It was all I could do to keep from tearing her clothes off right there. I figured it'd be bad form in front of one of her co-workers though. Especially one who could cut me in half with a paperclip if he wanted to.

"Thanks again, Mike. Take good care of him," said Madison.

"That's not my job. My job is to try and break him," said Mike, patting me on the back a little too hard.

"Oh, well in that case, Taylor, it was nice knowing you," replied Madison, winking at me and walking away.

"So, Mike, you got a last name?" I asked.

"I forgot it," he said.

"Right. So what are we doing?"

"Well, I was thinking about giving you a sixty second head start. Then I'd come after you."

"Wait, seriously?"

"Fifty-nine, fifty-eight... "

"Oh crap!" I said, running as fast as I could away from the house and into a nearby forest.

It was a really good thing that I was in shape. I knew that Mike was in better shape than me, so I needed to make the distance count. He was probably fifteen years older than me, but that also meant he was fifteen years smarter. I had no doubt that he would be able to hunt me down unless I kept moving, or came up with a better plan.

I didn't realize at first that he hadn't set any rules about what I could do and where I could hide. Once I reached the trees, I looked back to see him walking toward me, but not all that fast. So I ran deeper into the forest. I started thinking about what I could do to avoid him. Then I thought, well, I still have my phone, my wallet and my car keys. Could any of those things help?

I had an idea that I thought might work. I decided to make a wide arc through the forest by running in a huge circle. It took me about 20 minutes to make the complete circle without being seen, but it worked. I came out of the forest about where I'd started. I could see the house, the barn and my car. I looked around to make sure no one was following or watching. When I was sure that the coast was clear, I sprinted for the Challenger.

Once I reached the car, I quickly opened the door, slid in and tried to start it. It wouldn't start. So I popped the hood and kept a close eye on the forest, in case Mike had figured out what I'd been doing and took a shortcut. I got the hood open, and someone had pulled all the spark plug wires out. I figured Mike had done it, but didn't do a very good job of disabling the vehicle. He must have either known only a little about engines, or thought I knew nothing, because it only took me about 30 seconds to replace all the boots over the spark plugs. He hadn't even bothered to move them away from where they normally hooked up, so that I would have to guess the firing order.

I finished the wiring and hopped into the car. The engine roared to life. I peeled out, shooting gravel into a rooster tail behind me, and the Challenger eventually shot forward. I took it back around to the front of the house, and after checking both ways I drove down the road as fast as the car would move.

I had nowhere to go in particular, but I figured home would be the first place Mike would look once he figured out I drove off. Madison's might be another place he'd check, just because it was next door, and it would be as good of a place as any. So I figured, hey, why not go do something fun. I'd left my pool cue in the trunk, so I decided I'd go shoot a few games until I got a phone call telling me I'd won.

The pool hall not far from my house was decent. Half the tables needed new pockets and re-felting, but other than that it was a pretty cool place. It was open to families, so there was no alcohol allowed on the premises. When I got there, I opened my trunk, pulled out my cue and went inside. I scanned the tables to see if anyone I knew was there. I didn't recognize anyone inside. Even the girl working the counter was new.

So I went up to her, got some balls and a rack and pulled up a table. I practiced playing nine-ball for the next 10 minutes, until Mike walked into the hall, looking pissed.

"What the hell are you doing? You're in the middle of an exercise!" he said.

"Hey, let's take this outside. Don't want to spook the norms," I said.

His pissed-off look got more intense for a second then he nodded to follow him. I went outside after I paid for the short time I'd been there.

"Kid, the point of the exercise was to get you used to being chased, and to see how you'd handle yourself out in the wilderness," said Mike.

"Hey, you didn't give me any rules to start. You just said you were chasing me. So I tried to think outside the box."

Mike thought about it for a moment.

"Okay, you're right. I didn't tell you the point of any of it. It was actually fairly clever that you went back for your car. It's pretty much impossible to find someone after they've driven off," said Mike.

"Then how did you find me?" I asked.

"Because you're still a dumbass teenager. I stuck a tracking chip on your back when I slapped it. I just followed the GPS signal until I found you."

"At least I didn't go home, or to Madison's place."

"That's true; you did something unpredictable. I have to admit, the tracking chip wasn't meant to be used to find you. It was just in case something went wrong, and we really couldn't find you. For your safety, nothing more. Maybe you aren't a complete idiot. But you still have a lot to learn. Anyway, I rode my motorcycle here, so go ahead and follow me back."

Driving back seemed to take forever, because Mike went exactly the speed limit. I'm sure that in the service of your country you don't want to get pulled over for speeding, but everybody I know goes at least five miles an hour over the speed limit. He drove like my Grandmother. For the record, my Grandmother doesn't drive.

There were a few times I got anxious and frustrated, and wanted to hit him with my car, but I somehow managed to keep a level head. Maybe this was part of the test, to see if I could be patient if I needed to. I would imagine it'd be a handy trait to have in the spy business. To not kill someone you really, really wanted to kill.

We arrived back at the base, and Mike carefully drove his motorcycle to the back of the house. I pulled up right next to him. He motioned me to follow him back to the barn. I wasn't sure why, but I figured it must be necessary. He had me stand next to him on the platform as we were slowly lowered underground. When we got inside, Director Scott was waiting for us.

"So how did he do, Mike?" asked the Director.

"He evaded me," said Mike.

"Wait, he evaded you? Then how did he get back here?"

"I had to use the tracking chip to find him, sir."

"I thought you knew this area better than anyone, and could track just about anything."

"Well, I didn't really give him any rules, other than I was going to chase him. So he made a circle out in the forest then got in his car and drove off."

"Did he go home, or somewhere familiar?" asked the Director.

"No sir. When I found him he was shooting pool."

"Pool?"

"Nine-ball, sir."

The Director thought to himself for a moment.

"Well done then, Taylor. Not sure what to make of it, but I have to admit, you have good instincts. Didn't adhere to the spirit of the exercise, but that kind of thinking is what separates your average agents from your super-spies. I guess the next step, Mike, is weapons training. Make sure he can use a variety of weapons. At least a few handguns, assault rifles, and a couple of sniper rifles. He'll need to know how to use and maintain them. Go ahead and get started whenever he's ready."

"You ready, kid?" asked Mike.

"Ready like spaghetti."

"Spaghetti?" said Mike.

"Never mind. I'm ready," I responded.

23

I have to say, the highlight of my training was learning how to use a number of different weapons. I'd fired a few handguns before, and I shot a few clay pigeons with a shotgun, but I wasn't prepared for the guns they had in store for me. Mike took me outside and into the forest. He set up a table with a few different weapons and some paper targets about thirty feet away. He had me shoot into the side of a hill to make sure that a stray bullet wouldn't accidentally hit someone.

"This is your standard issue M9," Mike said, holding it up to show me. "It's an automatic, and fires a 9mm round. In this case automatic means that you can depress the trigger, and upon firing, the next round will move into place, so if you pull the trigger again, it will fire again. Any questions so far?"

"Not so far."

"Go ahead and squeeze off a few rounds."

I took my time and aimed at one of the targets. My first shot was a little high because I wasn't used to how the sights actually worked. I took my time and aimed my second shot more carefully. I was able to hit within an inch of the bulls-eye.

"Not bad," said Mike. "Go ahead and fire off several rounds in quick succession."

I fired four shots, the first hitting the target close to center. The next few were much higher.

"Notice the kick?" asked Mike. "It'll throw off your second shot quite a bit. If you can't figure out how to pull the gun down back in time for the second shot, I'd recommend first going lower, below center mass, then the second shot will end up being about where you want it to be."

I aimed for the target's stomach, and using the kick to my advantage I put the second shot within a few inches of the center of the target.

"Not bad. You don't flinch too much. This time try and brace yourself and fire a couple of times at the center of the target."

I took aim and fired a few rounds, trying to keep my arms braced. I didn't fire as fast as I could, but the bullets hit their mark, all in a small grouping.

"That's good," said Mike. "Okay, let's have you try out a few more weapons."

Mike next showed me how to use an M16 assault rifle, an AK-47, a Steyr Aug, and my favorite: the Barrett .50 cal. The thing I liked about the Barrett, besides the huge teeth-rattling boom, was how accurate it was. He had me set it up on the ground as a fold-out tripod and shoot at a paint can he'd placed about as far away as the other end of a football field. The scope on it was large and pretty incredible. I could easily see the paint can. I took my time, lined up the shot and pulled the trigger. I didn't have to move the trigger very much at all.

The paint can exploded, sending white paint everywhere. I was pretty happy with the shot, I'd hit it dead on, but the aftermath was the amazing thing. What remained of the paint can looked more like a pop can that had exploded. There wasn't much left of it, and the paint had made a beautiful spray pattern behind it.

"Looks like you're a natural," said Mike.

"I've played a lot of video games. I know it's not the same, but I think it helps with the nervousness, knowing I'm at least familiar with the look of the guns and the sounds that they make. So what are you going to train me on next?" I asked.

"Knives."

"Um, do you think that's a good idea?"

"Not really. But we need to prepare you for anything. It's also a lot easier to conceal a knife than a gun. So if you were captured, you might have a knife hidden on yourself. Maybe in your shoes, or in a belt buckle, or something like that. It could be the difference between being tortured to death and escaping," said Mike.

"Okay, then I'm definitely up for it."

Mike showed me how to use a couple of different knives. The first was a hunting knife, which he said was decent at slashing, but not as good at stabbing. The second was a switchblade, which he explained was good at jabbing and poking with, but unless you hit a major artery it probably wouldn't kill someone. The third knife had what he called a tanto blade. It looked like a very short katana, with a tip that formed a sharp, straight angle. He said it was the best for stabbing, and that it could potentially pierce body armor in the right hands.

I played around with the different knives for a while and tried throwing them at targets he'd set up. The hunting knife had good heft, and more often than not I could get it to stick in the wood target. The tanto knife generally bounced off unless I got really lucky, and the switchblade just didn't have enough weight to stick into the wood. It'd just bounce off the target like it was made by Nerf.

After Mike was satisfied that I was at least familiar with knives, he taught me some basic survival stuff. Things like how to use a compass, when I can and can't drink water from a natural source, how to start a fire with twigs; Boy Scout type stuff. After earning several merit badges, it was getting dark. And no, I never got the badges. A-holes. I should really email the Boy Scouts and ask them why. Anyway, Mike had a bright idea.

"Your first real test is to survive the night out here in the woods without help from me. The rules are you can't leave the forest for any reason, you can't have any help from anyone, and you have to fix your own meals. All you have to do is survive until morning. Oh, and you get to pick three items that you've been trained on to take with you," said Mike.

I looked at the tables he'd set up; at the guns, and knives and survival gear. I thought about what things would be the most and least important for surviving.

"Okay, the first thing I'd like to bring is the hunting knife," I said.

"That seems like a wise decision. Two items left."

"Yeah. I'm going to take the water canteen with my second pick. It's still filled with water, right?"

"It's mostly full."

"Good. My third pick is the rope and hook."

"Hmm," grunted Mike. "You haven't been trained on it yet. Can I ask why you picked that one?"

"Nope," I replied.

"All right then. Well, good luck. Hopefully the bears won't get you."

"Bears?"

"Or whatever else you find out there. Or finds you."

24

The canteen came with a carrying strap, which I'd pulled over my head and rested on my right shoulder. I slung the rope attached to the grappling hook over my head and stuck my right arm through it, so that I wouldn't have to carry it. The hunting knife came with a sheath and strap, which I wrapped around the upper portion of my calf. I was able to move at a pretty decent clip like this, leaving my hands free to protect my face from branches as I walked into the forest.

I wanted to get deep inside the forest, just in case Mike wanted to mess with me in the middle of the night. I figured under normal circumstances the forest would be safe. It was near a well-traveled road, surrounded by lots of farmland, and I knew there weren't many animals around of the dangerous variety. Thankfully, Mike was my only real concern.

I was getting kinda tired, so I found a tree that I thought looked about right and stopped to take a drink of water from the canteen. I could just barely see, since the canopy of trees blocked out most of the moonlight. There was just enough light to see the outlines of trees and branches, and see the ground. It helped that the time I'd spent walking into the forest gave my eyes a chance to adjust to the darkness. I capped the canteen and set to work on my trap.

It didn't take me long to get everything in place. The next part was what sucked. I hid behind another tree, making sure I could still see the trap I'd set. I kept an eye open in every direction that the tree didn't provide me cover from, leaning against the tree. I also listened, hoping to hear the sound of twigs cracking under Mike's feet. I waited. And waited. And then I waited some more. It was excruciating waiting for him to finally show up. I got so bored I decided to watch a movie in my head. I'd heard somewhere that it helps to keep you from going crazy if you're ever in solitary confinement. Just replay a movie in your head like you were watching Netflix.

It took what seemed like hours for him to finally show up. He was good, very good, but since there was no background noise to cover up what little noise he was making, and I wasn't moving, I could easily hear him approaching. I moved onto my stomach, looking around the tree I was hiding behind. I could see Mike staring up at the rope that I'd hung in the tree. I'd opened up the grapple and sent it into the air, swinging it around a branch. He must have thought I'd climbed the tree, because he yanked a few times on the rope to make sure it was anchored then tried to climb it.

Before he got more than a foot in the air, I launched myself from behind the tree and closed the gap. He hadn't expected me to get the drop on him, and he was so startled he forgot to let go of the rope. I used the strap from the canteen and wrapped it around his neck. Then I held on for dear life.

I have to say to all you kids out there, don't try this at home. Choking can kill people, even when done as a joke. Or as a friendly gesture. Or a more than friendly gesture. Bow-chicka-bow-bow. Seriously though, don't do it.

Anyway, I kept the strap really tight around his throat, and I could see him turn purple. He struggled against me, throwing elbows, kicking back at me, trying reverse head-butts. Nothing connected. I jumped around and did my best to keep the strap in place. After about forty-five seconds he passed out. I checked his pulse and breathing, and he seemed to be doing okay. I was really glad he was still alive. No one had ever trained me how to correctly knock someone out that way, and I was really scared I might hurt him. Mike wasn't a bad guy, he'd only ever tried to help me.

I did 'floppy arms' to Mike to make sure he was out cold. Ernie would have been proud. I didn't want him messing with me while I tried to work. He was also a pretty strong, and very heavy guy, but not large. Just really muscled. I dragged him up against the tree I'd been hiding behind then climbed the rope I'd strung up in the tree. After a few moments I was able to retract the arms on the grapple, let it fall to the ground and away. I dropped back down to the ground, then used the rope to tie Mike up to the tree.

I spent twenty minutes hoping that he'd wake up, and I was starting to get worried I'd hurt him. I splashed cold water in his face, which thankfully woke him up.

"What the hell are you doing kid?" yelled Mike.

"I'm tying the enemy up," I said.

"I'm not the enemy," said Mike.

"My ass, you aren't. I know you were out here to mess with me."

Mike didn't respond. I felt around his pockets. In them I found a compass, a tracker device for the GPS chip I had on me, matches, the tanto blade, a 9mm pistol, and four trail-mix bars. I ate three of the four right in front of him.

"Thanks Mike for the food delivery. Sorry I can't tip you," I said.

"Yeah, sure, have your laugh. Now let me go," he said.

"Yeah, I don't think so. As soon as I do, you'll kick my ass. And then you'll just keep kicking my ass. That doesn't sound too fun."

"Alright, I promise if you let me go now you can go back to the base and have whatever you want to eat, and sleep in the finest room money can buy," said Mike.

"What, you think you can bribe me?" I asked, surprised. "Sorry Mike, but you're stuck here with me until morning. And you better treat me well. I'm the only thing between you and the bears out here."

"I just made the bear thing up," said Mike.

"Unfortunately, it isn't a joke. I actually know this area, and I've seen dozens of bears around here," I lied. "I have a knife, and now a gun thanks to you. I have, well, had dinner. So what were you planning on doing to me?" I asked.

"The same thing you're doing to me. Make you regret setting foot in these woods."

"Well, at least you're honest. And I understand why, you're just trying to help me learn how to survive on my own. I really do appreciate that. I just hope that you can see the humor in the situation, and that I actually paid attention to what you taught me. I don't know if I'll survive all of this, but know that you did the best you could, and I'm a lot likelier to survive because of it."

Mike just looked at me, half-defeated, half-proud. What I'd said apparently changed his mood some.

"So why didn't you pick the compass, or the matches, or a gun when you were selecting your items? Those were the items I was pretty sure you'd pick," asked Mike.

"Well, the compass wouldn't be all that useful, since I figured I could easily find my way back. Just wait for the sun to come back up and use it to navigate by. Plus, I figured if I walked in a straight line long enough I'd hit a farm, or the road," I replied.

"That makes some sense," said Mike.

"I took the canteen both for water and to use as a weapon. I figured if it was filled with water, I could swing it around and hit you with it, or use the strap to choke you, like I did. And it would be a quiet weapon. That was the one thing I needed to be to beat you: quiet. That's also why I picked the knife, and not one of the guns. The guns are noisy and give away my position. The matches had the same problem, they'd give away my position. Plus, I might accidentally set the forest on fire, which would be bad. I can sneak up on you with the knife, or throw it. It also has about a million uses when you're out in the forest, from skinning animals to building shelter. I can even use it to make weapons, like spears out of tree limbs. I personally think the knife is the most important thing to have in the wild."

"You put a great deal of thought into it. You're more clever than anyone I've met your age, except for maybe Madison. She thinks the way you think. I couldn't tell you who would win in a mind-battle between you two, but I'm starting to figure out what she sees in you."

"Thanks Mike, but flattery won't work. I'm still not untying you," I said.

Mike got angry, and if I'd had a bar of soap to stick in his mouth, I would have. His language got pretty bad there for a while as he struggled against the rope.

"You know, if you don't calm down, I might not give you the last granola bar," I said.

"You can take that granola bar and shove it up your ass," barked Mike.

"Hey, it's not my fault you're in the trouble you're in. Actually, I take that back, it is my fault. Or at least part my fault. It's also part your fault for underestimating me."

"I never make the same mistake twice," said Mike, calming down a little.

"So, I suppose we're going to be out here a while. May as well get to know each other. What got you into the spy business?" I asked.

After a few moments of silence, Mike finally started telling me his story.

"When I was your age, I didn't really have any goals. My high school guidance counselor basically told me I wasn't good at anything, so I should go into the military," said Mike.

"I wonder just how many people's lives have been ruined by bad guidance counselors," I said.

"No joke," added Mike. "Anyway, it worked out okay for me. I kinda like the work, proving that I can survive on my own, even in hostile environments. I also thought I was helping save the world. That's kind of what led me here, to White Ops."

"Are you still a field agent?" I asked.

"No," replied Mike, in a very serious tone.

"How come?"

"No superpowers."

"That makes sense. Then how did you get involved with White Ops?"

"I had a run in once with Dantalion. I barely survived it. I ended up with thirty stitches across my stomach where he cut me. He thought I was dead, but I'm kind of stubborn like that. Never did fit into anyone's plans. Anyway, it's supposed to be a big secret that superheroes exist, so the government had to make a choice: either let me die or induct me. After some deliberating, Director Scott stepped in and said he'd use me. I agreed, because it seemed a hell of a lot better than the alternative. Scott's a good man. Haven't ever had a problem with him, so I'm loyal. It's not the threat of death that keeps me here. That's one thing you'll learn some day; the value of a good boss. I'd rather make peanuts and work for a good boss than make six-figures and work for an asshole."

"So wait, Dantalion used to work for White Ops, back when it was Gray Ops. Did you have to work with him after that?" I asked.

"No, I came in after Dantalion left the fold. I've only been working here about a year," said Mike.

"So then how old was Madison when she started dating Dantalion?"

"Sixteen."

"And he was?"

"Twenty-four."

"That asshole!"

"Yeah, that's how I felt. Anyway, they hid it from everyone. She was a young, very sweet and very naive girl. She had no idea what she was doing. He did though. He knew that he had her under his spell. Literally. I wouldn't doubt if he had some kind of charm power or something that made her lose all of her sense. Do yourself a favor and don't blame her for that relationship. It really wasn't her fault," said Mike.

I thought to myself for a moment.

"Thanks for telling me that, Mike. I'd already figured it was something like that, but it's good to hear from someone outside of the situation," I said.

"You didn't hear that from me. Madison would beat the crap out of me if she heard that I'd told you."

"No worries. I'll take it to my grave."

"Hopefully that'll be a long way off, kid."

25

I was able to stay awake by chatting with Mike the entire night. I found out that he'd never been married, but came close once, and didn't have any kids. He was a loner by nature and didn't feel like he'd really missed out. He isn't that old, so I guess there's still time for him, but time never stops or goes backwards, so he isn't getting any younger.

Once the sun started coming up, I went ahead and let Mike go. He stood up and took a swing at my head, but I easily ducked it. His body had been in such an uncomfortable position for so long that his arms and legs didn't work right. I landed a punch to Mike's gut, which doubled him over.

"Why'd you try and hit me?" I asked.

It took a moment for Mike to catch his breath and respond.

"Payback for keeping me tied up all night," said Mike.

"I thought the whole point was to survive."

"You weren't supposed to catch me so early and so easily. Actually, you weren't supposed to catch me at all."

"At least I gave you that extra granola bar. Didn't that help at all?"

"No."

"Yeah, well, get over it. Your job is to teach me how to survive, and I exceeded expectations."

"You want I should hum 'Pomp and Circumstance'?"

"The song they play at graduations? Nah, I'm good."

I helped Mike stand back up. Once he got fully upright he lunged for me. I ducked out of the way again and kicked him in the shin.

"Okay, fine, I've had enough," said Mike, rubbing his leg.

I took him at his word. I don't know if I should have, but I decided to. We walked back out of the forest and made our way to the base. Director Scott was inside waiting for us.

"So how'd it go, Mike?" he asked.

"I hate this kid. Within the first twenty minutes he had me tied to a tree, and tortured me all night with his constant yammering. He took my gun and my food. When he let me go, I tried getting revenge a few times, and he punched and kicked me. He's got heart, and the turd on top of his shoulders works pretty good," said Mike.

"That's great to hear," said Director Scott, smiling a too-big smile for Mike.

"Yeah, great, whatever," was Mike's response.

"Can I get some sleep now?" I asked.

"Sure, you can do whatever you want," said Director Scott. "I wouldn't recommend going home though. No telling if Dantalion will come after you or not. Madison's staying at a local hotel, so you might call her and see if you can crash on her couch."

Scott handed me my phone, wallet and keys, as well as a slip of paper with Madison's number on it. I went outside and gave Madison a call.

"Hello?" said Madison in her adorably sexy sleepy-voice.

"Good morning, sunrise," I said.

"Taylor! Is everything okay?"

"Yup, I survived a sleepless night in the forest. Any chance I could crash there?"

"Yeah, absolutely."

Madison gave me the directions to the hotel, which I memorized, then I hopped in the Challenger and sped off. The drive wasn't too far, but it was really tough keeping my eyes open. To keep from falling asleep at the wheel, I rolled down the windows and let the cool morning air slap my face like I'd insulted its mother. I also cranked up the radio, and listened to some AC/DC. I'm a sucker for classic rock, if you hadn't picked up on that. It's part of the reason I like the show Supernatural. That and I'm big into classic muscle cars, like the Chevy Impala they drive. Challengers, Mustangs, Camaros, 'Vettes, 'Cudas and Chevelles, too.

Anyway, I pulled up into the hotel named Luna Del Mar. It wasn't part of any chain, and it looked a little scary from the outside. There was a picture of a mermaid holding the moon like a beach ball on the front of the lobby. She had a knowing smirk that implied she knew something naughty was going down, which I imagine happened often in a seedy hotel like that. Once I got inside, however, I was amazed. It looked like the kind of place I'd have to sell a kidney to stay in.

As I walked in, one of the young women at the desk asked if she could help me, which made me blush just a little. I explained I already knew where I was headed and thanked her. She gave me a smile that honestly made me feel a little uncomfortable, especially considering I was heading to meet my girlfriend, who was gorgeous and didn't have her parents around. I guess it was one thing when her folks were just across the street, but it was different when we were going to be in the same hotel room. Together. Alone.

I walked over to the elevator and waited. It took a moment for it to finally reach the lobby. I saw my reflection in the brass doors and I realized just how crappy I looked. I must have smelled like it too, being active and outside for so long.

Eventually the elevator doors opened and an elderly couple got out. I smiled to them and held the doors open to make their departure easier. They thanked me and smiled as they left. I boarded the elevator, which was also wall-to-wall brass. It was kind of amazing how clean and shiny they kept everything. I pushed the button for the seventh floor then leaned back against the far wall as the doors shut and closed my eyes. I let out a big sigh, releasing some of the pent up tension I held on to. Kind of a lot had happened recently.

Six floors came and went, and the elevator mercifully made no stops. I got off the elevator and made my way to room seven-twenty-seven, the room Madison was staying in. Not having one of those credit card room keys I realized I'd have to knock. I gave it a quiet little tap to see if she was awake. I could see the light from the peephole disappear and I figured she was looking through it. The door unlocked from the inside and opened ever so slightly. I heard her move away from the door.

"Come in," said Madison.

So I came in. I opened the door, and standing about ten feet inside was Madison, completely naked. Just standing there. Nude. No clothes. Not even socks.

My jaw dropped. I closed my eyes for a second, took a deep breath and reopened them. She was still there. And she was still naked. I closed the door behind me and locked it.

Madison walked up to me slowly, kissing me on the lips. I started to kiss her back, but I realized how gross I must have been, so I stopped her.

"As much as I want to, I can't do this right now, baby. I need a shower; badly," I said.

Madison took the news well, but I could still tell she was disappointed. She stood there thinking for a second.

It took all of my self-control to turn away from her and shower. Have I ever mentioned that I hate having self-control? I made my way into the bathroom, started the shower then peeled off my dirty clothes. I unwrapped the little oatmeal-vanilla soap the hotel supplied and climbed into the shower.

I have to say, it was probably the most relaxing and energizing shower I'd ever taken. I was so tired and sore, and it made me feel like a million bucks. After about a minute of just letting the warm water run all over my tired body I heard the door to the bathroom creak open. Madison crept inside, pulled back the shower curtain and climbed in.

To say I was excited would be an understatement. She'd pulled her hair back into a ponytail to keep her hair from getting wet. I almost lost control of myself right there, but thankfully I didn't.

"I thought you might be too tired to wash yourself, so I thought maybe I could do it," said Madison, trying to act innocent but failing completely.

I smiled at her, letting her know it was okay.

Her eyes flashed in excitement. She reached down to the soap tray and lathered up the oatmeal-vanilla bar in her hands. Her smile had faded for a second, but when she looked into my eyes again, she couldn't help but smile. Madison saw the love and attraction that I felt for her in my eyes, and it made her just a little bit shy. She blushed and giggled then went to work.

She had me turn around, so that the water beat down on my bare chest as she ran her hands from the top of my neck down my shoulders, past my biceps and to my hands. She slipped her soapy hands in mine, gave them a quick squeeze then swept them back up to my shoulders.

Madison reached her arms around my chest and rinsed her hands off for a second then re-lathered them with soap. She took her time washing my back, and even more time washing my butt cheeks. It seemed that she enjoyed squeezing them as much as I enjoyed having them squeezed.

"Okay, turn around," she said in that sweet, sexy voice of hers.

I did what she said. I'd do anything she asked me to. Madison looked down and saw the effect she was having on me. This made her eyes flash again. After a few seconds of staring she embraced me, running her hands over my back and shoulders, rinsing the soap off.

Once she'd finished rinsing my back off, she coated her hands again in soap then rubbed them vigorously up and down my chest, working occasionally to my biceps so that she could give them testing squeezes. I couldn't help but smile, and she smiled back at me. Her teasing was the sweetest torture I'd ever felt.

It was too much for me to handle. I needed her. To feel what it was like to be one with her. I kissed her, held her in my arms, pulled her tightly against me so that there was no space between our bodies. They fit together so perfectly, so naturally; it was like we were made for each other.

She stopped kissing me for a second.

"Not yet. Not here," she whispered in my ear.

I love Madison, and I respect her completely. I would never ask her to do something she was uncomfortable with, so I stopped and moved my hands to her lower back, keeping her tightly against me. We kissed; our tongues probing each other's mouths as we let the water rain down on us, warming us. It was so intense, so amazing, that it almost didn't seem real.

I've never loved anyone the way I love Madison, and I never will. Everything I am, everything I will be, everything I was ever meant to be is because of her. I'd do anything for her, even risk my life for her.

Once we calmed down and relaxed we rinsed off. I took special care in cleaning all of her tender spots. I still didn't know what I'd done to deserve a girl like her, but I was hoping to earn her love, to prove to her that her faith and trust in me was well placed.

We used the hotel's big, fluffy white towels to dry each other. It was cool just getting to know each other's bodies; touching, rubbing and teasing. Once we were dry, I held her hand and walked her back to the bedroom.

"Baby, I think I'm going to pass out now. Feel free to take advantage of me if you want, but I've been awake the last thirty-six hours, and I'm about to slip into a coma," I said.

She kissed me, a very sweet, fun type of kiss.

"No worries. I'm absolutely starving, and they're serving breakfast right now. I'll go downstairs and eat, and you can rest." She kissed me again. "I love you, Taylor Swift."

"I love you, Madison Swift," I said.

She stopped dead in her tracks and blushed. Her mouth opened in surprise and she took a moment to think.

"Maybe someday, Taylor. Maybe someday."

26

T o say I slept a lot that day would be an understatement. I think hibernate would be a better word for what I did. I was so exhausted that my body shut down. I slept for ten hours, which was close to a record for me. When I woke up, I also felt somewhat taller. I was supposed to grow a bit more in height, and I think my body took the opportunity to add another half-inch to me while I slept.

Madison spent a good chunk of the day lying next to me in bed, watching TV quietly while I slept. She also went out a few times for groceries and shopping. I hadn't learned this yet, but Madison apparently loves to shop. It's almost a sport for her, like basketball is for me. She's pretty good about following sales and making sure the items that are on sale price are actually good deals. That's one thing I don't like so much about sales: a lot of times they inflate the retail price then make it look like a huge sale, when they're actually just selling it at regular price.

It's also kind of amusing, because it seems like there's always a reason to go shopping. I've heard everything from "it's a beautiful day out, so I'm going shopping," to "I feel really sad/bored/unhappy/tired/etc. so I'm going shopping." One time I even heard "it's Wednesday, so I'm going shopping."

Canada Day and Boxing Day are also two days she likes to celebrate with shopping, even though she isn't Canadian. And she usually gets things when she does go. Her shoe collection, or 'museum' as I like to call it, is filled to the ceiling with shoes. It's a good thing she makes a decent amount of money from her government gig. That's right, your tax dollars are going to making Madison's feet look adorable.

Anyway, once I woke up it was late-afternoon. I snacked on some of the foods that she'd brought back. I had a few of the best oranges I've had in my entire life and some beef jerky. I washed it all down with diet A&W root beer.

"So how did the training go?" asked Madison.

"Pretty good," I said with a smirk.

"Mike wasn't too hard on you, was he?"

"He cussed me out pretty good."

"Why?"

"Well, I kinda tied him to a tree."

"No way!"

"Way."

Madison laughed. A lot. It took a few minutes for her to calm down, and eventually started coughing from all the laughing. I just smiled at her. That content smile you have when everything is right with the world. She caught me smiling at her, and she came over and gave me a kiss. Just one small, perfect kiss, letting me know that she loved me. Nothing sexual about it, just love and appreciation. She also held my hand for a second and squeezed it.

It's amazing how much those little things mean to me. Her being so sweet that she got us snacks. Her kiss. Just the act of holding my hand. I know they seem like such simple, normal things. But I haven't always known normal.

Don't get me wrong, my parents are great, if not a little overprotective. My life hasn't been that particularly rough. I've dated a few girls who weren't so nice. Makes me appreciate the kind of person that Madison is all the more. Sure she's beautiful, and sexy, and makes my heart stop when she walks into the room. But it's the person inside that I love. I've known beautiful girls who were cold-hearted or mean and I can't stand them. I avoid them like the plague. No amount of beauty is worth that.

"So how were you able to tie him up?" asked Madison.

"I set a trap. Made it look like I'd climbed a tree. When he started to go up the rope, I ran out from behind cover and strangled him with my canteen strap," I replied.

"Wow, that's pretty impressive, Taylor. What I would've given to see Mike's face. How long did he stalk you before you got him?"

"I'd say less than an hour."

"I think that may be a course record."

"Really? How long did it take you?" I asked.

"A couple of hours. I did pretty much the same thing. I took off my bra and panties and hung them on a bush. He was so embarrassed when he found them, thinking that I might be in the forest naked, that he got distracted. I snuck up behind him and put a knife to his throat. He gave up quietly and we walked back to base together," said Madison.

"Yeah, I never thought to use my bra and panties to set a trap. I really should have thought of that," I said to Madison, winking. She giggled.

"He took it pretty well," she said, "but I got the feeling he was kicking himself for being distracted. He's actually a really good agent."

"I figured as much. My guess is it's easier being prey if you're well supplied, since you can just set a trap and wait for the enemy to come to you. If you're outnumbered though, you're probably screwed," I guessed.

"Yeah, it makes a difference. So did you guys walk back to base after you tied Mike up?"

"Uh, no. Actually, I left him tied up all night."

"Whoa. Um, Taylor, I think I'm starting to understand why he was cussing you out. Mike's a good sport normally. When he's been caught in a war game, he doesn't make a big deal out of it. I'm sure he tried to convince you that the exercise was over, right?"

"I didn't know if he was telling the truth or not. I was worried that if I untied him, he'd take my weapons and tie me up."

"Nah, he's not like that."

"When I did finally untie him in the morning, he tried to beat me up."

"I can't say I blame him too much. Hopefully you guys get along better next time," said Madison.

"Yeah, hopefully. So when do we start looking for Angela?" I asked.

It took her a moment to respond.

"Soon. We were hoping to hear from Dantalion by now with ransom demands, but we haven't heard anything yet. We figure that if we don't hear from him in the next 24 hours you and I can start looking for him."

"You know, Madison, you're taking this awfully well considering your sister's been kidnapped. I think if I had a sister and she was held hostage, I'd be freaking out right about now."

"Unfortunately, it kind of comes with the territory. I'm trained not to let those kind of emotions get the better of me or cloud my judgment. Plus I know Dantalion isn't going to harm her."

"I thought he was a really bad guy."

"He is, but he wants me to work for him. He probably wants to try and take what he wrongly thought was his too."

"And that is?" I asked.

"My virginity," said Madison.

"That asshole!"

"You don't know the half of it. Anyway, if he hurt Angela at all, he knows I'd rip him apart with my bare hands. Literally. I'd tear his arms off and beat him to death with them."

"That's a scary thought. Remind me not to get on your bad side."

"Don't worry, I don't have much of a bad side. Only for people that threaten those I love. So as long as you don't try and hurt my family, or yourself, we should be good," said Madison, giving me a smile.

27

We watched a couple of DVDs that Madison had brought along: Anchorman and The Losers. I'd seen Anchorman with a friend who didn't have a sense of humor, and it ruined it for me the first time I saw it. Watching it with Madison was perfect. We both laughed at the same stuff, and I had a blast watching it with her. My favorite line in the movie, which I quote a lot, is 'sixty percent of the time it works every time.' Those are some powerful words to live by.

I hadn't seen The Losers yet and it was pretty awesome! I'm surprised I hadn't heard more about it before. Every once in awhile a great movie slips through the cracks, and I think that was one of them. I was really impressed with it, and I don't impress easy when it comes to movies. Was it the Godfather or Raiders of the Lost Ark? Nah, but it was a really solid action flick.

While watching the movies, Madison and I held hands. She rested her head on my chest, and I could smell the scent of her shampoo mixing with her perfume. It was one of those perfect moments you wish you could stay in for the rest of your life. Like the world couldn't possibly be a happier place. Unfortunately, this was the eye of the storm. Everything was deceptively calm and perfect, but underneath the surface was Angela, still kidnapped, and Dantalion still free to hurt people and do what he wanted. Man I hate that guy.

Once we finished the two movies it was getting kinda late, so we went downstairs to the hotel's restaurant, The Green Penguin. I thought it sounded like an old TV show about a superhero that battled ill-tempered fish and climate change. Not a show I'd really be interested in watching. I like my heroes to come out guns a-blazin', defeating bad guys that are actually bad.

Anyway, Madison got chicken fajitas while I got a BLTA that was pretty awesome, the 'A' being avocado. If you've never tried one I highly recommend it. Mine came with a side of fries that I just kind of picked at, and hers came with a side of refried beans that she avoided, probably because she didn't want to be stinky if we were going to be spending the night together. I know what you're saying: girls don't fart. It was a widely spread rumor that I'd heard too when I was a kid. But they do. I saw it on MythBusters.

I tried to pay for dinner, but Madison reminded me that we were on White Ops' dime now. She paid with a credit card they'd given her. I thanked her, and we made our way back up to the room.

When the elevator doors closed behind us, I leaned in and kissed her; a warm, wonderful kiss. As our two bodies came in contact, she reached around my back and gave one of my cheeks a squeeze. It was fun and playful and sexy all at the same time. So I returned the favor by squeezing one of hers. She chirped a little in surprise then went back to kissing me, this time with more passion.

As we kissed, the elevator ascended. I ran a hand through her hair, and as the familiar ding of the elevator finally came, I pulled away from her only inches so that we could look into each other's eyes. Her green eyes picked up the reflection of the brass elevator walls and sparkled like gold. I took her hand and guided her out of the elevator.

The hallway was filled with people's room service trays, set just outside their doors. One of the wait staff walked past us, nodding his head and smiling. I pinched one of Madison's butt cheeks right after he passed by, and she turned to me with a partially shocked, partially smiling expression on her face then playfully hit my chest with her open hand. I just smiled back and winked at her.

She pulled out the plastic credit card style room key, slipped it into the slot for room seven-twenty-seven and opened the door. I looked both directions down the hallway, and as I stood there she grabbed my shirt and yanked me inside.

The room was just how we left it: lights off, curtains open, with snacks and candy scattered on the bed and on the nearby table. Pulling me closer toward her, Madison kissed me. After a brief moment, she pulled away.

Her lips mouthed "I love you", and I mouthed back "I love you too." She smiled again, the biggest smile I'd ever seen, and she said two words that nearly killed me "I'm ready."

"You mean... are you sure?"

"Taylor, I love you, and I want you."

I couldn't tell you why, but I was so touched by it that I started to tear up a little. Here was this perfect angel, and she wanted to be with me. An actual angel. She wanted to give me something sacred, something precious. A gift you can only give once. And she'd chosen me.

After taking off my shoes and socks I shed my jeans; crumpling them on the floor and kicking them away. While she watched, Madison removed her clothing then leaned back onto the bed again. I stood there, looking at her, soaking in her beauty. I bent over and kissed her, and she kissed me. The kiss was filled with innocence and uncertainty.

"Are you sure you want me to do this? I would understand if..."

"Shhhhh, it's okay, Taylor. Yes, I want this more than anything. Just... be gentle."

"Okay. I love you, Madison."

"I love you too, Taylor."

As we became one she cried a little, but smiled at me. I leaned down and laid on top of her, kissing her on the lips as gently as I could. Her kiss was a kiss of reassurance, letting me know she was okay despite the pain, and despite the tears, and that she was glad that I was sharing this experience with her.

I reached for her hands, lacing my fingers between hers, moving them up towards her head. I kissed her perfectly formed mouth, which was traced by a moonbeam that cast an unearthly blue haze in the room.

Taking things as slowly as I could, Madison winced in pain but seemed to enjoy the sensation. Her breathing started to pick up as our bodies danced together. Madison's eyes were electric; reflections of blue lightning arced within them. She made her sexy little grunting sound as I moved faster.

Her skin glowed; white light reflecting off of the walls, casting a shadow of me on the ceiling. Madison started making these very sweet, sexy and feminine 'unh' sounds then lost herself fully to the sensation. As our bodies shook in unison, the strangest thing happened: I started to glow.

It's hard to explain, but it was like being bathed in warm soda. The sensation tingled, and comforted and heated me from within. It was as if part of Madison's essence flowed into me, joining the two of us into a single being.

I kissed her, with more love and passion than I'd ever kissed anyone with before. I imagine it was the same awe I would feel if I could touch the stars. Madison finally opened her eyes and looked at me, shocked by my glowing body. After my body had calmed down, the glow slowly dimmed then disappeared, as did Madison's. Madison just stared at me, not knowing what to say.

"Taylor, are you a... "

"Angel?" I said, finishing her sentence.

"Yes," she replied.

"No baby, I'm not. At least I don't think I am. I'm pretty sure you are the source of my light. I've never done that before."

"I've never had that effect on anyone. I wonder if you have powers now."

"How can I tell?" I asked.

"You can sort of feel them, somewhere in the back of your mind, like something's there burning inside you."

"I'll try, but we should probably get cleaned up a little first."

"Oh, right. I'm just sort of in shock right now. I think we should probably take a shower," suggested Madison.

"Sounds amazing," I said in return.

The shower was more sweet than sexy. Madison and I took turns washing each other's bodies, kissing each other occasionally, and holding each other. I let her shampoo her hair, and because of the possibility of soreness, I let her wash her most tender areas. She seemed to appreciate my concern for her, and she subtly let me know that everything was okay, and that she wasn't in pain anymore.

Toweling off was a little sexier, because I could see all of her body thanks to the large mirror that hung over the bathroom sink. I pulled her close to me. After a brief moment of holding her against my body, she very politely asked me to stop.

"Taylor, I would love to do things again, but I'm just a little sore at the moment. We also both need to get some sleep," said Madison.

"Yeah, you're probably right. Can't blame me for trying though," I said.

"No, I can't blame you at all."

"I love you, Madison, with all my heart."

"I love you too, baby. Let's go get some sleep."

Madison and I were reasonably dry, except Madison spent another ten minutes towel drying her hair before we went to bed. It was late enough in the evening she didn't want to wake up the neighbors by running the hair dryer. While I waited, I popped on the TV. The hotel had a few cable channels to pick from so I watched Storage Wars for a while. I'm not really into the whole buying locker thing as much as I want to see the cool things people find. I kind of think of it like Indiana Jones, where people are in search of long lost treasure. That and Barry cracks me up.

Once Madison finished drying her hair, she came over to the king-sized bed I was lying on and had me move to the right side of it. Climbing into bed next to me, naked, she scooted herself close to me. She rested her head on my chest as we watched Dave and Jarrod get into a bidding war. By the time the auction was over, Madison was already fast asleep, breathing lightly. She twitched a couple of times and eventually rolled onto her left side, away from me. I slid in next to her, draped my arm across her stomach, and drifted off to sleep as I held her in my arms. Just before I drifted off I whispered "goodnight, angel."

28

I woke up a couple of times during the night, realizing that Madison was talking in her sleep. I couldn't really make out much of the conversation she was having with herself, but the names Angela, Dantalion and thankfully Taylor all made appearances. Even though she'd been so focused on me the previous day, it was nice to know that Angela and her safety were still the most important things to her.

I was able to get back to sleep quickly, so that when seven-in-the-morning finally rolled around I'd gotten a reasonable night's sleep. We'd shifted positions a lot in the middle of the night; as it turns out we're both active sleepers. She'd pushed the covers over onto my side, so that she was lying next to me naked and completely exposed save for her feet, which were partially covered by the sheets. I noticed her stir a little but not open her eyes.

We eventually got out of bed and took showers, this time separately. It was my idea, because I knew she needed time to deal with the soreness of her new discovery, and I figured we wouldn't be able to keep our hands off of each other long enough to get clean. Trying to be a gentleman, I let her shower first.

While I waited for her, I tried tapping into whatever powers she may have given me, if any, when she made me glow. Some of her essence had become a part of me, and would never leave. I've heard people say they carry around a part of their loved one with them. I'm blessed to be able to say that's true for me too.

Anyway, I wasn't able to do anything. I didn't seem to have any powers. I tried lighting the carpet on fire with my mind. I tried to tear a phone book in half with no luck. It still hurt when I pinched myself. I couldn't even float the Gideon Bible with my thoughts when I pretended to be Yoda lifting an X-Wing out of the bog. I guess he was right, 'there is no try'.

I was a little disappointed, because I thought it would be cool to be like Madison. Be a superhero, rescuing people, saving lives; making a difference in the world. It's taken me awhile to realize that I could've been doing those things all along, even without powers. I've learned CPR. I donate blood. If I see someone who needs help, I do whatever I can to help them, even if it's just to give them a few bucks.

When I donate blood, it really does make me feel like a hero, and it makes me feel like I'm in the presence of other heroes. It's a pretty selfless thing when you think about it. Donating is a bit of a process to go through, but you get a few things out of it. Juice and a cookie, which honestly kick ass, but I could also get those at 7-11 just down the street. And I get a sticker, which sadly to this day I still find cool. But I get two things that really make it worth it: I make new friends, and I get to help save someone's life every time I donate. It's one of the best ways you can help another person. It really is the gift of life. If you're able to do it, I hope you consider it.

Once Madison had finished getting ready, we made our way downstairs for breakfast. It was a buffet, so I loaded up on protein as much as I could. I had a plate full of scrambled eggs, some bacon, a few sausage patties and I had some orange juice to drink. Madison had eggs too, which she poured Texas Pete on, as well as a pastry that had what looked like raspberry filling in the middle. The breakfast was extremely well made, especially for hotel food. Even their coffee was good, and after Madison raved about it I had a cup too.

With breakfast behind us, we left for White Ops' base of operations. I drove Madison in the Challenger because she didn't have a car and had to take a cab to the hotel. On the way there, Madison called her folks and told them that we didn't have any news yet, but that I'd passed my training with flying colors. I could tell from Madison's end of the conversation that her parents seemed to like me more, now that I was helping with the search for Angela.

It seemed like Angela was a sweet girl, but that wasn't what motivated me. What did motivate me was my love for Madison, and I'd do anything for her, including helping her family. They seemed like decent people who cared about their daughters, but didn't have any experience with this sort of thing, and no superpowers of their own. Otherwise, I have no doubt they'd be out there looking for her.

The trip was spent mostly in silence. I turned on the radio for a change, and we listened to a station that played the top twenty songs of the week over and over and over again. I'd say I like three to five of the songs that repeat and the rest drive me a little crazy. The day was warm but overcast, and made things seem just a little gloomier than normal.

As we neared White Ops, I could tell that Madison's mood had changed. Maybe the reality of the situation started to finally sink in, that her sister was nowhere to be found. I think that she was able to push away her feelings about it when we were together, since there was nothing we could do about the situation, and that Dantalion wouldn't dare kill Angela. Or would he? Not at least until he had Madison in a dangerous position she couldn't get out of. But his ultimate goal was to get Madison back, and hurting Angela would only hurt him. I still wasn't sure if Dantalion was a normal enough person though to make decisions that made sense.

I parked around the back of the house that was falling apart and we got out. Madison came to my side of the car and gave me the greatest hug I'd ever been given. It was warm and fierce.

"Thank you for doing this, Taylor. You have no idea how much it means to me that you're helping out. I want you to know, if at any point you don't feel like you can do this, I want you to go. And if it wasn't for my sister being in danger, I never would allow you to risk your life, especially for me," she said.

"Madison, I have no problem risking my life for you. I love you and I want to help. I want to protect you. I want to be with you."

"You really are the sweetest guy in the world, aren't you?"

"Nah, I'm pretty sure Mr. Cinnabuns is," I said, jokingly.

"The guy on the cinnamon roll packages?"

"Damn straight."

That actually got a smile out of Madison. I was glad that even in the face of everything that was going on I could still make her smile.

"C'mon, we better get inside," I said.

I kissed her once to let her know I loved her, and that I'd always be at her side. I took her hand and walked into the barn with her, stepped onto the lift, and descended into darkness.

29

$\mathbf{M}$ike, Dr. Zumwaldt and Director Scott were at their desks when we got inside the secret underground lair. Their mood was as dark and serious as ours was. We could tell the news wasn't going to be good.

"Madison, Taylor, we haven't been able to figure out where Dantalion's been hiding Angela, so we're going to have you contact some of Dantalion's known associates, and check out some of his old safehouses and pray we get a lead. I've uploaded the information to these two smartphones you'll take with you. They're more than just smartphones. Yes, they have standard functionality like GPS, Angry Birds, and you can even make phone calls with them. Some of the things we've added are a small cutting laser, a composite knife that should be able to make it past most security, and a feature that should only be used in absolute emergencies: it can be detonated to open a safe, a door, or blow up a vehicle when placed near its fuel tank," said Director Scott.

Madison didn't take the news very well, and I could tell she was fighting back tears. I was starting to realize that since Dantalion hadn't contacted White Ops with a list of demands, or tried contacting Madison directly, that the possibility of Angela being in serious trouble had grown significantly. I reached over to Madison and took her hand, giving it a gentle squeeze. She looked at me and I could tell she was on the verge of falling to pieces, so I looked away. I figured if I gave her a shoulder to cry on, she might never stop crying.

The best thing I could do for her was to be strong for her. She nodded her head in understanding, squeezed my hand back firmly and swallowed her pain. Being sad wouldn't help Angela any and we both knew it. It's a testament to Madison's strength that she was able to control her emotions under such difficult circumstances.

"I've put together kits for each of you," said Mike. "They contain some basics like water, granola bars and hiking gear. They also contain handguns, knives and various other equipment. The bags are diplomatic pouches, which means you can take them into any of the countries we consider friends and they won't look inside the bags. So make sure that you don't unseal them while you're traveling. I wish both of you the best of luck."

"Thanks, Mike," said Madison, swallowing hard.

"I've also made you a gift, as it were," said Dr. Zumwaldt. "Inside the diplomatic pouch you'll find a few beakers of acid that may come in handy. We also constructed body armor for young Mr. Swift here. He's not immune to bullets the way you are, Madison."

"Thank you," I said, as I took the vest out of the Doc's hands.

"Just make sure you don't get shot in the face, Taylor. The body armor won't stop a head shot."

"That's good to know. Maybe a little obvious, but I'll keep it in mind," I replied.

I put on the armor and it fit like, well, armor. I felt like if Mike Tyson punched me in the chest, it'd probably knock me on my ass, but at least it wouldn't hurt much when I landed. I did think I looked pretty cool though. And it was pretty impressive they got the size right. It was fairly comfortable, even if it was a little bulky.

"Oh, and another thing Taylor: remember that some knives can penetrate body armor. Don't assume you're invulnerable to everything," said Mike.

"That's also good to keep in mind. Thanks, Mike," I responded.

"Sure kid. Just do me a favor and embarrass that Dantalion prick the way you embarrassed me in the woods. It'd make me feel a hell of a lot better about it."

"Will do."

"Is there anything else we should know?" asked Madison.

"Yes, you'll need to go to the airport straight from here. We've booked a private plane to fly you to Atlanta, and from there you'll be flying to Paris," said Director Scott.

"Wait; Paris, Texas?" I asked.

"No, dumbass: Paris, France," said Mike.

"Madison and I get to go to Paris? Together? That's outstanding!" I said, doing the world's worst job of hiding my excitement.

"It's not a vacation. The two of you will be looking for Angela the whole time," said Director Scott.

That snapped me back to reality. I hadn't been thinking clearly about our mission, because I was too wrapped up in the cool spy gadgets we were going to start using. That, and I love Madison so much the thought of being in the most romantic city in the world together was exciting.

"Yeah, I know," I said.

"It's okay, Taylor. The initial allure of the spy business makes everyone a kid for a few moments. Once you're out in the field though, reality will set in. You'll begin to understand what being a spy is really about. The shine wears off quickly. Anyway, I hope that both of you stay safe. Take care of each other, find Angela and bring her home," said Director Scott.

Madison paused for a second then in turn gave Dr. Zumwaldt, Mike and Director Scott a big hug. It made me just a little more serious about what was to come. I imagine the hug was both a hug of thanks for helping her, and possibly a goodbye hug if things went sideways with our mission. I shook each of their hands, and Mike swung an arm around me and patted my back.

I turned to Madison and struggled to give her a smile. She did her best to return it. We spent a few moments collecting our supplies, slinging bags over our shoulders, when Mike remembered something.

"Take this guitar case. It also has diplomatic markings on it, so that you'll be able to travel with it. Inside is a .50 cal Barrett that I've broken down for you. Taylor, you remember how to assemble it?" asked Mike.

"Yeah, I should be able to," I replied.

"Good. My guess is you won't want to get too close to Dantalion if you can help it. You'll want to provide support for Madison, not fight by her side. She's a lot tougher than she looks. Believe me," said Mike.

"I more than believe you, Mike; I know it. She's the strongest woman I've ever known."

"Damn straight," said Madison.

We all chuckled a little. I turned to Madison, took her hand and walked with her out of the lair, up the lift then into the bleak, sunless sky.

30

"**I'**m driving," said Madison.

"Um, should I be upset that you're demanding to drive my car?" I asked.

"Nope," she said, putting her hands in my pockets in search of keys.

I have to admit, the search made it all worthwhile.

"A little to the left," I said.

"Oh, you mean here?" replied Madison.

"Yeah, that's the place."

Madison gave me a kiss that could kill. After a few seconds of comfortable torture she broke away, taking the keys out of my pocket.

We both hopped in the car, and after she brought up the GPS system on her phone, Madison backed up then popped it into drive, kicking up loose gravel as we sped off. As we were driving along, I noticed she was really pushing my car to its limits.

"Baby?" I said.

"Yes?" she replied.

"You know how you're all indestructible and stuff?"

"Yeah..."

"Well I'm not. Can we keep it under one-sixty?"

"Don't you like to live dangerously?" she asked.

"Oh, sure, I tip cows and cut the tags off of mattresses. Sometimes, when I'm all alone, I drink straight from the milk carton."

"Wow, you really are a stud, aren't you? I bet on the weekends you even sleep in!"

"Damn straight, baby, damn straight. Seriously though, could you slow down just enough that we don't end up going back in time?"

"Wouldn't we need a DeLorean for that?"

"Any car that has a flux capacitor should be able to do it."

"Does yours have a flux capacitor?" she asked.

"Nope, but it has some really nice cup holders," I replied.

"That's VERY impressive," she said, teasing me.

We kept driving, and I did my best to keep her mind off things so that she wouldn't get down about Angela. I knew she was really anxious to get on with the search for her sister. We had no idea whether or not we were going to find anything in Paris, and at this point we didn't have much to go on. Searching was a lot better than just sitting still.

We made it to the airfield in record time, and thankfully they were nearly done refueling the plane. The airport, if you could call it that, had a small control tower run by one person. It was a secret government airstrip, and it was so secret that if you used Google Maps to try and locate it with satellite images, you'd simply see a blank square where the airport should be.

Madison parked the car in the one slot marked 'Long Term Parking.' I have to think it was put there as a joke. We both got out of the car, and got the bags and guitar case from the trunk. Closing it and making sure it was locked, I pocketed the car key after Madison handed it to me. One of the ground crew came up to us.

"Hey, we can valet park your car," said the ground crew guy.

Madison looked at me expectantly.

"Uh, sure, that'd be great," I said, tossing him the keys. He unlocked the car, dropped the keys on the seat and closed the door without locking it. Then he ran back over to us.

"Did you just throw the keys in there?" I asked, wondering what the hell was going on.

"Yeah."

"Shouldn't you like, take it somewhere safe?"

The guy just smiled. The ground started rumbling a little and the parking spot started lowering into the ground, swallowing up my car. It was a platform, just like the one at the White Ops base.

"Oh, okay, never mind, I'm cool," I said. Madison just rolled her eyes at me.

We took our bags over to the plane. It wasn't very big, something that might be called a puddle jumper if I remember correctly. Walking up the steps with our arms full wasn't easy, but we both managed to get up them.

The inside of the plane was freakin' amazing! It had really large seats that were all leather. It also had cup holders and small tables next to each chair. It totally did look like something out of a spy movie. I looked down, and thankfully there wasn't any shag carpet. It was more of a plush really. And no, I don't know how I know what plush is. Just go with it.

Anyway, there was also a self-serve mini-bar, a sound system that could play either music or whatever was being shown on the 40 inch TV. There were no other passengers, and once we'd stowed our bags and sat down, the pilot emerged from the cockpit then pulled up the staircase, sealing the plane.

"You guys can make yourselves at home. Technically, since you're both with the military, and technically, since we're on a military base, you're allowed to have whatever you like from the mini-bar. I just wouldn't recommend getting drunk. The flight will only be about three hours long. Then you'll need to board a commercial airliner, and they might not let you on the plane if you're intoxicated. Anyway, we have forty channels of TV to choose from, so feel free to watch whatever. Is there anything you two need? Because once I get this plane in the air, the door to the cockpit locks and I won't see you again until we land," said the pilot.

"Um, nothing I can think of," said Madison.

"Me neither. Oh, actually, can the seats be used as flotation devices, and do masks drop from the ceiling?" I asked.

"No, but up front here, in the compartment above where you stowed your bags, are two parachutes. If something goes really wrong, put them on and jump out of the plane. You'll know if something is going wrong if I start to cuss over the PA system," said the pilot.

"Great, that's reassuring. At least we'll get away from the crash landing," I said.

"You guys will. There's only two chutes."

"Why wouldn't there be enough for everyone?"

"It helps motivate me to want to land the plane safely," said the pilot.

"I imagine it would," I replied.

"Okay, I'm going to go fly this thing. Buckle up until we're airborne then feel free to move around."

"Thanks," said Madison as the pilot went back to the cockpit, closing the door behind him.

Madison and I sat down in our seats, clasped our belts around us and held hands while we waited for the plane to taxi into position for the takeoff. I noticed the TV remote sitting between us in a cup holder, so I pulled it out and handed it to Madison so she could pick what to watch. Yup, I love her THAT much!

Madison turned on the TV and started flipping through channels. There was a Burn Notice marathon on, so we watched it for a while.

"You know, Taylor, they do a pretty good job of getting things right on Burn Notice. Not always, but most of the time," she said.

"Like what kind of stuff?" I asked.

"The spy stuff."

"Oh, that's kinda cool, actually. And I guess you would know, huh?" I said, smiling.

"Obviously," she said, seeming slightly annoyed with me.

We sat in silence for a few minutes.

"Baby," I started, "are you doing okay?"

"What do you mean?" she asked.

"I dunno. You seem a little... off right now."

"Oh, I'm sorry. I'm just not the biggest fan of flying. On top of that, I'm starting to get more and more worried about Angela. I seriously don't think Paris will pan out, and I hate the thought that she might still be here in the States while we're halfway around the world."

"I can totally understand that."

She turned to me and gave me a sad smile.

"You're fine," she said. "And I'm glad you're with me. I don't know if I could do this alone."

"I'm glad I'm with you, too."

31

The plane was in position, and after a few seconds the engines roared, pulling the plane forward. Madison gripped my hand tightly and closed her eyes. She has the softest hands I've ever felt. So delicate and so tiny in comparison to my big mitts. My hands were calloused from working out, and felt like sandpaper, the way a guy's hands should feel. Hers were the opposite in every way.

That's one of the things that I love most about her: that she can be genuinely tough when she wants or needs to be, but when it's just me and her, she's very, very feminine. I wasn't lying when I told Mike she was the strongest woman I'd ever known. She has an inner strength, an inner confidence that lets you know she's seen everything, and can handle anything.

The plane eventually got up to speed then lifted into the air. The momentary feeling of weightlessness made Madison a little uneasy, but once the plane steadied she relaxed her grip.

The pilot's voice came over the PA system.

"Okay guys, you can feel free to move around the plane. Just remember, don't do too much drinking, for your own sakes. If you really need my attention, there's an intercom next to the cockpit door. I hope you enjoy your flight, and thank you for choosing Clandestine Air."

Madison laughed a little at what the pilot had said about the name of the airline. She knew that there really wasn't a name for the 'airline' we were on. I had no clue one way or the other, so I just smiled. We unbuckled our belts and got up and walked around. Madison went straight for the bathroom, while I made my way to the mini-bar. It also had a fridge, which I opened and found Bloody Mary mix, orange juice, ginger ale, Sprite, Coke, maraschino cherries, pearl onions, olives, lemons, limes and a bottle of champagne.

I'd never had a Bloody Mary before and I'd always wanted to try one, so I poured the mix into a glass sitting on a rack next to the fridge. I remembered it was supposed to be mixed with vodka, so I looked at the rack of bottles on the other side of the fridge. I found a bottle of Smirnoff Vodka, so I poured some into the glass. I had no idea how much I should put in it, so I just kind of guessed. I looked around for something to stir it with, and in a tray lower down in the fridge was a bunch of celery sticks. I pulled one out and threw it in my glass. I used it to stir the drink around then took a sip.

It was the first time I'd ever had alcohol. After I took a big swig I realized that the vodka was kind of bitter. Not a lot, it didn't change the flavor of the spicy tomato juice much, but I definitely could tell the difference. My face got warm for some reason and I could feel my cheeks and my ears turn red. After my second sip, Madison came out of the bathroom. She was a little surprised to see me drinking, but she didn't say anything about it.

"I figured since we're here, and we're not driving or doing anything dangerous, that it might be okay to try a little. Don't worry, I'm not going to get drunk or anything. I just thought that since it's legal and all, and free, that I'd try it once. Would you like to try it?" I asked.

"No thanks, I don't think a Bloody Mary is my kind of thing. I might try a margarita though," she said.

"I'll see if I can find the fixings."

I looked in the fridge, and tucked in the back was a bottle of Margaritaville margarita mix.

"I think I found it," I said.

I poured the mix into a glass for her and looked on the back of the bottle for a recipe. I realized too late that I was supposed to put lime juice around the rim and coat it with salt, but I figured I would have made a big mess with the salt anyway if I'd tried. It looked like it was a mix of about 3/4 margarita mix and 1/4 tequila. I found a bottle of tequila called Patron, which I pronounced 'pay-truhn'. This made Madison giggle, and she informed me she had heard it pronounced 'pah-trone' before.

"Wow, I guess we know who the drunk is in our relationship," I joked. She just laughed and shook her head in disapproval.

"I think the name's Spanish," she said.

"Well that makes sense I guess. Do you speak Spanish?" I asked.

"Si, muy bien Senior," was her response.

"I only know one phrase: mi pantalones es su pantalones!"

Madison just laughed. Have I mentioned I love her laugh? It makes me feel warm all over when I hear it. I know, I know; on with the story.

I sliced up a lime into wedges and stuck a thick wedge on her glass then handed it to her. She took a sip and her eyes got REALLY big. It was the first time she'd ever had alcohol before, and just like me her skin flushed. It was pretty effing cute. Then she took another sip, and another. I must have done a decent job on it because it didn't take her long to drink the rest. It took me another few minutes to down the Bloody Mary and eat the piece of celery I'd put in it.

I like celery; it's kind of nature's tooth floss. Oh, and the best smell in the world is Christmas morning when my Mom cooks up diced celery, onion and butter to make stuffing for the turkey. On a scale of one to ten of smells, it's easily a twelve-thousand.

Anyway, Madison asked me for another.

"Um, Madison, are you sure that's such a good idea? Remember, we probably shouldn't get drunk. And we don't know how much we can drink before we start doing crazy stuff, or dangerous stuff, or stupid stuff," I mentioned.

"We're locked in this room, and don't get me wrong, it's a beautiful room, but it's for the next three hours. I think I'll be fine by then. Also, I have you to protect me. My beautiful knight in shining armor," said Madison.

I thought about it for a minute. She was probably right, it probably wouldn't hurt her to have another. I just wanted to make sure that if something did go wrong, she'd be able to react to the situation. I just love Madison so much that I don't want her to be injured or worse. I imagine it's the same thing that spouses of police officers go through; worried if they'll come home at night. It's a crazy world out there, and life is short, and I know people say it a lot, but we really need to treat every day like it's our last, because it always could be our last.

I've come close to death a number of times in my life, and it's really inspired me to try and do the best I can with the time I have. I try to tell people what I mean. Tell the people that I love and respect that I love and respect them. Deal with issues between me and other people when they happen, and not leave them stewing in the background.

"Okay, Madison, I'll make you another one but not as strong. How about that?" I asked.

"Sure. That sounds like a wise idea. Wow, looks AND brains. RAWR!!!!" said Madison.

It totally made me blush and look away, smiling. So I mixed another margarita up for her, this time with only a very small amount of Tequila in it. I added a little water from a bottled water to it, just to make sure the flavoring wasn't too strong. I handed her the glass, and she started gulping it down.

"Almost as good as the last one," she said.

"Well I'm glad you still liked it. So what do you want to do, baby?" I asked, sitting back down in one of the seats.

"Hmmmm, well, I did have an idea."

"Oh, really? What would that be?" I asked, curious what she was thinking about.

"You ever heard of the mile-high club?" she asked.

"I think I have, but I don't know what it means," I admitted.

"Well, let's just say that only a small and exclusive group are members. Speaking of members... " she said, coming so close to me I could feel her lime flavored breath on my face.

She reached down and started to rub me through my jeans. I was kinda surprised she wanted a little bit of the Taylor while we were flying. I was glad she was over her fear of flying, but this I didn't expect.

Madison reached in and kissed me, warm and wet. I learned something interesting about women that day. Apparently when women drink, they have a tendency to also get... excited. Not all of them, but definitely most of them. I desperately tried to fight her off. No, not really. I loved the attention, and the sensation, and more importantly I loved Madison.

She pulled her tank-top up over her head and down her hair and undid her bra. This one clasped in the back. It was this beautiful blue color with sparkly things on it that reminded me of the night sky. Then she let it slip down her arms, catching it and throwing it aside.

We spent the next hour together: moving, feeling, and caressing. It was amazing. As we slowed down and eventually stopped, I kissed her neck. We relaxed and enjoyed how tired and in love we were.

I breathed in the deepest breath and felt alive. Madison's glow eventually faded, but her smile did not. Neither did mine. You couldn't have wiped the smile off my face with a sledgehammer and a blowtorch.

32

Eventually, Madison stood up and pulled away from me, but turned around and gave me a sweet, warm, perfect kiss. Even after what we'd just done it made my heart pound. She walked to the restroom to clean up, and eventually returned with supplies to help me clean up as well.

The rest of the flight we just sat next to each other holding hands, watching more Burn Notice. What got me watching it in the first place was Bruce Campbell. My Dad had me watch Army of Darkness with him. I spent an hour and a half laughing uncontrollably. Some of my favorite movie lines come from that movie. Every once in awhile I'll turn to Madison and say "give me some sugar, baby", or I'll pull my pants down and say "this is my boom-stick!" And yes, she gives me about the same reaction you just did.

Eventually the pilot came on the intercom. And by 'came on the intercom' I just mean that he talked on the intercom. Don't be weird.

"We'll be landing in the next fifteen minutes. I'd appreciate it if the two of you were fully clothed by the time we land, since I'll have to help you out of the plane," said the pilot.

Madison and I looked at each other and we both laughed. Madison's face turned a very beautiful deep pink color, and her mouth was wide open in shock. I just started laughing at her. That caused Madison to slug my arm playfully, and thankfully she wasn't glowing at the time. I figure if she ever powered up and hit me, she'd rip a hole clean through me.

The good news was we were already clothed and had been for the better part of an hour, so even though the pilot may have suspected we were up to something sexy, he couldn't see or hear what we were doing, so he didn't actually know. That made it slightly less embarrassing, but only slightly.

We buckled our seat belts after putting all of the drinks and other stuff away then went back to holding hands. Madison seemed to be handling flying much better now that she had a good experience on a plane, but she still squeezed my hand firmly as the plane landed. It took another ten minutes to taxi over to the gate once we landed at Hartsfield-Jackson. It all went smoothly, and once we came to a stop we unbuckled our belts and collected our things.

Madison looked at me, smiled, set down her bags then gave me the biggest hug I'd ever had in my life. She squeezed me so hard I was worried about breathing, but I dropped my bags and hugged her back. It was nice just standing there, holding her. It's funny how sometimes a hug can have as much, if not more meaning than a kiss. I've always been a big fan.

Anyway, we heard the door to the pilot's cabin unlatch and he came out smiling, pretending to be relieved that we were fully clothed. The pilot opened the door, allowing us to climb out and down a set of stairs, but not before we both gave him a handshake of thanks.

I did however notice the pilot checking out Madison's butt as she made her way down the stairs. I can't exactly blame him, it is beautiful, but it still made me want to punch him. It's funny how someone that can make you feel all soft and warm and squishy and sweet inside, like Madison, can also make you want to murder people.

We had to walk a ways to get to our connecting flight: first up a set of moving stairs to enter the building then down a long hallway to gate 23. I hadn't looked at our tickets yet, but I jokingly thought to myself how weird it would be if the company that we were flying with was Oceanic, like on the TV show 'Lost'. Then I started having images of crashing planes in my head, mixed with polar bears and killer clouds of dust. Not good.

We sat down in the terminal only briefly before they announced that our plane would be boarding. White Ops had been nice enough to provide us with VIP boarding, so we were able to get on the plane almost immediately. We stowed our luggage in the overhead bins, and aside from a few well-dressed suits we were alone in our section. I offered Madison the window seat, but she thought that she'd rather have the aisle seat instead.

I found it ironic that someone who could fly disliked being on planes so much. But I guess I can see how they'd be different, since when you're using your angel wings you're in complete control of your movements, and you're also glowing and invulnerable at the same time. I'd also come to realize she was worried for me, since I wasn't invulnerable, and I couldn't fly. If something happened to the flight, my one chance would be for her to protect me, jumping out of the plane with her. But I held her hand and squeezed it, and reassured her that the flight would be anything but exciting.

Once the plane was full, but before we started to taxi to the runway, I got up and got into our bags. White Ops did something extra cool and gave us Kindles to use on the flight. They were the black and white touch kind, which weren't quite as cool as the Kindle Fire, but the batteries lasted longer, so we could use them during our trip without having to recharge them.

An announcement came over the intercom telling us to stow our electronic devices until they announced they were safe to use, and even then we had to turn the Wi-Fi off. I tucked my Kindle in the pocket of the seat in front of me and leaned back. The seats were fairly comfortable, which is something you want on an eight and a half hour flight. I squirmed around a little, making sure I was as comfortable as I could get.

The flight attendants eventually went over the rules and safety features of the plane, something I'd heard before but tried to pay attention to, especially since there was someone out there wanting to kill me. It's funny how that makes you extra careful. And actually, I didn't know that Dantalion wanted to kill me for sure, but I took it on faith he did. Just like I take it on faith that when I step outside my home, I'll be able to breathe the air.

Madison and I held hands again as the plane took off, and I stared out the window as we left the ground. The sky was sunny and blue, and I could only see a few scattered clouds off in the distance.

I turned to Madison and smiled, and she returned my smile, only this time it was a more comfortable smile. She seemed less afraid of flying than she had, which was a really good thing. She leaned over and gave me a very sweet kiss, but kept the sexy out of it, since we didn't have any way to enjoy ourselves more without being obvious about it.

After a few more minutes the pilot came on the intercom and let us know we could start using electronic devices as long as we had them in airplane mode. I pulled the Kindle back out of the pouch and started looking through the books that were preloaded on it. There were a few that grabbed my interest, but the one I decided to go for was 'Hunger Games'. I'd seen the movie and thought it was really cool, so I figured I'd give the book a shot. I could have jumped to 'Catching Fire', but generally the book is filled with a lot more than the movie. I wanted the full experience.

I glanced over at Madison and saw the digital cover of the book she was about to read on her Kindle. It was '50 Shades of Grey'. I looked over at her with big eyes and a shocked look on my face, which she turned and saw. Her face went bright red. It made me want to push the recline button on her seat and lie on top of her sexy body.

"I so totally caught you!" I said.

"I don't know what you're talking about, Taylor," she replied, squinting at me.

"I can't believe you're reading that," I said teasingly. "I've heard there's all kinds of dirty stuff in there."

"Maybe I like the dirty stuff. Are you complaining about me liking the dirty stuff?"

"No ma'am, I most certainly am not."

"Well, then just be glad that you have a girlfriend with an open mind. Maybe you can be a boyfriend with an open mind, too."

She had me there. I love that she is so adventurous. Believe me, I love the normal, sweet love-making, but every now and again it's fun to push the limits. Try new things. I would be willing to do anything that Madison wanted to do. I love her that much. She's also just that sexy.

33

I went back to reading and let Madison read her smut. I say that jokingly of course. Or semi-jokingly, anyway. I have to say, I really loved reading about Katniss. The book is better than the movie, but I have to say for an adaptation the movie was extremely good.

I read for a few hours, and eventually the flight attendants rolled a cart down our aisle. I opted for a can of ginger ale and a turkey sandwich with cheddar cheese. The sandwich was kind of bland, but not bad considering it was airplane food. I almost always get ginger ale when I fly. When I was eleven, I was in this team competition thing in Colorado. On the flight there a girl on my team that I had a crush on asked for a ginger ale, so I decided I'd try it too. It was pretty damn good. That summer she changed schools. It broke my little eleven year old heart into a thousand pieces, but I still like to have ginger ale on flights.

Madison ordered a ham sandwich with Swiss, and gobbled that sucker up like she'd been starving for a week. Can't blame her after all the calories we'd burned on the previous flight. Her drink of choice was Diet Coke, and she made these tiny girl-burps as she drank it.

I spent the rest of the flight reading, totally enjoying the book. I was nearly finished by the time the plane started its descent into Paris. The pilot asked us to turn off our electronic devices so I did my best to speed read through the last two pages before turning it off. I held Madison's hand as the plane landed in Paris, where it was very early in the morning and still dark out. We probably should have slept on the flight, but she was too worried about the plane, and I was too worried about her.

Charles de Gaulle airport wasn't terribly busy that early in the morning. I guess people don't like flying in the middle of the night. As we walked down the gate hallway, Madison reached over and held my hand and smiled at me. I could tell though she was worrying again as the smile quickly faded. I squeezed her hand, and we made our way to the baggage claim. It took forty-five minutes for our bags to finally come through the conveyor belt, along with everyone else's. We had to get one of those roll cart things to move our luggage because of the diplomatic bags we'd been given.

I have a feeling the holdup with the bags was due to us, and my guess is that someone had taken a peek inside our bags despite the diplomatic tags on everything.

So we took the cart outside to a row of taxis. One of the drivers, who looked kind of like Jean Reno, waved us over. If you don't know who Jean Reno is, you should find out. He's an incredible actor, and he's been in movies like 'Mission Impossible', 'Ronin', and one of my absolute favorites 'Leon: The Professional'. He has a pretty cool deep voice. When I looked over at Madison it was like she could read my mind. She smiled with her mouth open and nodded her head up and down.

Anyway, with help from the driver we got the bags into the trunk. Madison and I sat together in the back seat, which wasn't very roomy. The car was just big enough to fit a family of four garden gnomes, including their evil pointy hats. I couldn't tell you why, but I think if it all ended tomorrow, the gnomes would take over the world. They scare me, with their pink cheeks and beards, and tiny gnome boots. I should have a t-shirt printed up that says 'Must Kill Gnomes.' Gnomes are way scarier than zombies. You can run away from zombies, but you can't outrun the gnomes!

Madison handed the driver a slip of paper with an address I couldn't make out, and started talking to him in what sounded like fluent French. She had the SEXIEST French accent when she spoke! I almost lost control of myself. When Madison was done speaking, I turned to her and whispered in her ear.

"I didn't know you could speak French."

"You never asked," she replied, smiling.

"Sometime, when we're making out, you HAVE to use your French accent. It is so incredibly sexy!" I said.

"We'll see," she said, wearing a huge smile.

I watched out the window as we went speeding down narrow streets. Buildings rose up on both sides of the road, making me feel a little claustrophobic. The architecture was pretty amazing. Everything looked like it was a few hundred years old. The entire city was lit up like the Fourth of July. I started getting a little carsick from all the crazy driving the cabbie was doing.

Ten minutes into one of the most uncomfortable drives of my life, we arrived at the Hotel Fouquet's Barriere. I know I don't have the right little squiggles over the letters, but bear with me. The taxi driver was nice enough to help us pull out the luggage, and a bellhop standing outside took our bags immediately, placing them on a luggage cart and wheeling it inside. Madison gave the driver a really nice tip, and he got in the car and sped off down the road.

Walking inside, my mind nearly melted. The front area had this amazing lighted mirror display, framed against a black curving desk. The white marble floor reminded me of something you might see in a James Bond film; super polished with a few simple black stripes. Beautiful wood panels lined the wall behind the desk, making the whole thing seem both fancy and warm.

We went up to the desk and Madison spoke sexy to the concierge. Hey, now that I think about it, that's a French word. Okay, Wikipedia says the word 'concierge' comes from the phrase 'Comte Des Cierges' which means 'The Keeper of the Candles'. Wow, even the meanings of French words are fancy!

Madison received a card key from the concierge. As we walked away, a woman came from a door near the desk and she pushed our cart to the elevator for us. I turned and whispered to Madison.

"Baby, why is she moving the luggage for us?" I asked.

"It turns out we get our own personal butler," she said.

"Seriously? What does she do?"

"She buttles. Duh," said Madison, playfully.

I snorted. The three of us got onto the elevator.

"So did they give us a good room?" I asked.

"The best: the Presidential Suite. "

"I'm guessing that was expensive."

"Very. It costs more than twice what your car is worth to stay here."

"Wow."

"Per night."

"Oh, holy crap!" I said, finally letting it sink in. "Why is the government willing to pay for all this?"

"They aren't entirely. France owes the US a few favors. I've helped stop a few terrorist plots here."

"Dang," I said. I pointed to a bulge on the butler's side. "Wait, is she packing?"

"Yes, everyone here doubles as security. When you have a fortress, especially one that caters to the cream of the cream, you have to protect them. Even the people at the front desk were carrying," replied Madison.

"I totally missed that. I was probably too distracted by the light up mirror desk downstairs," I said, smirking.

"Well, you are a guy. It's lucky you can even remember your own name."

"Yeah, what with all the grunting and leg humping us guys do."

"Exactly."

The 'Butler' apparently spoke enough English that she snickered when she heard the leg humping comment. It was good to know ahead of time that our conversations may not be entirely private. Of course I figured a place so concerned with security might listen in on our conversations. I also figured that the people that worked as staff could probably each speak a half-dozen different languages.

So we all got off the elevator on the top floor and made our way to our suite. The 'Butler' pushed the cart near the room, but left it in the hallway as she opened the door, escorting us inside. As we walked in, my jaw dropped right off of my face and fell onto the floor. It was the most incredible room I'd ever seen, real or imagined. The furniture was in some ways crazy, where no two styles of furniture matched, but in a weird way they worked. Some of the fabric patterns were so strong I couldn't stare at them very long or I'd get dizzy.

"The room is nearly twenty-seven hundred square feet," the Butler said in very clear English. I turned and whispered in Madison's ear that it was bigger than my parents place, and my parents have a pretty decent sized house. Madison whispered back that it was bigger than her home too. It was nice to know that even with the money she was paid, Madison still lived in a fairly decent but humble home.

The Butler continued, "There are two bedrooms if you need them, both with spectacular views. In fact you can see both Champs-Elysees and the Eiffel Tower depending on where you're standing in the suite. It also comes with a six person dining room, a very large living room, a walk in wardrobe, double-sized spa bathtub, and TVs with surround sound in both the living room and master bedroom. I stay in a room that's next to this one in case you need anything. It comes with a fully stocked pantry in case you get hungry. Just use the phone and I'll be here as soon as I humanly can. Is there anything I can get you now? Maybe some breakfast?"

"That would be wonderful," said Madison excitedly.

"Then I will have it brought up to you immediately," replied the Butler.

The Butler wheeled our bags in then placed them carefully down inside the walk-in closet in the master bedroom. Madison tipped her graciously, and the Butler was off in a flash to get us food. I thought to myself for a second.

"So why didn't she ask us what we wanted for breakfast?" I asked Madison.

She smiled a very knowing smile at me, like she was the cat that swallowed the canary. "You'll see," is all she said.

"Madison, have you stayed here before?" I asked.

"No, this is my first time."

"But you stay in nice places like this a lot?"

"Actually, no. Normally I'm lucky to find a Motel Six to stay in."

"Well, I'm glad then that I get to share this experience with you," I said, smiling.

"Me too, Taylor," she said, smiling back at me.

I walked up to her and kissed her. She stopped me and told me that the Butler would be back soon with food, and she also wanted to wait on kissing until after we'd brushed our teeth. I could totally understand that, especially after our long trip. So I took Madison's hand and we walked to the master bedroom.

It was bigger than my parent's living room. Madison and I laid down on the bed, still holding hands, resting next to each other. I popped on the TV and was immediately embarrassed that I had. On the TV was a female newscaster that apparently forgot to wear anything on the upper half of her body. I quickly changed the channel to sports to keep from getting hit by Madison.

After a few minutes of checking the scores, we heard a knock at our door. Still holding hands, we made our way to the front door of the suite and let the butler back inside. She came in with a service cart completely filled with food. We watched as the butler carefully laid out each dish on the dining room table for us, and set forks, knives and spoons next to plates.

The food looked incredible. There were muffins and fresh fruit, eggs done three different ways, sausage links and patties, waffles and pancakes, elaborate pastries, coffee, juice, water, and tea. Pretty much anything you could think to have for breakfast was now sitting on the table. After filling my plate with a variety of foods, I sat in a seat at one end of the table, and Madison sat at the other end.

I looked up briefly to see Madison enjoying a few pieces of mango and honeydew before I poured hot maple syrup all over a massive chocolate chip waffle. After I was done soaking the waffle, I took a bunch of cut up pieces of banana and placed them on top. I have to say, it was one of the most incredible eating experiences of my life. I felt like a king. It was so exciting staying in a place like that. I recommend you do it at least once in your life. Save up and go; it's so totally worth it!

Anyway, the butler stayed and watched in case we needed anything. It was a bit unnerving having someone watch us eat. To be as kind to the butler as she'd been, I decided to invite her to share our breakfast with us. At first she politely said "no thank you," thinking it was bad form to eat with her guests. Eventually I got her to agree though, and she added another place setting and set to work on filling her plate.

The butler's idea of eating a lot was way different than mine. I figure she ate about a quarter of what I normally eat. But she went for a few particular fruits, and had some of the more exotic pastries. It was kind of fun sharing the experience with a third person, but I definitely ended up preferring spending time just with Madison. Thankfully, Madison's sweet and she didn't have any problem with sharing our meal.

Once we'd absolutely stuffed ourselves, we said a temporary goodbye to the butler and went and laid down on the bed. After only a few moments we were both fast asleep.

34

After sleeping only a few hours I woke up, my bladder screaming at me. Flushing the nearly silent toilet still woke Madison. She stirred in bed and looked over at the clock on her nightstand.

"Baby, we should probably start looking for Angela," she said.

"Yeah, I think I'm awake enough," I replied.

"We'll need to get you set up with your gear."

"Can you help me get ready?"

Madison and I spent the next twenty minutes loading ammo into clips, getting me into my bulletproof vest, concealing my weapons and checking my earpiece communicator. I felt really dangerous for some reason. Well, I know the reason: it's because I was armed better than some third-world countries. But because of the seriousness of what might go down, I took a deep breath and kicked out all the thoughts of excitement and adventure. What we were in for was a life-and-death situation, and I shouldn't treat it like a video game.

I kissed Madison on the lips to reassure her, because I could tell she was nervous having me out in the field. I knew that with the training they'd given me, and the brains in my head, and my faith in Madison, that I'd be alright. And even if I wasn't, I knew I'd go down swinging, and I'd do it by Madison's side. I loved her that much. I'd die for her. She only needed to ask.

I got dressed in a suit that they'd custom tailored for me. I'm still not sure how they figured out my dimensions, but my guess is some computer somewhere took a picture of me and calculated it all out. It's amazing what computers can do these days. And I looked like mother-effing James Bond! I even got to wear spy sunglasses with a built-in targeting display.

I pulled out one of my handguns and aimed it. Somehow the glasses figured out what I was pointing the gun at, even though I wasn't looking down the sight. It put a little red target wherever I aimed.

I put the gun back in one of my holsters and covered it back up. I didn't need to help Madison get ready because she didn't need armor or weapons. She is a weapon, and she's as strong as a tank.

We made our way to the front door of the suite. I took a deep breath and let it out then opened the door. Madison walked through, and I followed her down the short hallway to the elevators. The butler came out of her room then walked over to us. She looked me up and down as Madison pressed the button for the elevator.

"Nice body armor. Can barely tell you have any on," the butler said, looking at me.

"Thanks," I said, not knowing what to say.

"Don't worry. Your secret's safe with me," she said.

I just smiled at her. She got on the elevator with us and we made our way down to the lobby. Our butler walked up to the entrance then talked into her hand.

"Please bring Ms. Wheatfield's car around," said the butler, speaking to her thumb.

We waited less than a minute, and a bright orange Lamborghini Gallardo Superleggera pulled up. If you're not sure what kind of car that is, you should do a Google image search on it. Basically, imagine the sleekest, fastest, sexiest car you can think of. It's ten times sleeker, faster and sexier than that.

The valet got out of the car and tossed the keys to Madison. I couldn't breathe for a moment. Seriously, I got dizzy just thinking about getting into this amazing car.

"Can I drive?" I asked Madison.

"Let me think... nope," she said, smiling.

"Damn."

I opened the door and it swung upward. I knew they did that, but I couldn't help laughing because of how cool it was. As I got into the car I was shocked. The inside was just as amazing as the outside. Everything inside was black and expensive looking.

"Do you know how to drive this thing?" I asked.

"Sure! No problem."

Madison spent a moment typing the address that Director Scott had given her into the GPS system. I started to worry a little that she might not know how to work the paddle shifter. I watch the TV show Top Gear, and I've seen them use the paddles instead of a stick. But I shouldn't have worried. Madison had us off and running in no time flat. She smoked the tires a bit as we rocketed away from the hotel.

The drive was both intense and fun. I started to trust that she knew what she was doing. The French drivers seemed even crazier than her, since most of them seemed to want to run other drivers off the road.

It took about an hour to get to our destination, even with Madison driving as fast as she could. We ended up in a town called Houdan, which reminded me of Disney World for some reason. Madison pulled up to the curb in front of a split-level home with the number 13 on the front. It had old blue shutters and a dirty look to it that made me want a tetanus shot. Madison parked on the sidewalk. It was going to take me a little while to get used to the way they do things in France.

Thankfully, the Lamborghini's doors were easy to get out of, so I didn't bump into the wall. Madison nearly got hit by a speeding taxi, but thankfully she got out of the way and didn't have to use her superpowers. If people weren't already looking at us funny, they definitely would be if she powered up.

I followed behind her, since she's the indestructible one. I pulled one of my pistols out, an M9, and pulled the slide back on it to chamber the first round. Madison motioned me to stand just to the side of the door. She pulled out her cell phone, pressed a few buttons, placed it near the door, and after a few seconds I could hear a series of locks inside the door move.

She looked over at me, made the universal hand gesture for "sit" then "good dog," so I stayed. She pushed the door open quickly and started glowing as soon as she got inside. I peeked around the doorway to make sure she wasn't being ambushed. I never heard any gunfire, nor an explosion, so I crept in behind her, trying to stay as low to the ground as possible. I kept moving my gun around in every direction like they do on cop shows.

Madison let out a sigh of relief. I could tell she was worried she might find them here; her sister hurt, or worse. I walked up behind her and put a hand on her shoulder. She shrugged it away, covered her face, and started to cry. I tried to hold her, but again she pushed me away. Not remembering she was still glowing, her push was a bit harder than she'd meant. I slid backwards a few feet, rubbing a thin layer off the bottoms of my shoes. The Kevlar vest helped absorb the shove, but it still knocked the wind out of me. I coughed a few times.

"Madison?" I said.

It took a few seconds for her to respond.

"I'm sorry, Taylor. I just hoped she'd be here. In some ways I'm glad she isn't, because that would mean Dantalion was here, and I don't know if I'm really ready to face him yet. I think my emotions are finally catching up with me. I'm scared, Taylor. For the first time since I've joined White Ops, I'm really scared. Angela means the world to me, and if anything happens to her, it's my fault." Fresh tears streamed down her face.

This time I approached her slowly, holding out my arms for her. She stopped glowing and moved into my embrace. I held her as she sobbed into my chest, finally letting out all the fear and frustration of her sister's kidnapping. After I was sure she'd let the last few tears out, I kissed her on top of the forehead and rocked her back and forth in my arms, whispering to her, telling her it was going to be okay.

After a few moments, she finally broke our embrace, pulled back and rubbed the tears from her puffy eyes. She still looked beautiful, or at least I thought so, and I told her as much. She managed a small smile that quickly disappeared.

"Let's look around, maybe we can find some clues as to where they might have gone," I suggested.

We looked around the apartment. She went back to the bedrooms while I checked out the living room and kitchen. The apartment was well decorated; very subtle, unlike the strong colors in the hotel. I noticed something in the kitchen that would give Madison some hope.

"Madison, you'll want to come here," I yelled.

Madison came running into the room.

"Did you find something?" she asked.

"Yeah, they had to have been here, and not long ago. Look," I said, pointing to the cutting board. On top of it were a jar of preserves and a jar of peanut butter, and a half finished loaf of bread. I squeezed the bread and it was still soft, even though the package was open.

"See, it's still soft," I pointed out. "My guess is they left in the last day or two. Just a guess anyway."

"Yeah, it's totally like Dantalion to just leave food lying around. Asshole," said Madison.

"I like it when you call him that," I said.

"Me too. It's kinda liberating."

"Well, I wouldn't mind at all if you burned your bra," I said, deliberately staring at her chest. She gave me that cute little squinty-eyed look of fake disgust she gives me.

"Taylor, we should probably keep looking around. Maybe there will be something that will tell us where they've gone to," suggested Madison.

"Sounds like a brilliant plan," I responded.

We spent another twenty minutes searching through the apartment. I looked through all the cupboards, and except for some SPAM, cocoa powder, Keebler Club crackers and a bag of sugar, they were bare. The fridge had very little to offer; just some eggs, milk, coffee grounds, some bologna and some Brie cheese. I was surprised to see so many American type groceries instead of local French food. But I guess it made sense, since a guy like Dantalion probably wasn't interested in cooking or dining out with a captive.

When I searched the living room, I did find an earring between the couch cushions.

"Madison, is this your sister's?" I asked, as she walked down the hallway to me.

She took the earring and held it up to the window to look at it.

"Yes, it's Angela's. Do you know what this means? It means that she was definitely here, and definitely alive. She hid this here for me to find. Where did you find it?" she asked.

"Between the couch cushions," I replied.

"Did you look under the cushions, maybe further back but still between them?"

"No, I didn't."

"I'm hoping if she was smart enough to leave me this, she was smart enough to leave me a message. I'm sure that Dantalion would keep a very close eye on her, so the message may be subtle," she said, moving to the couch and pulling off the cushions.

Madison inspected the cushions, looking for clues. I looked down at the couch, now naked. Underneath where the cushions were, written in strawberry preserves, was one word: Bern.

"All right, Angela!" I yelled.

Madison dropped the cushions and looked at me.

"What is it?" she asked. I pointed down at the couch.

Madison stood in stunned silence and smiled.

"Thank goodness she's so smart," said Madison.

"And courageous. She was probably afraid when she did it. If Dantalion had found out, he could have hurt her, or worse," I pointed out.

"But she was smart enough to hide the message in a place he'd never look. If someone were just to feel around the cushions or underneath them for a note, they wouldn't have found anything."

"Remind me to give her a gold star when we find her," I said.

"Make that two; one from both of us," she responded.

"So what does 'Bern' mean anyway? I assume it's pretty important if she wrote it. Is it a code word?" I asked.

"Let me guess, geography isn't your best subject," questioned Madison.

"I like it pretty well, but it doesn't seem to like me so much. So Bern is a place?" I said.

"Yeah, it's in Switzerland. It's like the capital."

"Ah. Sorry, haven't learned that yet. So are we heading to Bern then?" I asked.

"Nah, we'll just go home."

"Oh, uh, okay."

"Of course we're going to Bern, Taylor. Do you think I'm just going to let my sister stay hostage?"

"No, I don't. Sorry."

Occasionally, Madison's sense of humor isn't all that funny.

"Sorry for the yelling," said Madison.

"It's okay. Do you think there's anything here worth taking?" I asked.

"No. Knowing Dantalion, things we take might hurt us. He could have poisoned the food, put tracking devices in the furniture. That kind of thing," she responded.

"Did you think he might have booby-trapped the house?"

"Oops."

"What does 'oops' mean?" I asked.

"It means I didn't think about it before. Sorry, Taylor. There are some things you take for granted when you're practically invincible. I really should have thought about that first before I let you follow me inside."

I stewed for a bit.

"That's okay. I know you're just worried about your sister. It has to be at least a little distracting."

"Try a lot. I've been trying to hide it, but I think it's just making things worse. Thank you, Taylor, for being there for me. Not just for coming along, helping me, and risking your life, but for being supportive and understanding. Decent."

"Of course. I do things because I love you and want to be with you. And I want to always help you, however I can," I explained.

"One of the many reasons I love you," said Madison.

"I only love you for your boobs," I said jokingly.

"I can't blame you, they are pretty incredible," she said, pushing her chest forward. Damn, I love that woman.

35

"Taylor, I'm gonna need to call in to White Ops and let them know we've made some progress. Can you drive while I do that?" asked Madison.

I just stood there, staring at her, dumbstruck by the thought of getting to drive the Lamborghini.

"Seriously?" I asked.

"Yes, this time seriously. I don't think it's a good idea for me to drive while talking on the phone. I need to concentrate in case what they have to tell me is important," said Madison.

"Um, hells to the yeah!" I yelled.

She tossed me the keys and I followed her out of the apartment. I was kind of sad to leave, because it really was a pretty cool place. The first place in Paris that reminded me of home. Not that I'd been gone long, but I'd never been that far from home before. Not even close. In a land where I don't speak the language. I guess it was a pretty cool country, but unfortunately we hadn't had time to really enjoy it.

I helped Madison into the car, because I'm a gentleman like that, and got into the driver's seat. It was surprisingly comfortable. I'd always heard that exotic cars, especially Lamborghinis, were uncomfortable to ride in. I guess they'd gotten better over the years, or I was the exact right height for the seats. I pulled the door down, and Madison explained to me how the paddle shifter worked. It seemed pretty intuitive, and after a few minutes of slowly driving down side streets I figured I'd gotten the hang of it.

Madison placed her call while I followed the GPS back to the hotel. It was kind of insane how fast the car was. I got it up to about 120 MPH, thinking I was going maybe 70. When I looked down at the speedometer my jaw dropped. Madison noticed how fast I was going and she looked over at me and winked. As she talked on the phone, she put her hand on my thigh and crept it slowly toward my... Eventually she finished her call with White Ops.

"Um, baby, as much as I would LOVE for you to do that, I really think I should be paying attention to driving. I mean, if this was a Yugo or something, no biggie. But this car is worth more money than I'll probably make in my lifetime. So can we wait at least until we get to the hotel?" I asked.

Madison smiled and kissed my cheek. I slowed the car down to a less insane ninety miles per hour. Apparently I have a need for speed.

We spent the rest of the drive to the hotel in happy silence, both of us wearing dumb grins on our faces. There were a couple of times I thought to make small talk, but I figured with her emotions so high in so many directions, it wasn't a good plan.

The drive was at least a beautiful one, getting to see a mix of farmland and city. It kind of struck me how odd it was that France's landscape wasn't all that different from what it was like at home. The people, the food and the culture were very different, but the natural world around me was the same. It was kind of comforting.

We eventually made it back to the hotel. I pulled up to the valet and gave him the key. Madison was still smiling as we made our way inside.

When we got to the room, the butler was standing at the door waiting for us. As we walked inside, we noticed a complimentary snack basket filled with all sorts of candy, nuts, croissants, jellies and biscuits. Madison turned to the butler.

"Was this brought in from the outside, or was this put together here at the hotel?" Madison asked the butler.

"It was assembled here. I've personally inspected it to make certain there was nothing dangerous in it. Believe me, this is not the first time we've had guests with targets painted on them," replied the butler.

"Oh, I didn't mean anything by it," said Madison. "I just didn't know if someone was sending a subtle message or not. Apparently not."

"Actually, the basket was purchased online for you. I believe there was an accompanying message that we printed out. Of course, we respect your privacy, so no one has read the message. Is this something the hotel should be worried about?" asked the butler.

Madison thought to herself for a moment.

"No, it should be alright," she replied.

Madison walked over to the basket, found the note then read it. She closed her eyes and nodded her head in understanding.

"What does it say?" I asked.

"All that's written on it is 'You for her.'"

"At least it sounds like he's willing to play ball, finally," I said, just now realizing the butler had left the room as soon as Madison reached for the note. "So what are we going to do? What's the plan?"

"I give him me," said Madison.

"Wait, what? No, that's not gonna happen," I said.

"Taylor, I think it's the only way. I don't know what else to do. Angela didn't sign up for any of this, and she doesn't have any powers. At least if I turn myself over to him, she'll be safe. He won't have any more need for her, and he'll let her go."

"So then what happens to you?" I ask.

"I do what he wants. I work for the dark side."

"You can't do that! No effing way! I won't let you."

"I don't have any choice, Taylor. He's too dangerous. He'll kill my family, and he'll kill you. This is the only way to make sure that everyone is safe."

"Madison, listen to me: if you give yourself over to him, then he might ask you to kill people. Innocent people. And you'll never be rid of him. Can't we just pretend like you're joining team Dantalion and then you can rip his head off?" I asked.

"My guess is it won't be that simple. He's probably put some sort of device on her that he can trigger remotely to kill her. It's the only way to guarantee I'll follow his orders," she said.

"Will he make you have sex with him?"

It took her a moment to respond. "Yes."

"No, I can't let you do that. I can't!"

"Taylor, it's sweet of you, it really is, but this ultimately isn't your decision. It's not your fight."

"Like hell it's not. If you somehow forgot, I love you. You think I can just ignore that? To send you off to a life of slavery? There's no way," I said.

Madison walked over to me, wrapped her arms around me and gave me a kiss filled with love and despair. She started to glow, and before I realized what was happening, she hit me over the head. Everything went dark.

36

I don't know which hurt worse, Madison hitting me on the head, or Madison leaving without me. When I woke up my head was pounding. I looked over at the clock and realized I'd been out for five hours. Five hours lost. Five hours that Madison had been on the move. The only thing I knew was that she'd gone to Bern to trade herself for her sister. Like Dantalion would really give Angela up when he could continue using her to manipulate Madison. I understand why Madison did it. She loves her sister and would do anything for her. But I don't think Madison was thinking clearly.

At that point I don't know if I was either. I went into the bedroom and picked up the phone next to the bed. The concierge answered, recognized what room it was, and politely spoke to me in English.

"Concierge desk, how may I assist you?"

"This is Mr. Swift. Can you please put me in touch with White Ops?" I asked.

"I'm sorry, who?" asked the concierge.

"You *know* who," I said.

"Uh, one moment, sir."

It took a few moments for Director Scott to come on the line.

"Scott here."

"Madison's gone. She knocked me out and left," I say, panic in my voice.

"Wait, hold on. Taylor? You say she knocked you out?" asked Director Scott.

"Yes."

"And you're still in Paris?"

"Yes."

"Do you know why?"

"She received a gift basket from Dantalion, with a note saying she could exchange herself for Angela."

"That sounds like Dantalion, although he'll never let Angela go."

"My thoughts too, sir."

"Damn. Well, you better come in then, Taylor. I actually sent Mike there to keep tabs on the two of you. He'll be there in an hour to pick you up and get you home," said Director Scott.

"No offense, sir, but I'd like to stay. I'd like to get Madison back," I said.

"No offense, son, but against Dantalion, alone, you don't have a chance. With Madison, you might have stopped him. Even that was a question mark. You're outgunned more than you realize."

"Again, no offense sir, but I don't care about anything else in this world right now. I don't care if I die trying. I have to get her back."

"I admire your spirit, but that's all you have. He has powers that you just can't match. I'm sorry," said Director Scott.

"Are you going to send in a team to extract her then?" I asked.

"First, I'm going to try to contact Dantalion and go from there. See if he's just trying to hold her for ransom. The government may not be as interested in saving the sister of an asset, as it is in saving the asset themselves. Especially when that asset can be manipulated to work against us. So we might get some help. The question is whether or not Dantalion is willing to play ball. If he isn't, we're screwed. We don't have any assets that could hope to fight the two of them together. They know how to work as a team, and they're very, very good at what they do. We could send in an infantry battalion against them, and Madison and Dantalion would carve through them like a hot machete through margarine."

"So what am I supposed to do, sit on my ass and not help?"

"I don't know, Taylor. I wish there was some way you could help, but you're just one guy, you're green, and you're more of a liability than an asset right now. I promise you, I'll do my best to bring her home. Just stay put, and Mike will be there shortly. Scott out." With that, Director Scott hung up the phone.

I started cussing at the top of my lungs. A knock came at the front door. I hurried over to it just in case Mike was already there, but instead it was the butler.

"Is everything okay, Mr. Swift?" asked the butler.

"No. She hit me over the head then left," I replied.

"I'm sorry to hear that sir. Is there anything I can get you? Maybe some Ibuprofen and an ice pack?"

"Yes, please. Oh, also, can you bring dinner for two? I'll be having a friend stop by shortly. His name is Mike; please send him right up when he arrives," I said.

"Absolutely, Mr. Swift," responded the butler.

"By the way, did you see Madison leave?" I asked.

"Yes."

"Do you know where she was headed?"

"I'm sorry sir, I have no idea. She said not to disturb you; that you were resting."

"Like hell I was."

"Was there anything else?" asked the butler.

"No. Oh, yes, actually. What's your name?"

"It's Calandre."

"That's a beautiful name."

"Thank you. I'm named after my Grandmother. She and I were close. She passed away last year."

"I'm really sorry to hear that."

"Thank you," said Calandre, turning to leave the room. She stopped then turned back to me. "You know, if there's anything I can help with, please let me know. And I don't just mean with food or amenities. I really am more than just a butler."

"That's very kind, but I don't know that I could ask you to help. Hell, I don't even know if there is a way anyone can help," I replied.

"Can you tell me what happened? Is Ms. Wheatfield in trouble?"

"I honestly don't know if it would be a national security breach to tell you. They might hang me."

"I don't think they do that anymore, Mr. Swift."

"Call me Taylor."

"Alright then, Taylor. Just keep me in mind."

"I will. And again, thank you."

Calandre gave me a sad smile, nodded then left. About twenty minutes later, Mike arrived. One of the people at the front desk escorted him up. I heard their knock and opened the door.

"Hey kid, Scott told me what happened. Sorry she got the drop on you," said Mike, entering the room.

"Yeah, I'm not too worried about that right now. I'm just worried about Madison," I said as I closed the door behind him.

"I don't blame you. She's an amazing girl. Stubborn, thinks she knows what's best. Sometimes it makes working with her tough. There's been a time or two she's knocked me out for what she thought was my own good. Once she did it when I was about to go out on a date with this girl she didn't approve of. She's funny that way; protective to a fault."

"Yeah, I get that. So what's the plan?"

"What do you mean? The plan's to get you on a flight home," said Mike.

I shook my head 'no'. Another knock came at the door. I went over and opened it. Outside was Calandre the butler, standing with a cart of food for us. I moved out of the way and let her wheel it into the dining room. I started to say something, but Mike made a motion with his hand to stop talking. I ignored him.

"Mike, she's actually offered to help," I said.

"How do you know you can trust her?" he asked.

"I don't. It's a hunch. But since you have to be highly trained and approved by the French Government to work here, I'd guess she's on our side. She has no motivation whatsoever to interfere, and if she was working for Dantalion, my guess is she would have already killed me. She's had plenty of opportunities," I said.

"Thank you, Mr. Swift, for your vote of confidence," said Calandre as she dressed the table.

"You're welcome. I can't see any reason not to trust you," I said.

"I don't like it," said Mike.

"You don't have to. Anyway, I'm not going home. I'm going to try and rescue Madison. Do you want in?" I asked.

Mike thought about it for a moment.

"You're one stupid kid, Taylor, for thinking you might have a chance against Dantalion. Without me you'll be dead in seconds. With me, well, you may last minutes. I'll help," said Mike. "Besides, I owe Madison my life, several times over. Wouldn't be fair to let her be a slave like that."

"So Ms. Wheatfield's being held hostage?" asked Calandre.

"Something like that," I said. "By the way, Calandre, this is Mike. Mike, this is Calandre."

Calandre walked over to Mike and shook hands with him. I saw Mike blush a little as she smiled at him. I saw her stand up a little straighter, subtly thrusting her chest out. Good lord, just what I needed: old people flirting. I hoped that maybe it would make them trust each other.

"Calandre, would you like to stay for dinner?" I asked. "There should be plenty of food."

She turned and looked at me, finally breaking eye contact with Mike.

"Certainly, Taylor. I'd love to."

And like that, our team was born.

37

The three of us sat down at the dining room table together. Before we ate, Mike said grace for us, since he was a serious Catholic. Calandre had brought us duck, ham, a couple soufflés, a baguette to share, and a whole lot of other things I couldn't pronounce. We talked about specifics while we ate.

"So what's your background, Calandre?" asked Mike.

"Do you mean where did I grow up, or where did I serve?" asked Calandre.

"Where did you serve?"

"Technically, I still serve the Directorate of Protection and Defense Security. I've been an agent for nearly ten years."

"Nice," said Mike. He was obviously impressed, which meant I was impressed, because Mike doesn't impress easily, and I had no idea what the DPSD was. I now know that it's the DPSD instead of the DPDS, because in French it's 'Direction de la Protection et de la Securite de la Defense'. That is one long-ass name. I imagine they have to use bookmarks instead of business cards.

"So do you specialize in anything?" asked Mike.

"I do field work; mostly intelligence gathering. Occasional wet work. Isn't that what you American's call it?" asked Calandre.

"We do. It's a messy business," said Mike. "Do you have any favorite weapons?"

"I'm partial to the SIG P226 when it comes to handguns, even though it's not officially sanctioned by France. I believe your Navy SEALS carry them."

"They do," said Mike.

"I also favor the MP5. It's lightweight and effective; perfect for clearing rooms."

"A woman after my own heart."

"Um, I'm sorry to interrupt," I said, "but I'd like to talk about rescuing my girlfriend now, if that's alright with you two."

"Oh, yeah, sorry kid. So do you know where she was headed? Director Scott didn't fill me in on every detail," said Mike.

"Yeah, she's headed to Bern, Switzerland. Angela left us a note in jam that just said 'Bern'."

"Okay, I think I may know where he's holing up there. In fact, I may be the only one, other than Madison, who knows where he is. I think he uses an old warehouse-sized building there as a safe-house," said Mike.

"What's the place like? Is it guarded?" I asked.

"He doesn't have any guards, but he has extensive security. It won't be easy getting inside. It's safe to assume that no matter what we do, he'll know we're coming. So what are our primary objectives?" asked Mike. "We should figure those out first."

I thought about it for a minute.

"Our first primary objective I think should be to rescue Angela," I said.

"Why not Madison first?" asked Mike.

"Because Madison won't fight Dantalion if Angela's still in danger. Speaking of which, Madison thinks that Dantalion may have put something on Angela that could kill her remotely. Like some kind of small bomb or microchip or something. If we get Angela back, would you be able to protect her from that?" I asked.

"Normally you could just put her in a shielded van that blocks out any radio frequencies. But with Dantalion, he might make it so that the bomb is activated when the signal is lost. That's just how sick he is," said Mike.

"What about using an EMP device?" asked Calandre.

"That might actually work," said Mike. "Beautiful and brilliant." It was Calandre's turn to blush.

"So what's an EMP device?" I asked.

"You need to watch more movies, kid. EMP stands for electromagnetic pulse. It basically fries circuit boards when it goes off," said Mike.

"Oh, that thing in 'Ocean's Eleven'?" I asked.

"Yeah, that thing. We have them, only much smaller. We'd need to be within a few feet of Angela to set it off and not damage other systems. I actually have one in my watch," said Mike.

"That's pretty cool," I said.

"The downside is it makes the rest of my watch useless. No more laser, no more explosive device. I can't even tell time on it anymore. Any electronic device within about fifty feet will be useless," explained Mike.

I thought about this for a while.

"You two will need to hide your headsets somewhere away from the EMP when you use it. I'll need to know when you've rescued Angela," I said.

"Why, where will you be?" asked Mike.

"I'm the distraction," I said.

"Do you have a death wish?" questioned Mike.

"No, but I can't think of another way. The two of you are both better at this spy stuff than I am. If I can distract Dantalion long enough, you might be able to free Angela. Then you call me up on my headset and tell me she's safe. I'll let Madison know so that she can turn on Dantalion."

"You must really love her," said Calandre. "I've actually heard of Dantalion, although most of what I've heard I thought was ghost stories meant to keep us agents in line. I did some research on Ms. Wheatfield, since I was assigned to protect her. It turns out the truth about Dantalion is far worse than what I'd heard. Apparently, he can torture a person psychically. He finds your deepest fears and turns them against you. One touch from his dark tendrils, and they burn your skin right off."

"Great, that really helps my confidence," I said sarcastically.

"You should know what you're up against, Taylor. If you go in like that, you go in alone. I may be able to get us a few items that could protect you from Dantalion's powers," said Mike. "It will still be impossible for you to beat him, but we might be able to stack enough odds in our favor that you can survive the fight."

"Okay, that makes me feel a little better. So do you guys know how Dantalion got his abilities?" I asked.

"No one's quite sure, although I've heard about experiments on children that both the US and Russians were performing. Not our country's finest hour," said Mike.

"I think there are moments in all of our countries' pasts we'd like to forget," said Calandre.

"One thing I want to mention, that I heard in history class, is that France and the US have a long history of helping each other. If it weren't for France, the US wouldn't be a country. And if it weren't for the US, France would still be occupied by the Germans. It's nice we were able to repay the favor. I even read somewhere that the French gave us the Statue of Liberty," I said.

"That is very true, Taylor, we did. Like you, our country believes in liberty and freedom. It is entirely too bad that our countries have had a more difficult time getting along lately," said Calandre.

"Well, on behalf of the US, I'd like to improve 'relations' with you," said Mike.

OMG, I just about threw up in my mouth. What a horrible line. The sad thing is it seemed to work. Maybe French women aren't as jaded as American women when it comes to pick-up lines.

"So what's our next step?" I asked.

"We'll need to do some recon work. Determine where he's hiding Angela, where you can set up your distraction, and see if there's any chance you might be able to take down Dantalion yourself," said Mike.

"You really think I could do that?" I asked.

"I think you're willing to die trying," said Mike.

"Gee, thanks," I said.

"In all seriousness, Taylor, what you're planning takes a lot of guts. If you didn't have my respect before, you have it now."

"Thanks, Mike. That actually means a lot."

"Don't go gettin' all soft on me now, kid," said Mike.

"Never," I replied.

"I'll make arrangements for a flight to Switzerland for three," said Calandre.

"Are you sure you want to do this Calandre? You don't have any ties to Madison. You would be risking your life for a virtual stranger," I said.

"I like the excitement. Plus, it will give me a chance to improve 'relations.' Isn't that how you put it, Mr. Mike?" asked Calandre.

"It's just Mike, baby doll. Just Mike."

I hate old people.

38

Calandre left the room, and Mike and I talked specifics on what kind of devices I would have to carry to protect myself from Dantalion.

"You'll need protection from his psychic powers. I have a safe house nearby with some equipment, including a helmet that might just keep him from frying your brain," said Mike.

"Cool, kind of like how Magneto's helmet protects him from Professor X's telepathy," I said.

"Yeah, somethin' like that. Also, standard Kevlar body armor should be thick enough to protect you from his tendrils. They're strong, but to do real damage they need to come in contact with your skin. Hell, you could be wearing a spandex leotard and it would keep the burning sensation at bay."

"You sure do have a way with words, Mike."

"Yeah, I'm a regular Shakespeare."

"So you got anything else that might help?" I asked.

"Maybe a few things. I have flashbang grenades that should stun him. I also have devices that emit a loud noise that make it hard to concentrate. I can calibrate a headset for you that will block out the frequencies they emit," said Mike.

"That's pretty cool. Is it like noise canceling headphones?"

"Exactly like that. It generates a secondary sound wave that cancels out the first one. Pretty clever idea if you ask me," said Mike.

"It's a good thing nobody did," I reply.

"Nobody did what?"

"Ask you," I said, laughing.

"Smart-ass."

Just then Calandre walked back into the room.

"Well, I've done some research on traveling to Bern. We can either take a flight from Charles de Gaulle Airport to Bern, and it'll take four hours and forty-five minutes to get there, costing us $1,000 each, or we could take the train, which will be faster, arriving in four hours and fifteen minutes, and it will only cost us $300 each," said Calandre. "Oh, and it'll probably be easier to transport our gear on the train. I have the ability to carry anything I need on a train, but they won't allow me to carry weapons on a flight."

"So it's faster, cheaper, and better to take the train? Uh, yeah, I'm thinking that might be the better of the two options," I said.

"The downside is no free peanuts on the train," said Calandre, matching my smart-ass comment.

"Normally that would be a deal breaker, but it just so happens I've cornered the black market on honey roasted peanuts," I said. "The first bag is free, but the second will cost you. Someday you may have to sell your bongos just to score another package."

"Uh, right. Anyway, thanks Calandre for looking into that for us," said Mike. "So when do we leave?"

"First thing tomorrow morning. I'll come wake you when it's time to get up, and I'll give you time to eat breakfast and shower," said Calandre.

"Um, Calandre," started Mike.

"Yes?"

"I was wondering... if maybe you could wake me up... by nudging me," said Mike. He was trying to use a line from the movie 'Sneakers' I think, but he said it kind of sheepishly. Calandre blushed, but for some strange reason, relented to his request.

"I can nudge you," said Calandre, smiling at Mike.

"Wow, you two are quick. Jump in the sack much?" I said.

"Taylor, something you'll find out quickly in the spy business is that you never know if you'll be coming back from a mission. You have to enjoy life when you can, take chances when you can, and share an evening with a beautiful woman when you can," said Mike.

Calandre smiled again.

Sigh.

"Okay, you two gross old people go sleep together or whatever, just let me get some sleep. Try not to make too much noise," I said.

"I can't make any promises."

I was surprised when those words came out of Calandre's mouth, and not Mike's. I will say that Calandre's quite a beautiful woman. I don't blame Mike at all. And Mike's kind of got the rugged outdoors thing goin' on. Kind of reminds me of the guy on the Brawny paper towel rolls.

Calandre took Mike's hand and guided him out of the room.

"Goodnight, kid. It might be tough, but try to get some rest," said Mike.

Calandre pulled a little harder and Mike laughed. He followed her quickly out the door and shut it behind him. One nice thing is that I couldn't hear them through the room's walls. For all I know, they could have both passed out the minute they got in the room. In some ways I'd hoped that was the case. I wanted them sharp and well rested for the mission. The mission was the only thing important to me at that moment.

I actually thought about it and realized it wasn't true. I started to wonder about my parents, whether they'd tried to call, or worse yet come home. So I picked up the phone next to the bed and had the operator put me through to where they were staying in Chicago. A minute later, my Mom answered.

"Taylor, where are you calling from?" she asked.

"You wouldn't believe me if I told you. All I can say is that I'm healthy, and I'm chasing after a girl," I said.

"The one you told me about?"

"Yes, that one. I love her, and she needs my help. So I'm doing the best I can to do that."

"She isn't pregnant, is she?"

"What the hell, Ma! No, she isn't pregnant. I'm gonna go now. Tell Dad I love him, and I love you too," I said.

"Love you, sweetheart," said my Mom.

I hung the phone up then rolled onto my back. I started thinking about Madison and what that a-hole Dantalion might be doing to her right then. After a few minutes I finally broke out of my worrying and turned on the TV, wiping the wetness from my eyes. I tried watching everything from Chopped (I love competitive cooking shows), to Tom and Jerry, to the news in an attempt to distract myself from missing and worrying about Madison. Nothing worked. In a lot of ways I'm glad it didn't. What kind of boyfriend would I be if I could be so easily distracted, when the person I love more than anyone else in the world was in serious trouble?

I tried my best to fall asleep normally, but couldn't. I went downstairs to the hotel's workout room, ran a few miles on the treadmill as hard as I could, lifted weights and swam a few laps in the pool. I'd exhausted myself to the point where I could barely lift my arms to shampoo my hair in the shower.

All of the exertion had done its job, and I was finally able to fall asleep. Passing out is probably closer to what I did. But I needed it badly for what lay ahead. I seriously thought I knew what I was getting myself into. I thought I'd be able to easily handle Dantalion if I hit him hard enough and fast enough. Nothing had prepared me for the showdown that was to come.

39

As good as her word, Calandre woke me up the next morning. The sun was just starting to come up over the horizon. I love that time of day, where it's cool out, and the air is crisp and filled with promise. On any other day I would have stood in the first beams of sunlight that came through my window, but today wasn't a good day. Madison was with Dantalion now, having turned herself into a slave to save her sister.

The only good thing about the situation was that I had Mike and Calandre on my side. I trusted them both completely. Two professionals to help me with my suicide mission. I wonder if it's easier or harder for them not being the ones creating the distraction. To not be putting themselves directly in harm's way. Sure, they'll probably have their hands full with security, but my guess is they would have an easier time with that than having to go up against Dantalion.

Anyway, I hopped in the shower while Calandre grabbed our breakfast. Mike showered in Calandre's room. I took a cold shower to wake up. I still felt a bit tired going in, but the shower took the fuzzy edges off of everything.

Calandre came back with the standard breakfast that the hotel served. I had eggs, bacon, what I would call French toast, but what Calandre just called 'toast'. Actually, that's not true. She called it 'pain perdu', which translates to 'lost bread.' If you don't believe me, Google it. Anyway, I poured a ton of real maple syrup all over my French toast and ate the stack like I hadn't eaten in weeks. I was hungry because my stomach was filled with worry and acid, and the food seemed to help with the pain.

Once we had finished our breakfast, I packed up all of my gear. Calandre mentioned that Madison had left the Lamborghini, but Mike pointed out there was no way in hell we could fit three people plus gear into it. He'd brought a surveillance van along, so we took that to his hideout. It really sucked, because the van had been designed solely for surveillance, and not for transport, so there were no seats in the back. Mike drove, and being the gentleman I am, I offered Calandre the passenger seat. So I got bounced around pretty good in the back of the van as Mike tried keeping up with the morning traffic.

Thankfully, the drive to Mike's hideout wasn't long. It took about ten minutes to get there. I only suffered a few bruises while being tossed around in the back. I was shocked when we pulled up to the place. It was a very beautiful bakery. I don't know that I'd ever seen a bakery that fancy. There were a ton of people inside, too.

"Um, Mike, you sure this is the right place?" I asked.

Mike laughed. "Yeah kid, this is the place."

I hopped out of the side of the van and started walking toward the front door when Mike stopped me.

"This way," he said, as Calandre and I followed.

He took us around the back to a covered flight of stairs. I inhaled the smell of fresh bread and pastries and was almost overwhelmed by it.

"Man, it smells incredible here," I said to Mike.

"That's the reason why this is my favorite hideout," said Mike.

We followed him up the stairs and into a loft just above the bakery. We could hear all sorts of noises below. The ringing of the service bell, people yelling out their orders over the noise of the crowd. The wordless music being pumped in. If it weren't for the heavenly smell of baked goods, Mike's hideout would be a really annoying place to stay in.

That and it wasn't very comfortable. There were a couple of military style beds toward the back of the large room. I could see a bathroom tucked even further back, which looked only large enough to accommodate a stand up shower, toilet and sink. There was also a small TV mounted on the wall. It would have been a very empty room if it weren't for the dozens of racks of both low and high-tech equipment stacked to the ceiling. Guns, body armor, electronic devices that looked older than my folks, as well as some brand new things I'd never seen, filled the shelves. Mike was excited to show off his stash; not so much to me, but to Calandre.

Mike showed us some small communication devices that weren't easily noticeable when you put them in your ear. I tried a pair out by walking outside. After a few seconds Mike's voice came into my ear, totally clear. It was pretty amazing. I went back up the staircase and inside.

"Yeah, that worked really well, Mike. And you can program them to cancel out the noisemakers you were telling me about?" I asked.

"Shouldn't take more than a few minutes. Just need to update the firmware," said Mike, as I handed him back the ear pieces.

Mike then started showing off some of the weapons. He had a few sniper rifles, a number of assault rifles, sub-machine guns and pistols, but he saved showing us the best for last. I'd seen one in the movie Predator. Mike had a Minigun.

"Wow, that's... impressive," was Calandre's response to the Minigun.

I noticed her face turning bright pink. I also noticed she was looking down in the general vicinity of his... yeah. It was understandable, since he was holding it in a way that the Minigun was covering it up for the most part. But it was still obvious what she was referring to.

"Okay Mike, are you done showing off your massive gun to the lady?" I asked. "Because I'd really like to go rescue my girlfriend and her sister now."

Mike and Calandre laughed at the first comment, but got quiet about the second. When I mentioned Madison and Angela, their mood turned back to business.

"So what weapons do you think we should carry?" asked Calandre.

"I'm planning on taking everything I can carry, and then some," I said. "I'm hoping to take a sniper rifle I can sling on my back, an assault rifle with a mounted grenade launcher, a number of pistols, and whatever Mike thinks will distract Dantalion. That's my biggest goal: just to keep him busy while you guys are doing your thing."

"That sounds like a reasonable list. Oh, here, try the helmet on. This is what I was telling you about. It should protect you no problem from Dantalion," said Mike, handing me the helmet. "His effective range thankfully isn't very far with his psychic powers. You have to be within about 30 feet for him to be able to mess with your head. You can keep your helmet off when you're using the sniper rifle. Up close, you'll need it on."

"Good to know. Hey, that kinda looks like the Styg's helmet," I said.

If you don't know who the Styg is, you should totally check out that TV show I mentioned, "Top Gear." It's pretty funny. It's basically a comedy show that also happens to be about cars. Some episodes are more serious than others. I'm not as big on the cars as I am about the comedy, but the cars are pretty cool too.

Anyway, I tried the white helmet on. It was comfortable and had good visibility. I was actually surprised at how clearly I could see out of a helmet that covered my entire head. I looked over at Mike and noticed his mouth moving. I couldn't hear anything. I took the helmet off.

"Mike, I can't hear jack in this thing," I said.

"You're not supposed to. It's another layer of protection for your ears. It has built-in headphones as well as a speaker built into the mouth, but you have to turn it on by flipping the switch inside the back of it," said Mike.

I flipped the helmet over, saw the slide switch and turned the helmet on. Sticking it on my head, I could now hear everything clearly.

"That's much better," I said.

I started laughing, because the helmet made me sound exactly like James Earl Jones.

"No Luke, I am your Father," I said, and Calandre and Mike cracked up.

"I added the Darth Vader voice just for fun. Turns out there's an app online that changes your voice, so I uploaded it to the helmet," said Mike.

"Effing awesome!" I said.

"Yeah, well, if you can't have fun while trying to save the world, what's the point?" said Mike.

"Maybe it'll scare Dantalion. Or make him laugh at least. Maybe if I start off with a comedy routine, he'll be too distracted to kill me," I said.

"Yeah, I don't think that's probably a wise tactic. I've never seen Dantalion laugh, let alone smile," said Mike.

"What about a cute kitten? I could walk up to him holding a cute kitten. No one can resist cute kittens."

"Pretty sure that wouldn't work either. For kittens to work, you have to have a soul. I don't think Dantalion qualifies."

"Well, it was an idea."

"Yeah, it was an idea."

"We better get going if we want to make the train," said Calandre.

"Wow, didn't realize we were cutting it so close. Alright, help me load up the van. Remember, we can only take what we can carry," said Mike. "But feel free to help yourselves to anything you want or need. This mission's a top priority, and not just for White Ops. There are more than just US agencies that have an interest in keeping Madison alive."

I decided to grab a bunch of extra things that I figured might help out. I put everything I could in duffel bags and struggled to carry all of it, but I knew we wouldn't be coming back here anytime soon, so I had to take what I needed. I picked through the stacks as quick as I could, grabbing weird things I wasn't even sure I'd seen before, just in case they might help out.

Calandre was very serious when she went through the stacks. Very focused. Picked up a few guns here, a few tech devices there. When she was finished, I realized she had only mostly filled a single bag. But she's the professional, so I figured she knew what the hell she was doing.

Mike grabbed a bunch of stuff, like me. Tried packing everything that he could. Only thing he left was the Minigun. Makes sense. Not that I think it's worthless, it's just extremely heavy. Not something you can be sneaky with either. So for his part of the mission it'd be a total waste.

It would have been cool to take for me to use though. I can just imagine how fun it would be blasting away at that a-hole Dantalion, ripping him to shreds. My guess is most of the bullets would bounce right off of him, but I wouldn't care. It'd be worth it just to be able to fire sixty-six rounds a second into him. That's roughly four-thousand rounds a minute.

Anyway, I realized the error of my mistake when I tried to carry everything down to the van at the same time. I nearly fell down the stairs a couple of times, but was able to somehow keep myself upright long enough to make it to ground level. If you ever transport bags full of explosive devices and firearms, make sure they're easy to carry.

After loading everything into the van, Mike let Calandre drive since she knew the streets and traffic better. Calandre got in the driver side, took a look at Mike in the passenger seat and winked. She then peeled the van out, sending me falling backwards against the rear door, and sending pain through my back.

"Ow!" I yelled out.

"Oh, Taylor, I'm sorry. I forgot you were back there," said Calandre.

I thought about it for a second.

"Well, I'm basically committing suicide trying to save my girlfriend, so I guess I can't fault you for being so distracted by love you forgot about me. Well, I can a little, but not a lot," I said.

"That's very considerate of you, Taylor," said Calandre.

"Yeah, I'm a regular Mother Theresa."

"Hey now, remember I'm Catholic," said Mike.

"Yeah, how could I forget?" I responded.

40

The drive to the train station didn't take very long, thankfully. This time, since the bags were so heavy, the only thing bouncing around in the back of the van was me. As we pulled up, Mike got out and wheeled a large luggage cart over. We worked together to fill it up from the back of the van. Calandre went inside to get our tickets, which she'd phoned ahead to order. It took both me and Mike to push the cart since it was really friggin' heavy, but eventually we got it inside.

Calandre reappeared and took out a bunch of special tags to mark the bags as diplomatic so that they wouldn't be searched. After she'd tagged the last bag, she had us follow her to a door that wasn't marked. I thought it was strange that it didn't even have a sign that said 'keep out' or 'employees only.' It was a lot more mysterious seeming since there were no markings at all. In fact, there wasn't even a door handle.

Calandre pulled out a plastic ID card and slid it into a slot next to the door. Once she pulled it out, I heard a click, and the door swung open slightly, just enough for Calandre to get her hand around. Pulling it aside, she held the door as Mike and I pushed the cart through the doorway and into a small room.

A pair of soldiers were inside. I couldn't tell what kind of soldiers they were since I didn't know the branches of the French military too well. They picked a couple of the bags up off of our cart so that we each only had one bag to carry. We followed them through another door leading out of the side room, and down a long tunnel going under the station.

It kinda freaked me out to be honest. Not that I get that claustrophobic or anything, just not knowing where we were heading was a bit unnerving. I felt better having Mike and Calandre there, and I had a whole bag of weapons under my arm in case things got sticky. Thankfully, nothing bad happened.

The tunnel curved back upward, and I could see at the end of it what looked like the opening of a train compartment. As we got closer, I could tell it was the train we were supposed to be on, and for the most part the space between the tunnel and the train was completely covered. We couldn't see anyone else boarding, and thankfully they couldn't see us.

Boarding the compartment, I also noticed that the windows were tinted so that people couldn't see inside the cabin. We would be able to see outside, but not quite as well as through normal clear glass.

The compartment itself was pretty amazing. Lots of space for us; places to store our bags. It wasn't quite as nice as the first plane Madison and I flew on, but all things considered it was pretty cool. I also noticed that there weren't any doors on the compartment leading to the other train compartments. Apparently, once you were in this particular compartment, you couldn't leave it until the train stopped. There was a restroom, thankfully, and a fully stocked kitchen, so we wouldn't die of starvation or holding it in. That much was good.

There were a number of bench style seats with backs, and a table between each. They were kind of like sitting at a booth in a restaurant. Calandre sat down at one, and I decided to sit across from her.

"Wow, this is pretty fancy," said Mike. "You guys want anything from the kitchen?"

"Yeah, can you get me a Coke?" I asked.

"A James Bond, please," said Calandre.

"The martini?" asked Mike.

"That's the one. It was actually originally called 'The Vesper', after the character Vesper Lynd in the book 'Casino Royale'," replied Calandre.

"Wait, Casino Royale was a book? I loved the movie, and the martini in the movie sounded really good. Can I try one too, Mike?" I asked.

"Yeah, I can make up a couple," said Mike, unhappy at being our bartender. Or at least my bartender.

Mike walked off to the kitchen and out of site.

"So why do they call it the 'James Bond' instead of the 'Vesper'?" I asked.

"Probably because people don't remember the character Vesper as well as they remember James Bond," said Calandre.

"Yeah, that does make sense. So is the drink pretty good?" I asked.

"No, not really. It's kind of like drinking hairspray," replied Calandre.

"Oh, that sounds REAL tasty," I said sarcastically. "So why are you drinking it then?"

"Well, I'm a spy, and it's a spy's drink. What can I say?" said Calandre. "It just always puts me in a certain... mood on a mission. Makes things seem a little classier, a little more romantic than they actually are. Are you sure you're really up for this Taylor? No one would think less of you if you didn't go through with it. You don't have real fighting experience yet, you've only been minimally trained. You're very young. Sure, you've got heart, anyone can see that. But Mike and I have been doing this for years, and we're both a little nervous about the mission. Dantalion really is worse than anyone you've ever met. He'll try and kill you for real."

"I couldn't live with myself if I didn't try, and I want Madison back. It's pretty simple to me. I guess it comes down to the fact that I'm willing to give my life for hers," I said.

"I really hope and pray it doesn't come down to that," said Calandre.

"Me too. I'm not looking forward to dying, even if it would be noble. Heroes don't really get any of the benefits of being a hero unless they survive," I said.

Just then, Mike came back carrying two martinis. He handed one to each of us. Calandre and I both took a sip at the same time. I looked over, and Calandre's face had wrinkled up like one of those pug dogs. I must have looked pretty funny too, because both Mike and Calandre were staring at me and laughing.

"Yeah, that's... smooth," I said with a painful, raspy whisper.

"I don't really like it either," said Mike. "It's very good at getting you very drunk very fast. That and taking the paint off an old car. But it's not that great of a drink."

"Thanks for warning me ahead of time, Mike," I said. "Boy, I sure feel like a special agent now. Blech!"

"Hey, at least it puts hair on your chest," said Mike.

"I sure hope not," said Calandre, who was coughing through her laughter.

"So is there anything we can be planning or doing right now to get ready for the fight?" I asked.

"Actually, yes," said Calandre, pulling out a few folded sheets of paper she'd kept with the boarding documents. "My contacts were able to get me floor plans for all of the buildings at the complex that Dantalion is holed up in."

"That's great," I said. "Thanks for getting those for us."

"You're welcome. Anything I can do to help," said Calandre.

The three of us spent the next couple of hours going over the plans, trying to figure out where Dantalion would most likely be hiding Angela, and where he would be staying. After we came up with a list of possibilities, we divided the locations up so that we'd each take a few.

One rule we had was that we shouldn't engage under any circumstances, no matter what we saw, because it was important that we worked together as a team if we were going to pull it off. That was a lot easier said than done. After we'd gone over our plan four times, we all took a break and ate some food.

I just fixed myself a sandwich out of some ham and a croissant I'd found in the kitchen. I couldn't find any mayo, so I used some fancy mustard stuff on it instead that was pretty good. I also had some very soft white cheese with it that reminded me a little of mozzarella, but wasn't.

Instead of having an adult-type beverage, I opened up a bottle of Coke. That's right, a bottle. You don't see them as often as you used to, obviously. But I prefer the bottled kind because they use real sugar in it instead of corn syrup. Nothing against corn syrup, it's just that I prefer the flavor and subtle texture of real sugar. Yes, apparently I'm a soda snob.

We watched some of the local news. I couldn't follow any of it of course, since I don't speak French. Eventually Calandre changed the channel over to BBC Europe, which was being televised in English. English-English, not American English. So every now and again I had a hard time understanding what the heck they were talking about. Apparently there were some explosions in Afghanistan, oil prices went up, and the Dow had gone down.

For whatever reason, Calandre turned it to a Jerry Lewis movie. I don't understand why the French love him so much. I mean sure, he's a decent enough actor and comedian, but it's weird that it seems like it's so universal there. Kind of like the Germans with David Hasselhoff. Just don't get it.

Anyway, I talked with Mike for a while about the ins-and-outs of recon work. How to be patient, how to use the spy equipment we brought, and what kind of things I should be looking for. He pulled out his iPad and showed me pictures of what hidden security cameras might look like and how they would be disguised.

He also explained that generally the most heavily secured areas won't look like they're secure at all. It's human nature to assume that if someone was hiding something really important, they'd have razor wire and electrified fences and cameras everywhere. Guys with sub-machine guns, dogs; you name it. But for those people that are smart, like Dantalion unfortunately, and have been trained, you want to hide your assets somewhere inconspicuous.

It made sense to me. I've had friends who worked in software and knew where the video game companies were. Generally, not always, but generally the video game companies don't mark their buildings with any signs. They aren't flashy or cool looking like you'd expect. In fact, they're the opposite. Boring structure outside, boring lobby inside. No office directory signs inside the building. No way of knowing what was hidden inside unless you actually open up a door to one of their offices. It totally makes sense. If you don't want people to know where you are, don't advertise.

So I was supposed to look for the most normal, boring, unprotected building I could find. And I was supposed to do it so that I wouldn't get noticed. That was the other thing that Mike drilled into me. Move, but move slowly. Look for any kind of sensors or devices on the ground that could alert someone to my presence. Avoid cameras at all costs. Avoid making loud noises.

A lot of it seemed obvious, and a lot of it wasn't. Like don't drink or eat much before you go, or you'll have to go. I wouldn't have thought about that. Also, try to cover up as much skin as possible, since there are cameras that can see heat, not just movement. It made me think of Predator again. Don't bring gum. Wear black, not camouflage. That one made sense at least since we were going in at night.

There's an upside to going in at night. Normal cameras will have a much harder time of seeing you, as will guards. The downside is that heat sensors will work extremely well. The upside to going in the day is that if it's warm enough, the heat sensors won't see you, but you'll be much easier to spot moving around.

It was all great information to know, and it was kind of cool learning it. I finally started to look at things the way a spy would. How to avoid detection. How to assess security. How to be like Michael Weston, or Jason Bourne.

Anyway, once Mike filled me in on how to be sneaky, we had to change trains. Apparently there's no train that goes straight from Paris to Bern. When we switched, we went through another tunnel like the one in Paris, but this one had an entire hub of connecting tunnels attached to it. Our new armed escorts, who were nice enough to help us carry the equipment, took us down a long tunnel that ended at our next train.

This one was similar to the last one, since it had tinted windows, a similar setup with kitchen and booths, but the colors were much more like they came out of a 90's music video. Sadly, this one was missing a TV, but I had Mike and Calandre to keep me busy.

I decided to speak with Calandre, and she gave me a few pointers on how to take down a person with only your bare hands. Mike was good at hand-to-hand combat, but he was outclassed by Calandre. When she showed me some of her moves, using Mike as sort of a fighting dummy, it was obvious she'd learned how to be quick, and vicious, and move in a way that was hard to react to. I could tell she'd been training in martial arts for years because it was all automatic. No thinking, just instinct and will.

Calandre showed me a few things she thought I might be able to use. Where the best places are to punch or kick someone, how to use someone's momentum against them, and how to disarm them. We spent the rest of the trip to Bern practicing what she'd taught me so that when push came to shove, hopefully my reflexes would take over and they'd save my life.

41

We arrived in Bern a little after lunchtime. None of us were very hungry since we'd been snacking the entire trip there. As we pulled into the station, I put away some of the gadgets I'd been playing with, and the weapons Calandre had tried improving my skills with.

I'm really glad she hooked up with Mike. I think they make a good couple. Are they gross? Hell yes. But still, it's kind of sweet in that disturbing 'my parent's still kiss each other' sort of way.

Mike had some connections with the CIA, and even a few friends that were working out of Switzerland. After we got off the train and into the main terminal, one of Mike's friends showed up with an odd shaped vehicle. It looked like a mini-van mated with an SUV, and had an ostrich for a godfather. Apparently, different parts of the world have different views on what's cool and what's weird.

The inside of the SUVanEgg, or whatever you want to call it, wasn't so bad. It had a big cabin, seats for each of us, and plenty of room to store our equipment. Mike's friend Burton drove, while Mike shotgunned. Calandre sat in the middle with me, while all of the toys rode in the back.

Burton seemed like a good enough guy. He kind of sounded like John Wayne, which seemed completely out of place for the rich feel of Switzerland's cities. I couldn't imagine why the guy was stationed there, other than he was either an exceptional agent who picked where he worked, or he was a bit of a troublemaker that was stationed somewhere relatively boring. I don't know why, but I don't see Switzerland planning on taking over the world anytime soon.

It took about an hour to get to our new headquarters, an old CIA hideout that had been abandoned a long time ago. Burton showed us inside, and for being abandoned it wasn't in too bad of shape. There was a thin layer of dust covering everything, and cobwebs had formed on the furniture and in the corners of the different rooms that made up the building. It'd been designed to hold about a dozen agents, and the computers it had looked like they were about ten years old.

"You can still use them," said Burton. "They should be able to get you on the Internet, but they probably won't let you play any new games on them."

"Good to know," said Mike. "We probably won't need them much. Should be able to do everything we need with the equipment we brought, but thanks Burton."

"Hey, no problem. I still owe you for that one time in Tijuana," said Burton.

Mike laughed. I looked puzzled. Calandre looked a little angry.

"Consider the debt paid in full," said Mike.

I was surprised to hear that Mike had been cool enough to use one of his favors to help out the 'Save Madison' effort. I added it to the list of things about him that impressed me.

Mike and Burton talked for a while as Calandre and I did an inventory of all the equipment we'd brought. It didn't take long to do, and thankfully everything had made the trip safely. I watched as Mike and Burton walked outside. They seemed like best friends, like two people who grew up together, but I figured that wasn't the case. I guess when you're in life-and-death situations with someone, you tend to form a strong connection with them.

I wondered if Mike and I would ever be that way. I felt more like a kid brother to him than someone he could count on in a firefight. Maybe if I proved myself to be brave, and with a lot of luck survived rescuing Madison, he might treat me as a friend and someone he trusts. I knew at the time that Mike respected me some for wanting to help, but I hadn't yet earned his full respect.

I decided to go ahead and start dusting off the computers and furniture. I found the bathroom and got some wet paper towels to finish the job. With Calandre's help, it didn't take too long to make the place look better.

I did some looking around. There was a very small kitchen in the back of the building, and the refrigerator had thankfully been emptied out a long time ago. I'd hate to think some leftover food had gone bad and came to life, and was now waiting to eat us. The thought kind of reminded me of 'The Thing', that movie where they're in the snow and monsters are after them. I highly recommend the John Carpenter version; it's awesome!

While I was looking, I also found a meeting room with a long black table and shiny chrome chairs. It had a TV screen mounted up on the wall, and a few pieces of artwork that I thought I'd seen in a hotel before. Next to the meeting room was a small utility room with several washers and dryers, and a sink.

I did find a storage room that reminded me of Mike's apartment over the bakery, because it had a number of metal shelves in it. I figured this must have been where the people who used the place previously stored their equipment. I showed Calandre, since Mike and Burton were still outside chatting, and she helped me load up the shelves with what we'd brought with us.

After we put the equipment away, I searched some more. I found a workout room that still had a weight bench and free weights, some wrestling mats, a chin-up bar, a treadmill, and a few other items. I didn't bother to clean that room since hopefully we wouldn't be staying long enough to use it.

The last area I found was the sleeping quarters. There were twelve rooms, each one about the size of a jail cell, with a bed, a dresser, a small nightstand and a lamp. Each one also had a window, thankfully, but they were frosted so you couldn't see outside. I guessed the windows were probably bulletproof, but didn't want to shoot one to find out.

I picked a room and shook the sheets and blankets outside, getting all the dust I could out of them. The room itself was a little cold since the walls were concrete. It also didn't have any vents for heating or cooling, other than some vent holes on the door. The room made me feel a little trapped, so once I'd unpacked my stuff I left it.

I passed by Calandre cleaning up her room. I figured Mike would share a room with her, but the rooms were just too tiny for two people to fit in comfortably. I'm sure that's why the beds had been the size they were, to prevent people from sleeping together. You could probably still figure a way to have sex on them, but it wouldn't be very comfortable.

Walking back into the large room at the front of the building, I saw Burton and Mike shake hands. I went up to Burton and thanked him, offering my hand. He shook it firmly, and with a very grave expression nodded his head. It was my guess that Mike had filled him in on at least some of the details of the plan. It wasn't completely abnormal to have someone out in the field as young as me, but generally they wouldn't see any real action. Under normal circumstances, I would have been left behind, either coordinating things or doing tech-stuff during the mission.

I swallowed hard, trying my best to not look rattled by his gesture. It did cement for me the seriousness of what we were about to do, and how dangerous Dantalion was. Once Burton left, I asked Mike what our next move should be.

"We should probably get some groceries and some medical supplies," said Mike. "I've been thinking about it, and we don't know how well Dantalion's been taking care of Angela and Madison. My guess is Madison's been eating okay, but all Dantalion needs to do is keep Angela alive. It's amazing just how little food someone can survive on if they have to. And I imagine the worse the conditions that Dantalion is keeping Anglea in, the more Madison is willing to do what he says. For all we know, he could be keeping Angela on an IV drip instead of feeding her."

"Do we have a vehicle then?" I asked Mike.

"Yeah. Apparently there's a small garage filled with some military vehicles around here. They're unmarked of course, so that people can't tell they're from the US. He said we can use what we need as long as we refuel them when we're done. Burton gave me a key to the garage, and another key for the security box holding all the keys. Oh, and he said there was a Jeep that should work for daily driving. I'll go get the supplies we need back in town, and you can stay here and try to get those computers working," said Mike.

"What should Calandre do?" I asked.

"Stay beautiful."

Whatever.

42

As soon as Mike left I went and told Calandre what he'd said about her 'staying beautiful.' She of course smiled and went about her business. I turned around and went back to the computer stations, firing each of them up and making sure I could get on the Internet without any problems. Thankfully, only one computer wouldn't turn on.

I went ahead and started surfing the net for information about Dantalion. It was kind of creepy what I found, actually. Apparently Dantalion had a website filled with pictures of Madison and him doing various things, and in various places around the world. There weren't any pictures of them fighting enemies or anything like that.

One thing that started to bother me though was that Madison actually looked happy in some of the pictures. I knew they'd had a relationship, but I figured that since he was such an asshole, she would have barely tolerated him. There were even a couple of pictures of them kissing. If blood could actually boil I'd have looked like a giant Christmas turkey right then.

Calandre walked up behind me.

"Taylor, are you okay?" asked Calandre.

"Yeah, why?" I replied.

"Because you're bright red, and it looks like you're about to crush your mouse in your bare hand."

Realizing she was right, I calmed down a bit. It also helped knowing that Madison loved me, and not him, and that holding her sister hostage would pretty much guarantee that she hated him. I would have felt better about it if she'd been there to hold and to kiss, but hopefully in just a few days' time I'd be able to do that again.

"I'm okay now, Calandre. I just found some pictures of Dantalion and Madison together, back when they were a couple. But I'm calming down," I said.

"I can understand why you'd feel that way. Especially since Dantalion, if he wasn't evil, would be quite good looking. He's tall, muscular, dark, with amazing hair," said Calandre.

"And what am I, chopped liver?" I asked.

"I happen to like chopped liver, so... yes," responded Calandre.

All I could do was laugh. It helped lighten the mood.

"Taylor, you have something that Dantalion will never have: Madison's heart," said Calandre.

I sat in silence for a moment.

"Thanks, Calandre. I hope when I finally fight Dantalion, that I'll still have her heart," I said.

"If you don't have it now, you will when she sees you trying to save her. A lot of girls want to be rescued by a knight in shining armor," said Calandre.

"Even the powerful ones that can punch through a school?"

"Even those girls."

I smiled at her. Calandre was incredibly sweet for a super-spy.

I gave up looking at normal websites and instead focused on news reports. I figured that maybe someone had captured some information on him that could help me kick his ass. Some bit of information from a botched mission, where someone had gotten the better of him somehow. But the more I looked, the less I found. It seemed that this guy was pretty much invincible.

They say the bigger they are, the harder they fall. My guess is that means if you think too highly of yourself, when you lose at something, your ego is damaged much worse than someone who isn't so stuck up. Or something like that. But I'm going to reuse the same phrase. What I take from it is that if they seem big and powerful, they probably are, and it's going to be a lot harder to take them down. The harder it is to make them fall. So yeah, once I was satisfied there was no information on a weakness, I gave up. I was going to try and stick to the plan as much as possible, using the weapons and gadgets Mike suggested. I just hoped they'd be enough.

Since I didn't have anything else to do, I went ahead and checked out the vehicle hangar. I wasn't ready for what I found when I went inside. It was three times bigger than it looked like from the outside because it had been built into the side of a hill. There were helicopters, tanks, trucks for transporting soldiers, Jeeps, a mobile missile launching truck, and vans that looked like the A-Team would jump out of them at any moment. There was also a plane that looked like it could take off by launching straight into the air. I think I remember seeing one in a Pepsi commercial when I was a little kid. Jump-jet or something like that.

Thankfully, Mike had left the box that contained all the vehicle keys unlocked. They were marked, so I grabbed a set of keys for a vehicle that sounded interesting. I first opened a large bay door by pressing a button near the key box. I ran as fast as I could to a tank and used the key I'd found on the hatch after climbing on top of it. I was able to pry the hatch open and climb inside.

I'd never driven a tank before, but figured it couldn't be that different from driving a car. Boy was I wrong! It took me several minutes just to figure out which button turned the damn thing on. Once I did, its engine roared to life. All sorts of screens and displays came to life. I started playing with controls one-by-one to see what they did. Eventually, I was able to get the tank moving slowly toward the door. I was just about to drive out of the hangar when Calandre showed up.

She appeared on one of my monitors. I watched her mouth moving, but couldn't hear what she was saying. I saw a button next to the screen marked 'External Audio' and I pressed it.

"What are you doing, Taylor?" asked Calandre, yelling as loud as she could at the tank.

I found what looked like the thing on a CB Radio that you talk into. I picked it up and pushed the button.

"I'm just taking it for a test drive." My voice came out of a loudspeaker on the top of the tank and echoed in the hangar.

"How about you don't," said Calandre, worried.

"We may want to use this thing. Better I learn how to use it," I said. "Wouldn't it be cool if I showed up at Dantalion's doorstep with this baby?"

Calandre thought about it for a second. She hung her head down, shaking it, and I could tell I'd won her over.

"Alright, fine Taylor," said Calandre. "But whatever you do, don't try to pilot any of the helicopters, or the Harrier."

"What's a Harrier?" I asked over the loudspeaker.

"The jet. Anyway, stick to the ground equipment. Helicopters are really difficult to pilot, and the Harrier isn't much easier. They take years of training before you're safe with them."

"Okay, I won't."

"Thanks, Taylor. Oh, and by the way, don't fire any of the weapons. We don't want to start a panic around here. Stick to driving," said Calandre.

"Fine," I said, unhappy that I wouldn't get to fire the gun mounted on top of the tank. You know, the big gun on it that goes BOOM!

I went ahead and drove the tank out of the hangar once Calandre moved out of the way. It was kinda fun, actually. Once I got her outside she went pretty fast. The ride was bumpy, but I have to say I'd rather they work on keeping the tank from taking damage than on the suspension.

I drove it down a pathway to an open field near the base. After a few minutes I was doing figure-eights, circles, moving the turret on top of the tank so that it pointed in a direction different from where the tank was pointed. I basically just messed around for awhile until I felt comfortable in it. Once I was sure I knew how to pilot the thing I parked it back in the hangar.

I also tried the missile truck, but that was boring because I couldn't fire the missiles. I'm sure it would be awesome if I could have blown something up, but otherwise it was really lame. I didn't even bother with the soldier transport, because it would be more of the same.

I did drive around in a Jeep, which went fast enough to be entertaining. I was surprised how well it could turn, and I was even more surprised I didn't roll it as I tried taking some sharp turns at fast speeds. I wouldn't recommend trying it though in your normal Jeep. That's my 'Don't Try This at Home' disclaimer.

Once I was done fooling around with the land vehicles, just for fun I got in the Jump-jet. I didn't turn it on or anything, but I did strap myself in. There wasn't a helmet, so I didn't exactly feel like I was in the 'danger zone'. But it was cool playing around with the joysticks that controlled it. I admit, even at my age I made some sound effects for firing the guns and launching my missiles. A few of them even found their targets, and I made the explosion sounds too. I did make sure to get out of the cockpit before Calandre or Mike found me; I figured that'd be bad.

I closed the cockpit behind me as I climbed down the jet's ladder then made my way back to the key box. After putting the keys away, I turned back to look at all the cool vehicles we could use. Standing there for a moment, I eventually pressed the red button on the wall, closing the massive hangar's main doors then left.

43

As I walked back to the main building, I heard Mike pull up.

"What are you doin' out here, Taylor?" asked Mike, as he drove up next to me.

"Oh, I just tried out some of the vehicles," I said.

"Was Calandre teaching you?" he asked.

"Nope. Figuring it out on my own," I replied.

"Tell me you didn't mess with the Harrier."

"Nope, I left that one alone."

"Good. It's pretty hard to pilot. Same with the 'copters."

"That's what I'd heard."

"So, can you help me carry this stuff in?" asked Mike, pointing to the bags of groceries in the back.

"Can do."

I grabbed as many bags as my arms could carry. Between the two of us we were able to get everything inside. I started filling the kitchen's fridge with all of the stuff that needed to be kept cold. Mike had purchased a mix of foods: makings for sandwiches, cans of soup and chili, bagged salad, various breads, chips, Swiss chocolate, cheese for fondue, eggs, milk, and some random fruits and vegetables. He also had some basic first-aid supplies like bandages, gauze, ointment, splint materials, a neck brace, an air cast, safety scissors, thread and needle, ice packs, heat packs, syringes, morphine (not sure how he got that), saline solution in IV bags (or that), and a blood transfusion kit.

"Wow, you really did get a lot of stuff. Thanks, Mike," I said.

"Yeah, sure, no worries. Calandre doing okay?" he asked.

"Yup. She's been pretty busy getting stuff ready for our recon mission."

"She's an amazing woman," said Mike.

"I have to agree. Make sure you tell her that," I said.

"Don't worry, I will."

"So when do you figure we'll be going?" I asked.

"As soon as we're ready. No reason to waste time," replied Mike. "It's nearly dark out, and by the time we get to Dantalion's compound it'll be pitch black."

"I'm cool with that. I'll go get my gear ready."

I walked back to my room where I'd left my gear. I decided that even though we were supposed to be doing just recon work, it'd be best to wear something that would keep me alive. I would at least wear the psychic helmet that Mike gave me. I also loaded up on sonic grenades, and grabbed an assault rifle with a very good scope and heat-vision as well.

Mike stopped by my room briefly.

"Hey Taylor, one more thing: don't pack too heavy. We'll need to travel on foot a ways so that the Jeep won't give us away," said Mike.

"Yeah, that makes sense. Any other suggestions?" I asked.

"Bring some snacks; it could be a long night. And nothing that will upset your stomach. Last thing we want is a fart setting off a heat sensor."

I just laughed. Mike turned and left the room. It took me a few more minutes and then I was all suited up and ready to go. I waited for everyone else in the big front room of the base, but I didn't have to wait long. Calandre came out all dressed in black and wore a ponytail that made her look as sexy as she was dangerous. After a few minutes of standing around with her in silence, Mike appeared.

"You two ready?" Mike asked.

"Yeah," said Calandre.

"Me too," I replied.

"What, no jokes about being born ready?" asked Mike.

"Didn't want to beat a dead horse up a tree," said Calandre. Mike and I laughed.

We loaded up the Jeep with our gear. I noticed Calandre had pretty much the same equipment I'd brought, except for the helmet. Unfortunately, Mike only had one, otherwise we'd all be wearing them. Mike brought a sniper rifle instead of an assault rifle, and frag grenades instead of sonic grenades. He also had a number of knives strapped to his bulletproof vest, and two side arms, which both looked like the M9 I'd trained with. It seemed like he was more concerned with fighting offensively than defensively, which would be good if we got into a major firefight. Calandre and I could distract Dantalion while Mike could damage him.

The trip to Dantalion's base took a while. On the way there I checked my gear three times. Calandre eventually put her hand on mine at the start of the fourth time to get me to calm down.

"Taylor, they're fine. You've already checked them. Don't worry, we're just going to get a look at things. No fighting if we can help it," said Calandre.

"And what if we can't?" I asked.

"We'll deal with that when it happens. You know it's possible to over-prepare. Sometimes people work so hard at something, that when the time actually comes for them to use their skills they freeze. Sometimes they overcompensate. Like if they were going to fire at a moving target, and they were a perfect shot on a training course, when it comes time to fire at a real enemy they lead their target too much and blow the shot. Athletes do it too. They make their muscles too big so that they aren't useful in competition. Or they run much farther than they need to, to train for sprinting."

"I'd never really thought of it that way. I guess I'm just nervous. It's my first time going on a real mission like this, and there's a chance we all might die," I said.

"Oh, Taylor, it's okay to be nervous. Just remember you have two of the world's best soldiers backing you up," said Calandre.

"And best looking," said Mike.

"Wow, conceited much?" I said.

"Flaunt what ya got is what I always say," said Mike.

"You do have a nice butt," said Calandre to Mike.

"Ack! I'm not hearing this!" I said, putting my hands over my ears.

They kissed, and I just turned away and did my best to ignore them.

Eventually we came within about a mile of Dantalion's HQ. Mike had us get out of the car after he parked it off to the side of the road. We helped him cover it with tree branches, leaves; pretty much anything we could get our hands on. It took us about thirty minutes to completely hide it, and it was almost like it wasn't there. Apparently, Mike was quite good at concealing things.

"Will we be able to find it when we get back?" I asked.

"Yeah, I have a tracking device installed in it. That way if some kid stumbles onto it and goes for a joyride, I can find his stupid ass and smack him," said Mike.

"Sounds reasonable," I replied.

Mike led us a little ways into a forested area, and then ran us parallel to the street. That way we could keep an eye on traffic, but we wouldn't be seen. As we walked, Mike rubbed black makeup onto his face to darken it, and so did Calandre. I didn't need to since the helmet I brought covered up all of my face. It was nice to wear actually, since it was kind of cold out.

The walk was awesome in the moonlight. I could tell that the trees were kind of a bright green color, instead of the darker green I was used to back home. They were also really full, which at times made it difficult to walk through the forested area. A couple of times we had to go deeper into the forest to get around a few particularly bushy trees.

The air was cool and refreshing. A perfect night for a walk if you aren't carrying a small arsenal with you, which I was. I pulled out a granola bar and took a few bites, more to calm my nerves than because I was hungry. It wasn't long before we reached our destination. I really didn't expect what I saw when we got there. Not at all.

44

After about fifteen minutes of walking I could see Dantalion's headquarters. It wasn't at all what I'd imagined. I was thinking it would look like some simple buildings, square and uninteresting, like warehouses. Instead, it was a freakin' castle! It was huge, lit up like a Christmas tree and beautiful, and I couldn't believe I'd be doing battle in a castle. Well, I guess it's kind of fitting, if you think of me being a knight, and Dantalion being a dragon.

Calandre looked back and saw my mouth hanging open.

"What is it, Taylor?" she asked.

"Um, I don't know if you noticed, but it's a castle," I replied.

"And?"

"Oh. Never mind." Sigh.

"I think we're probably close enough," said Mike. "Remember, we're here to figure out where he's keeping Angela, and hopefully where Dantalion and Madison are staying. Don't engage Dantalion unless you absolutely have to. And don't use the coms in case he's monitoring radio signals. We meet back here in two hours. Taylor, always make sure you're hidden, and move slowly. Stick to the front of the castle, because I'm betting that Dantalion will want to stay toward the front so he can defend it. Calandre and I will scout around the sides of the complex and see if there are any other buildings in the back. My guess is that's where Angela will be."

"I'll do all that, Mike. And thanks again, both of you, for helping me try and rescue Madison. I wish I could do something more than just say thank you," I said.

"Don't sweat it, kid. I'm here for Madison as much as you are. Calandre is the one who really deserves the thanks," replied Mike.

"Then Calandre, thank you."

Calandre smiled at me, put a hand on my shoulder then started walking away toward the castle. Mike moved toward the road, which thankfully had trees on both sides, and making sure he wouldn't be spotted, he ran as fast as he could across it. I watched him make it to the trees and then disappear.

I stayed back. I wasn't going to need to get any closer to scout the front of the castle. I pulled the assault rifle off my back and set up the scope for normal viewing. The castle looked almost too perfect, like someone had gone in and washed every single stone by hand. Maybe they had, which was a weird thought. It started messing with my head a little, that Dantalion would have the resources to own such a large place. Of course, I guess with his powers, he could have just taken it by force.

After I came back to reality, I started looking for signs of security. I was easily able to spot a number of cameras that were placed along the castle walls. Mike and Calandre had told me to look for blind spots, places where someone might be able to sneak in without being seen by the cameras. I spent twenty minutes trying to figure a way in, but I never could find one. There were cameras everywhere.

The really suck thing I found out is that most high-end security systems now don't have a donut eating guard that you could distract, or hope didn't see you on the cameras. Nowadays they have software that can recognize a person's face and body, and send you a text message on your phone saying there are intruders, who they are and exactly where they are. It can also give you information from their Facebook or Twitter pages, so that you could go knocking on their friend's doors too.

I didn't see any guards, which made sense because Dantalion probably thought he didn't need any. When you're a super-powerful bad guy, you don't rely on others to do your dirty work, despite what the movies tell you. You enjoy hurting people, defeating people, so you do all the fighting yourself. Also, you would have less people around that could sabotage what you're trying to accomplish. Less people that you don't really trust.

Plus, who would want to work for a bad guy? I mean the pay couldn't possibly be worth it. You could get shot or killed at any minute. If you were lucky, maybe you'd only get arrested. And the hours would probably be horrible. I can't imagine anyone taking a job like that, unless they were desperate. And even then there are much better, safer jobs out there. Yup, I don't think I'd want to be a henchman.

I decided that if I wanted a better view, I would need to climb a tree. The nice thing about the bushy trees was that they had a lot of good limbs for climbing. I didn't plan to go too far, so I left most of my gear at the base of the tree. I opened up my backpack, pulled out my rope and another granola bar then took the strap of my assault rifle and slung it over my back. It only took me a few minutes to climb high enough where I could see through the limbs but still be hidden.

I carefully wrapped the rope around the tree to keep from falling out of it then tied the other end to my waist. I wasn't planning to be up in the tree for very long, but wanted to be prepared just in case. Also, I needed both hands to work the scope on my rifle. Once I was sure I wouldn't fall out of the tree, I pulled my assault rifle back over my shoulder and set the scope up for heat vision.

I was glad to have that kind of tech, because without it I think my recon trip would have been a waste of time. The first thing I noticed was all the lights that showed up in the scope. There were so many, it kind of looked like a weird colored connect-the-dots picture. I slowly moved the scope around, and I was finally able to see something through one of the castle's windows.

I saw what looked like two people, standing and arguing. I couldn't tell at first who was who, and if it was even Dantalion and Madison. Suddenly, what looked like a pair of wings expanded out of one person's back. Unless Dantalion had somehow stolen her powers, that was my baby.

I kept watching. After a few minutes of watching them move around the room, still arguing, they moved to an area covered by the castle walls. Unfortunately, the heat vision doesn't work through stone. I kept watching for a while, hoping to see them pass by another window, but I never did see them again.

With the gun still aimed at the room I'd seen them in, I flipped the scope back into normal vision mode then zoomed backward so I could see more of the castle. The window I'd been looking through was four floors up, and about three windows in from the left. I figured Mike and Calandre would want to know exactly where I'd seen them. I didn't know if the information would help much, but it couldn't hurt.

I looked down at my watch and realized it was time to meet up with Mike and Calandre again. I undid the rope, made my way down the tree, collected my things then walked the short distance back to the rendezvous point. Mike was already waiting for me when I got there, but Calandre wasn't back yet.

"Do you know where Calandre is?" I asked.

"Not a clue. I'm sure she's fine though. She's one of the best," said Mike. "Besides, if there was a problem, all hell would be breaking loose inside the castle. We'd know about it."

"That's true," I said. "So did you find out where they were hiding Angela?"

"Nothing I can confirm. I did find a smaller building out back that looked like it houses groundskeeping equipment. I'd put my money on that, since it had an HVAC system on the roof, and you don't normally need to heat or air condition a storage building," said Mike.

"Yeah, that makes a lot of sense. Too bad we don't know for sure," I said.

"Maybe Calandre had more luck," replied Mike.

Just then Calandre walked up to us with a smug look on her face.

"Talking about me?" asked Calandre.

"Maybe, baby," said Mike.

As much as I like Mike, right then I sort of wish he was stranded in an elevator very far away from me.

"You're rhyming now? Really?" I said.

"Well I think it's charming," said Calandre.

"Yeah, whatever. So what'd you find, Calandre?" I asked.

"Angela is in a building at the opposite side of the complex. Some kind of storage building," she said.

"Housing groundskeeping equipment?" I asked.

"Yes, how did you know?" asked Calandre.

"Because I guessed the same thing. Are you absolutely certain it's the right building?" asked Mike.

"Of course."

"How do you know?"

"Because I snuck in," said Calandre.

"Wait, you what?" I said.

"I snuck in."

"How the hell did you manage that?" asked Mike.

"I found a small blind spot in the security cameras there. I crept up very slowly to the building, and did my best to avoid making any noise. Once I got to the building, I used a gadget I brought along to hack the touch panel on the door. When I finally got inside, it was deserted and dark. Apparently, he didn't bother to install cameras on the inside, since he has so many on the outside. So I was able to walk around freely. I found the room he's keeping Angela in. She looks well fed, thankfully, and other than being tied up, she didn't seem to be in bad shape," said Calandre.

"Why the hell didn't you help her escape then?" I asked.

"Taylor, we're not ready to fight Dantalion yet. We don't have a credible diversion, and we don't have all the equipment we'll need. If we snuck Angela out, he'd know we were here in Switzerland. We also don't know if she has booby traps on her, or at the very least if we'd set off an alarm if we tried to get her out. It isn't the right time," said Calandre.

I thought about it for a minute and realized she was right. Even if we got Angela out, Dantalion might figure a way to use it against us. And if we botched things and he found us, he'd kill us. We just didn't have all the things we needed to take him out.

"Okay, I understand. I don't like it, but I understand. I'm glad you're the one that found her. I think I would have probably risked freeing her if I was given the chance," I said.

"And that's understandable. You're trying to save two people, and that would definitely solve half the problem, if you were lucky enough to get her out safely. But that's also part of the reason why we left you here to look for Madison and Dantalion. You're new to this, so you're bound to make mistakes. Speaking of which, did you find out where Madison and Dantalion were?" asked Calandre.

"Yeah, I saw them up on the fourth floor of the castle, three windows in from the left. They seemed to be arguing," I said.

"How certain are you that it was them?" asked Mike.

"Madison popped her wings out. My guess is it was out of anger at Dantalion," I responded.

"That's probably good enough. Not too many people out there walking around with wings, and even then, they aren't likely to be holed up in a castle in the middle of Switzerland," said Mike.

"Yeah, no joke," I replied. "So we done here?"

"Looks like it," said Mike.

We moved a little faster heading back since we were all hungry, tired, and less likely to stumble upon any surprises the further we got from the castle. I took off my helmet and carried it at my side, which was nice because it started to smell a little funny from wearing it for so long. I mean I brush my teeth and shampoo and everything, but even your head would start to smell funny after two hours.

It took us a few minutes to find the Jeep in the dark, once we got close to it, and another few minutes to remove all of the branches and leaves we'd used. I got in the back again, but this time Calandre drove and Mike rode shotgun.

I was happy to have survived my first mission, and it was a successful one. I suppose any mission you get to walk away from is a successful one. Live to fight another day and all that. But the main thing was that both Madison and Angela were alive and healthy. I was so glad to know that. The not knowing is what kills you.

45

When we got back to the base it was pretty late. Mike was cool enough to make us all dinner, which he threw together from the groceries he bought earlier in the day. It was some kind of soupy stew, which I'm normally not a big fan of, but somehow he made it taste good. I wish I would have had a little hot sauce to add to it, to give it some kick, but honestly it was good just to have a warm meal after being out in the cold.

We talked while we ate, and it kind of felt like we were becoming a family now. Mike and Calandre were both interested in what I wanted to do with my life. What college I might go to, what I might study, and where I wanted to work. I hadn't really put too much thought into it. My Dad of course wanted me to be a software developer, but I just didn't feel like that was what I wanted to do with my life. Don't get me wrong, I play around with writing software, and I'm fairly good at it. It's a decent living, with reasonable job security. If it's for you then go for it. It just doesn't fit me and my personality well.

I kind of want to be like Madison; a writer. I mean I'm writing this book, aren't I? It's been a lot of work. It's not easy stringing sentences together, revising them, making sure they not only explain what I'm thinking but sound nice. That's one of the hardest parts of writing: making the words sound nice. Madison has a magical way of writing. It seems so effortless. It's like watching a ballerina dance, moving smoothly, with grace and power. I so wish I could do that.

I also love art, but I've found that if I work on a piece long enough I start to get bored. It just doesn't hold my attention the way that writing does. Every single word I type is me creating something new. When I paint or draw, the creative portion is finished almost immediately, at the very beginning. After you've come up with a concept, it's a matter of executing it. That's where skill and experience come into play. The other thing is that it's more difficult to make money selling artwork than it is selling books. At least from what I've seen.

Anyway, I explained all of this to Mike and Calandre. They seemed impressed that I was pretty certain what I wanted to do with my life. I told them I'd thought about writing down my adventures, not that anyone would believe they were real, but I could just put it out as fiction instead of as an autobiography. They both liked the idea of being immortalized in my book. And they were both cool with me using their real first names. So the Mike and Calandre you're reading about are actually named Mike and Calandre in real life.

They also both admitted that James Bond was the reason they wanted to get into the spy business. It seemed so glamorous, and dangerous, and exciting to them. They also agreed that the reality wasn't as fun as what the books and movies make it seem like. But once you're actually doing the job, you realize just how important it is. You help keep bad people from doing bad things. It's a calling.

The pay certainly isn't that great if you work for the government. They told me the problem with working for a private company as a spy is that you don't know if you're working for good guys or bad guys. I really like that they can still see things in black and white like that. I see the world mostly as shades of gray, and no, not the book.

Once we finished up dinner, I went and took a shower. It was several minutes before the water got warm, but once it did, steam rose up from the water. I had to turn it down so I wouldn't get scalded. I let the water rinse all the stink off of me, especially my stinky head. It felt nice to get warmed up by the water. It's something I've always really liked. Makes me feel alive again. I toweled off, slipped on a t-shirt and shorts, and headed to bed.

I didn't sleep very well that night. It was a huge relief to know that the girls were alive and well, don't get me wrong, but I knew that I'd be fighting Dantalion very soon. There was a very good possibility I might die.

Anyway, when I woke up the next morning, I figured I was running on about four-and-a-half hours of sleep. Apparently I'd been moving around a lot in the night, because I'd kicked the covers off my bed. It was chilly in my room, so I changed into a pair of sweatpants and a long sleeve shirt and made my way to the kitchen.

No one else was up yet. I decided to go ahead and make up some coffee, eggs and toast. I'm not a chef or anything, but I have to say, it all turned out pretty good. I put some onions and some cheese in with the eggs and scrambled them. Mike had purchased some apple cinnamon spread stuff that I put on the toast and it was awesome.

Once the coffee was ready, I sat down and ate. I didn't enjoy eating alone so much. Being on vacation at home without my folks in some ways was nice, but I enjoy having people around. Thankfully, the smell of coffee made its way down to Mike and Calandre's rooms, and they got up to see what I was fixing.

Both Mike and Calandre came into the kitchen and poured themselves a cup. I made plenty, so it wasn't a big deal, and I figured it was the least I could do since they'd both been awesome, even if they'd been gross around me. I did tell Mike and Calandre over coffee that I wasn't sure I wanted to be a spy. That although some parts of being a spy I enjoyed, and that I really liked working with them, I just didn't know that I would want to do it for a living.

I honestly don't think Madison would want to do it for a living either. She just feels compelled to use her powers because she's a good person and wants to help in any way she can. That's why she's continued working for White Ops.

Mike and Calandre both had big bowls of cereal then took showers. I have no idea if they took a shower together, or just both happened to shower at the same time, but I REALLY didn't want to know. While I was waiting, I fixed myself a bowl of cereal too. Hey, I'm a growing boy!

In the meantime, I looked over the floor plans that Calandre brought along so that I'd know what the layout would be like. Once they were dressed, Calandre and Mike joined me at the kitchen table.

"So we know exactly where the two of you are going," I said. "And I think I know what I should do for a diversion."

"Oh yeah? What's that?" asked Mike.

"I think I should drive a tank up to the front of the building and fire at it with the gun," I replied.

"Uh, no," said Mike.

"Why not?" I asked.

"Actually, I'm with Taylor on this one, why not?" asked Calandre.

"You don't even know how to use it," said Mike.

"That was one of the vehicles I practiced with," I said.

"And he's decent with it," said Calandre.

"I thought you'd just driven the trucks and Jeeps around," responded Mike.

"Nope, I thought it might be useful to figure out how to use it, just in case. Honestly, I think it gives me my best chance for survival. Dantalion is strong, but I think he'd have a hard time getting into a tank, and I can do some serious damage to his headquarters with it," I said.

"That would definitely get his attention. Well crap, I guess that would work. We just need to figure out a way to get it down the road without him noticing it. Some kind of Trojan horse," said Mike.

"What if we went at dark, and I drove it with the lights off? It doesn't seem to make a lot of noise, and I think I've figured out how to work the night vision on it," I suggested.

"Actually it's FLIR, not night vision," said Mike.

"Wait, what's the difference?" I asked.

"FLIR is forward-looking infrared. It's based on heat, like the scope your assault rifle has. Night vision just amplifies the ambient light that already exists. So if it were pitch black out, you wouldn't see anything. With FLIR, you can still see things. For the most part, FLIR is better," said Mike.

"Ah, gotcha," I replied. "So anyway, I'd use the FLIR system to make my way to the castle, and then when I get close enough I'll open fire. I'll make sure you guys are in place before I let him know I'm there," I said.

"We need to figure out a way to signal without alerting Dantalion to our presence, which means avoiding coms. If he hears radio chatter, he'll know it's more than just you, Taylor," said Mike.

The three of us brainstormed some ideas. My idea was the simplest and seemed the most effective. Mike would just shoot a flare from the back of the castle to the front of it. It won't actually light up until it is right over my head, and when I'm lit up and visible, I'll go ahead and fire. Once Mike and Calandre hear me firing, they'll know it's time to rescue Angela. I just had to hope that Dantalion wouldn't notice the trajectory of the flare, going behind me instead of in front of me.

While we waited for the dark to come, Mike spent time with me practicing in the tank. He showed me how to use all the controls inside of it, showed me what not to touch, and how to drive it effectively. He also showed me the machine gun turret mounted on top of it, in case the gun was destroyed. I practiced using it without actually firing it, because we didn't want the neighbors realizing what we were doing. Sure, they were a ways down the road, but the noise would have traveled pretty far. Better safe than sorry.

Mike thought I was a natural. I just told him it was from playing video games, which was probably true. I had fun driving the tank around, even if it was kinda cramped inside. I got good enough with it that I could move the tank one direction while I spun the gun in another and fired. Well, if I was actually firing it.

We hopped out of the tank after Mike taught me how to parallel park it. He'd made me drive it over to the fuel depot, and he started refueling it, making sure I had plenty of fuel for the trip.

"Wait, Mike, won't it take me forever just to get to the castle in the first place?" I asked.

"Actually, it tops out at 45 mph, which isn't that bad. Not freeway speeds, but for the trip you're going on, it should be sufficient," said Mike.

"Oh, okay, no problem," I replied. "Will you guys be in the tank with me until we get there?" I asked.

"No, we'll take a second vehicle. That way we can get Angela clear more easily."

"That makes sense. Also, who knows if the tank will survive the fight? It'd be a long walk back," I mentioned.

For lunch we all ate light; stuff that would settle well on our stomachs. Calandre and Mike suggested we skip dinner altogether so that if I got nervous I wouldn't throw up in my helmet. Yeah, that was a pleasant thought.

We spent some time going over the battle plan; the timing. Who would take care of the different goals we'd need to accomplish. It wasn't really that difficult, since Calandre and Mike would work together, and I'd be working alone. They both said my biggest goal should be distracting Dantalion, not trying to kill him. The more general damage I could do, and the more chaos and havoc I could create, the better.

So I started thinking about it like it actually was a video game. I had a strategy from an old video game from the 80's that I thought would work. I tucked the idea away in the back of my mind, and we continued going over our strategy until we knew it forwards and backwards.

A few hours before we left I started having cold sweats. I'd never had them before. I could tell it was worrying Mike and Calandre. They suggested that right before we left I should grab a shower. If you haven't had the cold sweats before, basically think of yourself drenched in sweat after running a couple of miles on a hot summer day, only you aren't out of breath. The sweat actually ran down my sides. It was crazy.

Anyway, I spent some time before my shower reminding myself of all the reasons I loved Madison. Her heart. Her sweetness. Her body (hey, I'm allowed!) Her mind. And above all else, her smile. I would die for that smile.

I took my shower, and it did help some. It was both a good distraction, and a way to clean off all the saltwater I had sweat. I hadn't had much to drink, so I figured once I got cleaned up that would be the end of the cold sweats. And for the most part that was true.

I changed into my battle gear, and I had Calandre check me to make sure I'd done everything right. She gave me a 'thumbs up' to let me know everything looked like I'd put it on how I was supposed to. I went to the hangar and drove the tank up to the main building then loaded up all my gear. It was dark out, and finally time to go.

46

I checked to make sure Mike and Calandre were ready before I got in the tank.

"Any last advice?" I asked them.

"Don't get dead," said Mike.

"Wasn't that in a movie?" I asked.

"Hey, I didn't say it was original."

"Stay safe, Taylor," said Calandre.

"Thanks, you too. Let me know the second you get Angela out of there. I'll let Madison know, if I'm able to. If I die before you get Angela out, make sure that Madison knows that Angela's rescued. She needs to know," I said.

"We will," said Calandre.

I gave them both hugs, which surprised Mike a little. I just figured it was a good way to let them know how much their help meant to me. And I kinda needed a hug right about then.

"So am I following you guys?" I asked.

"Nope, we're following you," said Mike. "You offer much better protection from a frontal assault, and we don't want to get in the way of your gun if for some reason we run into him on the road. Also, it'll be easier to make sure you haven't driven yourself into a ditch."

"Ha frickin' ha," I said.

I turned and started to climb into the tank. Once I was about to get in I waved to them, not knowing if it'd be the last time I saw either of them. My mission was dangerous, but knowing how devious Dantalion was, their mission could prove just as deadly. Mike and Calandre put an arm around each other, waved back to me then got into their Jeep.

I climbed into the tank. I was really glad I spent all that time practicing with it, because I actually felt comfortable driving it around. I drove with the lights on the outside, more for other driver's safety than my own, because with the FLIR I could see everything just fine anyway.

The drive was long and boring, and it seemed to take forever. I was too nervous to do anything but drive, so I went over the different tank systems in my head, reminding myself of how everything worked. I figured there might be a moment when using one of the systems could save my life, and the faster I could get to it and use it, the better chance I had of surviving.

About two-thirds of the way there I saw a deer that was standing directly in front of us, eyes reflecting the tank light back at me. I stopped, and it just kept staring. Mike and Calandre had stopped behind me, but couldn't see what was blocking the road. I heard a crackle over the radio.

"Taylor, come in," said Mike over the radio.

I picked up the CB microphone thing and squeezed the button.

"Mike, there's a deer in the middle of the road," I replied.

"Can you get it to move?"

"I don't think so."

"Okay, stay in the tank. I'll take care of it."

I was able to look at one of the monitors in the tank and see what was behind me. I saw Mike get out and very carefully walk around the tank. Calandre also got out and moved to the driver's seat, leaving the engine on just in case. I watched as Mike made his way over to the deer.

As he approached, it kind of bobbed its head a little, not knowing what to do, whether to run, or to stay motionless. It looked young and didn't have any antlers. I didn't know much about deer, but I figured it was either a very young male deer, or a female deer. Great, now that song from 'The Sound of Music' is playing in my head. Sigh.

Anyway, Mike very carefully came within a few feet of it then started waving his hands up and down rapidly. The deer bobbed his head once more and bolted. Mike turned toward the tank, and I could see there was a very serious look on his face. He then made his way back to the truck as Calandre got back out and let him drive again.

A few seconds after Mike got in the Jeep I heard the radio crackle to life again.

"Taylor, you saw that?" asked Mike.

"Yeah, why?"

"Don't be the deer. It was too frightened to act. Thought that maybe if it just stood there, we'd give up and leave. Didn't even have the good sense to run when I got right up to it. It was lucky that we weren't out to hurt it. But Dantalion will be. He's going to do his best to kill you Taylor, and he's very, very good at it. Remember this. Sometimes all that matters is that you act. You move left, you move right. But if you stay right where you are, you're dead."

I let it sink in for a moment. I pushed the button to talk. "Thanks, Mike," was all I could say.

I got the tank rolling again. I kept those words running through my head as we continued down the road. 'Don't be the deer.'

The rest of the drive was as boring as the first two-thirds. When Mike thought we were close enough to the castle he flashed his headlights at me. I came to a stop then turned off my exterior lights and turned on the FLIR system. I could pretty easily see everything around me.

I looked in the rear-view monitor and I could see both Mike and Calandre putting what looked like night vision goggles on. It was kind of funny; they both looked like aliens now and I couldn't help but laugh a little. They also turned their headlights off. I got the tank rolling again. Now I had to be alert, because pretty soon Dantalion might know I was there.

I took my time, making sure that I was running as quietly as possible. I even avoided running over branches and rocks just in case it made more noise. But honestly, with a tank that size, it was making noise.

I came up over a slight hill and I could finally see the castle. It was lit up just like it had been the night before. Everything seemed the same as I'd remembered it. Dantalion must not have realized we'd been there, which was a really good thing. I stopped the tank so that Mike and Calandre would know we were there. I watched in my rear-view display as they drove off the road and into the forest.

Once I was sure they were out of sight, I got all of my gear ready in case I had to get out of the tank. I put on my helmet, made sure my body armor was still attached correctly, and that all of my weapons were loaded. Trying to see in the helmet was a little tough, but I knew that something could go wrong and I might have to leave the tank in a hurry.

I waited. My stomach was a big ball of nerves, and I could feel the cold sweats again. I said a prayer to myself. Hoped my parents would understand if I didn't survive. Hoped they knew I loved them. After ten minutes that felt like torture, I saw the flare.

The tank lurched forward as I gave her all the power she could handle. I aimed the gun barrel up slightly, but waited until I was sure I'd hit the main castle wall. There were two stone towers, one on each side that I passed as I entered into the protected area. Connected to them were long walls that surrounded the main castle and ran along to the back of the complex.

I drove straight through, right in between the towers, hoping that Dantalion hadn't set up any mines or other explosive devices under the cobblestone. I was starting to calm down a little now that I was actually on the move. Once I was absolutely sure I was on target, I fired.

It's amazing just how much force the gun had. Even though I had several things protecting my hearing, I could make out the loud deep roar. It also shook the tank a little when it went off. I checked my screen and I'd scored a direct hit to the middle of the castle. Stone flew in all directions, and I could tell that I hadn't just made a hole in it. It had caved in somewhat, forming a pile of rock below the hole.

I stopped the tank a few hundred feet from the castle wall. I turned the gun to the right and fired again. Direct hit, sending more stone flying. It made the front of the castle cave in even more, and I could see some of the furniture and paintings fall out of the hole I'd just made.

I turned the gun to the left and fired a third time. A tower that had been placed a few floors up crumbled down with the main castle wall, smashing into the ground. It helped cover up the hole I'd just made.

Once the dust settled, he emerged. He was dressed all in black, just like usual. What a douche bag. But what worried me wasn't so much Dantalion's appearance, as how he arrived. He was being carried by Madison, who had flown both of them down from a tower that was still standing off to the right. She dropped him on the ground then stood right next to him.

I couldn't tell by the cold expression on her face what she was thinking. It kind of worried me. Of course, there's no way for her to know that it was me, since I was in a frickin' tank. And inside that tank, I was covered in body armor and a helmet. To her, I could have just been some crazy person storming a castle for money.

Dantalion looked from the tank to the damaged castle wall. As he turned away, I aimed the gun and fired a shot directly at him. Madison, thank goodness, was still glowing and still alert. She jumped out of the way to safety as the round nailed him and sent him flying against the wall. As he hit the wall, the round exploded, sending stones raining down on top of him.

Being a kid, and still sort of seeing it like a video game, I cheered. I was pretty impressed with myself until I saw the pile of rubble move, and Dantalion emerge. He looked stunned. Unfortunately, he wasn't dead. His shirt was completely missing and his pants were torn to shreds. Seeing his overly ripped body made me want to puke. Thankfully, he was still stunned. This time I loaded a white phosphorous round then fired. Another direct hit. The tank was freakin' awesome!

Anyway, white phosphorous burns pretty much everything it touches. Dantalion was engulfed in a ball of flames. I could see the last of his clothes catch fire, as well as his long black hair, which had already been burnt from the first round I'd hit him with. Smoke poured from him like one of those Fourth of July smoke bombs. In a panic, Dantalion dropped to the ground, rolling as fast as he could to put out the flames. For a moment he just stayed there, on the ground, not moving.

I looked at Madison through one of my screens. She looked so beautiful, glowing like that, with all the destruction around her. She'd been smart enough to get completely out of the way of my shooting. I knew she was pretty much indestructible when she glowed, but I still didn't want to do her any harm. She was the only thing that mattered to me in the whole world.

I turned on the external speaker system and started talking.

"Madison, it's me, Taylor!" echoed around the castle in an almost robotic sound.

"Taylor? Taylor!" yelled Madison.

Madison's face had a look of happiness and surprise on it, until she thought about the situation. I could see an expression of horror form on her face.

"No, Taylor!" she yelled. "You have to leave, he has Angela locked up somewhere! He might kill her!"

I couldn't tell her that Angela was being rescued, just in case Dantalion had a way to kill Angela remotely. I couldn't risk it. So I talked.

"I love you, Madison!"

"I love you too, Taylor, but you have to go! Please, hurry, before he gets back up!"

I watched in horror as Madison walked over to Dantalion, still laying on the ground, and stood in front of him, preventing me from firing.

"Madison, baby, you need to get out of the way!" I said.

"I can't Taylor. Don't make me choose between you and Angela. Please don't do that. I know your heart is in the right place, but you have to go!"

I saw Dantalion start to move, first push himself up onto his palms and knees then very slowly stand back up. I could tell he was still reeling from the two direct hits he'd taken, but somehow he'd survived both. I have to say, it was pretty funny seeing him now though, completely bald and naked. At the very least I'd humiliated him.

I should have expected what happened next. Dantalion looked over at Madison and said something to her that I couldn't hear. I tried to turn up the sound of the external microphones, but it didn't help. I watched as Madison shook her head back and forth, got down on her knees and it seemed like she was begging to Dantalion. I never thought I'd see her cave like that. That wasn't good. She covered her head, and I could see her body move like she was sobbing.

I didn't like where things were going. I started to back the tank up some, when I saw Dantalion yelling at her. A dozen or so creepy black tendrils stretched out from behind his back and started to wrap around Madison. They seemed to writhe and burn in pain at the touch of her glow, and they retracted, but they had done their job. Madison stood up, turned to me, and with tears in her eyes soared into the air. I watched helplessly as she flew up several hundred feet. I actually lost sight of her on my screens for a moment. Then, she ripped the top of the tank off.

47

Thankfully, I was prepared for something like this. I watched her hover a few feet over the tank as she took the turret and threw it aside like it was made out of cardboard. I knew she was strong, but I'd never really known just how strong. It startled me. With only a half-second to think, I pulled out a sonic grenade, yanked the pin, and threw it above her. It took her a second to realize that I'd thrown a grenade, a second to decide what to do, and as it came back down she caught it, I assume to protect me from the blast.

She apparently wasn't familiar with the grenade, because she got a puzzled look on her face when she turned it over in her hand. Then it went off. Thankfully, Mike had done a good job with the helmet. I couldn't hear the grenade go off. In fact, it was like someone had blown a dog whistle. I panicked as I watched Madison cover her ears and roll up into a ball on the top of the tank. Even Dantalion, who had approached us but was still fifty feet away, covered his ears.

I stood up and climbed out of the tank, making sure I had all my equipment with me. Once I got on the ground, I pulled out another sonic grenade, yanked the pin then held it in my hand without releasing it, preventing it from going off. I could tell that the effects of the first grenade were starting to fade, so I released the second, throwing it closer to Dantalion, but just out of the a-hole's reach.

I moved to the back of the tank, putting it between me and Dantalion. Opening up my bag of toys, I pulled out my sniper rifle and got down on the ground. Looking between the tank's treads I could see him directly across from me, laying on the cobblestone. I flipped the scope open, lined up my shot, and sent a bullet straight at his head.

It didn't kill him, but it really, really hurt him. It actually caused him to bleed some. More like a deep scratch than what you'd expect from a sniper rifle. I fired a couple more rounds, causing his head to start bleeding pretty badly. After I got a fifth round in him, the sonic grenade stopped working. I could tell, because he was able to lift his head up and look at me. That's when I made the shot of my life. I sent a bullet directly at his left eye, obliterating it.

Dantalion screamed and writhed in pain, covering up the hole I'd just made in his head. I can only imagine how scary it would be to lose an eye. I had no idea if Dantalion had the ability to completely heal, so I didn't know if it was permanent. I could hear him cussing and crying and panicking, and I almost started to feel sorry for him. Almost. That's when Madison grabbed me. She picked me up and flew me high into the air.

"Taylor, you're going to make things worse! He's going to kill Angela for sure now!" said Madison, tears streaming down her face.

"Baby, you have to trust me. I've got everything worked out. Just believe in me," I said.

"I can't take that chance, Taylor. You're not only risking your life and my life, but Angela's life as well. I love you, more than anyone I've ever known. Obviously, more than I should. But she's my sister. I can't let her die. I'm so sorry, Taylor."

With that, Madison dropped me.

48

I panicked as I fell. I'd never fallen from that high up, and I didn't know if the body armor would help. I figured I was dead. Without thinking, I screamed out Madison's name in horror, flailed my arms around, and landed with a bone crunching thud.

I really don't know what hurt worse, that Madison wouldn't believe in me when I needed her to most, or the pain in my broken back. I just laid there, completely still. I could breath, but it was very difficult. I could move my eyes and my mouth, but I couldn't feel my arms and legs. They wouldn't move. I started crying. I couldn't stop crying. I was useless now. Dantalion could get his revenge on me, because I was completely helpless. And Madison wouldn't stop him, because she didn't know that in just minutes, Angela might be safe.

I coughed up blood, enough to coat the inside of my helmet, blocking out most of the light. It made it almost impossible to see. I just laid there. What else could I do? After a few minutes I stopped crying. I'd let out my emotions. By some small grace I couldn't feel anything below the neck, so I wasn't in that much pain. I was just afraid, more than anything else.

I watched as Dantalion walked up to me. I could see the evil bastard's eye socket. Yeah, that's right a-hole, I did that! Believe it or not, even though I'd kicked his ass, he was smiling. Not because he'd beaten me, but because Madison had betrayed me. Dantalion was a sick monster that got off on other people's misery.

I could also see Madison standing behind him, crying. I could tell how horrible she felt for destroying me like that, how much pity she had for me right now, as I lay motionless on the ground. 'Yeah, well, you kinda did this to me, baby,' I thought to myself.

All I could do was stare at her. That beautiful face of hers. Her glow. Those flowing waves of hair. I cried again, this time for her. I pitied her, because I didn't know how she'd be able to live with herself after this. How she could go on. I know if I'd done the same thing to her, I couldn't forgive myself. It's crazy the things we feel when we're dying.

Dantalion picked me up off the ground and held me by the neck, still smiling. That's when I heard a faint crackle in my com. I could just barely make out the words 'Angela' and 'safe'. I started smiling right back at Dantalion, which infuriated him.

"Why are you smiling?" asked Dantalion, in his deep, demonic voice.

I spoke, but he couldn't hear me. The speaker system in the helmet was damaged during the fall. I also couldn't speak very loudly because of the internal damage I'd suffered. And he was squeezing my throat as he held my limp body up in the air.

Dantalion used two of his tendrils to remove my helmet then dropped my body down on the ground. He leaned down near my head, and thankfully Madison did the same. My voice was faint. I almost couldn't hear it either. It made them move in even closer, within inches of my face. I said the two words that I'd been hoping to say for a long time. That I'd sacrificed myself to make happen. Two words.

"Angela's safe," drifted out of my mouth. What I could read on Dantalion's face was a mix of confusion and surprise. Madison looked skeptical. After a second of hesitation, Dantalion stood up straight and spoke.

"Computer, current location of Angela Wheatfield."

I could tell it was taking a second for his computer to search for her. I couldn't hear the computer's response, but I could tell it couldn't find her.

"NO!" yelled Dantalion at the top of his lungs.

I could see that Madison now realized Angela was safe, that I hadn't lied. That she could count on me. She started crying tears of sadness for me, tears of joy for her sister, and tears of anger for what Dantalion had done.

Madison reached over, grabbed Dantalion and flew him high into the air. She threw him at the ground as hard as she could, sending him crashing down to Earth. He hit with such force that it made my lifeless body bounce in the air, and left a large crater underneath him.

She used her angel light vision to burn out his other eye, flew down in a rage and stomped on his stomach. A burst of blood launched out of his mouth. She grabbed his arms and tore them free from his torso, more blood flowing from the sockets where they were once attached. She used his arms to beat him mercilessly, until all that was left of him was a bloody stump, crushed, mangled and smashed into nothingness.

That's when I died.

49

This is where you first came in; the part where I died.

Surprised that I could write my own story after I died? Well, so was I. Life is funny like that. You can't really plan for this sort of thing happening. Can't really expect everything to work out the way you imagine it will.

I have to say, I'm sorry that I'm drawing this part out. I bet you're wondering if I somehow reappeared as a ghost that only Madison could communicate with, Obi-Wan Kenobi style, and she wrote all of this down for me. Maybe Madison just wrote this story based on everything she could piece together from what she knew of me, and what Mike and Calandre had told her. But neither of those are the truth.

Madison.

She held my lifeless body.

Cried over me.

Tried desperately to use her healing powers on me.

She knew it wouldn't work.

Knew that she couldn't raise the dead.

But it turned out that something was different. This time my body did glow. The light that she had given me when we first made love had stayed inside me. Her essence was a part of me, and it gave me a chance. One small chance to live.

I could feel my mind wake up; fuzzy at first, but the pain was so intense that I couldn't ignore it. It consumed me. I could feel my bones one at a time snapping back into place, creating an eerie popping noise that was like walking through a field of dead crickets. As soon as I could breathe again I screamed in agony. It sounded like I was gargling, because I basically was. My lungs and throat had blood in them, and I violently coughed it out.

Madison continued holding me. Holding me as the most horrible feeling I'd ever felt made me pass out. Seconds later the pain shocked me back to consciousness. It was so horrible that I wished I'd stayed dead. I hope you never have to go through something that painful. I still sometimes have nightmares about it. I've even had a few flashbacks from it.

My body kept healing. I could finally feel my hands and legs again, move them around slightly. I also felt the warmth return to my body. I hadn't been dead long, but the cool air of the night had chilled me. That and the lack of blood pumping to my feet and hands. My skin was now glowing white, as brightly as Madison's. I could move again. I could see and hear and touch the world. I actually started feeling better. It was weird, but I could actually feel my internal organs moving around, repairing themselves. After a few more minutes of pain, I was healed.

I looked up at Madison, who was smiling down at me. I didn't quite know how to react. I loved her, I still love her, but it felt like she'd betrayed me. Like she didn't trust me. It hurt like hell. I wanted to be happy, I really did. We'd won, we'd survived, together. Angela was safe. As far as I knew, both Calandre and Mike were safe. Dantalion was dead. Shouldn't everything be good and happy and right with the world?

Only life's not that simple. It's never that simple. The world is shades of gray, not black and white. People aren't completely good or completely evil, they're somewhere in between. Things would probably be much easier if they weren't so complicated. Weren't so gray. But that's real life for you.

I cried. Not because I was in physical pain anymore, but because I didn't really know how to feel right then. Thankfully, Madison touched my cheek. Wiped the tears from my eyes with a bright, glowing hand. Kissed me on my forehead. Held me. That made me cry even harder. It all came out. I didn't even try to hold it back. I just sobbed as she held me, and I could feel her sobbing too. We must have stayed like that for minutes, just crying.

I cried until I really couldn't cry anymore. Eventually, I rolled more onto my side and sat up. It actually felt good to be able to sit up. I mean, moments before that I was dead, and a few moments before that paralyzed. It's amazing how something as simple as sitting up can be so important to you when you can't do it.

I wiped my face with the backs of my hands, and rubbed the salt out of my eyes. I looked at Madison, and she had such a look of loss on her face that it tore me apart.

"I'm sorry, Taylor. I'm so, so sorry," said Madison.

"I know you are," was all I could muster, trying to sound as sincere as possible.

"I should have trusted you," she replied.

All I could say in response was "yes."

We sat there in silence for a few minutes. Neither of us knew what to say. Eventually, she broke the silence again.

"Thank you, Taylor, for saving me. For saving Angela."

"You're welcome."

"How did you do it? How did you get her to safety?"

"I had help."

"Really? From who?" she asked.

"Mike and Calandre," I said.

"Mike! I should have known! But who is Calandre?"

"Oh, heh, that's our butler."

"Wait, our butler helped save Angela?"

"And she's kind of dating Mike now, or something."

"Seriously?" Madison couldn't help but laugh at the thought.

"Seriously. They make a good couple."

"So where are they now?" asked Madison.

"I imagine they are waiting outside the front entrance, in a Jeep we borrowed. Oh, crap, the tank was on loan, too. I don't know how we'll pay for it," I said.

"I'm sure we'll figure something out. Can you walk?"

"Yeah, I think so."

I stood up. It took a moment for me to stand up straight. My body didn't feel quite right yet. Everything was back in place now, but I still hadn't fully recovered in my mind from it. I turned and started walking towards the two towers that stood guard at the entrance. Madison stopped me.

"Wait, I have a better idea," she said.

With that she wrapped her arms around me from behind, stretched out her wings then flew me up into the air.

I panicked.

"Down!" I screamed, fighting against her.

She swooped back down to the ground, letting me stumble out of her arms.

"I... just... please don't do that. I can't handle that feeling right now," I said.

"Oh," was all she said. Fresh tears streamed down her face.

I turned and started walking toward the towers again. Madison caught up with me and stayed at my side as we walked. As we passed the two massive towers, I got a little lightheaded and stopped. I took a few deep breaths then continued walking. Eventually, Madison again broke the silence.

"Taylor?"

"Yeah?" I said, quietly.

"Can I hold your hand?"

I had to think about it for a minute.

"Yeah, you can hold my hand."

I put my hand out for her, and she held onto it. We walked that way down the road.

50

At the pace we were going it took us several minutes to meet up with the truck. I could hear its engine running before we could see it. Once we made it over a small hill, I could sort of make it out in the moonlight. Mike turned on the headlights and it disoriented me for a second. As soon as he saw both of us, alive and well and walking, he started honking the truck's horn in happiness.

Calandre, Mike and Angela all jumped out of the truck and ran up to us. Angela grabbed Madison and held onto her tightly, crying tears of joy and relief. Mike and Calandre both wrapped their arms around me. I was surprised that they were both crying too. I found myself crying. I guess we're just a bunch of wimps. The thought made me laugh.

Calandre was the first to ask, "Taylor, are you okay? You're covered in blood!"

"Yeah, I'm okay," I replied.

"Then whose blood is that?" asked Mike.

"Mine."

"How?"

"Oh, I died. Then Madison brought me back to life."

"Dantalion killed you?" asked Calandre.

"I..." I turned away from her. I couldn't meet her eyes. "Let's just go home, okay?"

"Oh. Sure," said Calandre.

I felt bad for her. She hadn't done anything wrong. She had no idea it was Madison who actually killed me. I hadn't even thought about it that way until right then. It kind of made things a little worse inside.

Angela came over and kissed me. Right on the lips. Apparently Mike and Calandre had told her what I'd done, and

I was her hero for distracting Dantalion long enough so that she could be rescued. It was a little embarrassing being kissed by Madison's sister right in front of Madison. Because of the circumstances though, Madison didn't say anything.

When Angela finally pulled away from me, I could tell that she was blushing. It was sweet, and innocent, and kind. I looked over at Madison. She just kind of smiled a sad smile at me. I got in the back seat, Madison in the middle, Angela on the other side. Calandre drove and Mike rode shotgun.

The drive back we spent listening to Angela talk about how Dantalion had treated her. Apparently he didn't seem to care much at all about whether she was there. Didn't really talk to her. Just left her tied up and gave her food occasionally; mostly sandwiches.

Madison told us about how Dantalion had sent her out on missions. He apparently hadn't just wanted her to be his girlfriend, he needed someone with her particular gifts to break into a few prisons for him. There were a couple of fugitives that escaped and were free because of her. Mike thought it would be a good idea to call it in, so he used a satellite phone and called White Ops HQ.

Mike also filled in Director Scott on the good news, that we'd saved Angela and Madison, and that everyone was coming back alive except for Dantalion. Nothing was mentioned of my death. I think that Mike picked up on the fact that something was wrong and decided not to mention it. I silently thanked him.

They tried getting me to talk about what it was like fighting Dantalion. Standing up to him. Madison mentioned that I'd shot his eye out. But I just didn't feel like celebrating. I felt like sleeping, for a very long time.

Eventually, we made it back to the base. I finally thought to tell Mike that the tank was trashed. He didn't seem to be bothered too much by it.

"I'm sure if the vehicles were important and necessary, they wouldn't have left them in an abandoned military complex for so long," said Mike.

"Yeah, I guess that's a good point. Still, I feel bad," I responded.

"Taylor, I don't think you realize, you saved one of America's most important assets. You seriously have no idea just how important Madison is to the United States Government. To most governments, actually. I think they'd have been happy to pay for a thousand tanks to get her back. She's a rare girl, with even rarer talents. Never forget that."

"Worrying about breaking someone else's stuff is just my upbringing. Can't really help it. But based on everything you just said, I guess I'll consider it something I shouldn't worry about."

As we made our way inside, Calandre had both Madison and Angela follow her to where they would be spending the night. I stayed behind with Mike for a moment.

"So what really happened, Taylor?" asked Mike.

I had a hard time trying to figure out what to say, if I should sugarcoat it, or just not tell him at all. Play it off like it was no big deal. But after everything we'd been through, everything that Mike had done for me, I felt I owed him the truth.

"Madison killed me, Mike," I said, looking him in the eyes, trying to get a read on what he was thinking.

Mike just slowly nodded his head in understanding of what she'd done. He could understand why she had done it, because he knew what was at stake. He was sure she hadn't really meant to kill me, just wound me to the point where I was no longer a threat.

"So how are you still alive?" asked Mike.

"Well, without going into too many specifics, Madison at one point shared some of her energy with me. I actually glowed when she wasn't touching me anymore," I replied.

"Oh. OH!" said Mike.

"Yeah," I responded.

"Right. So, uh, anyway, that made it possible for her to heal you?"

"You mean bring me back from the dead? Yeah. I guess technically that makes me a zombie. It's funny, but I'm not really craving brains right now. I was thinking grilled cheese sandwiches and soup might be good."

Mike looked at me blankly for a second then laughed. It was good to hear him laugh.

"I think I could do that for you, Taylor. A dinner fit for a hero. Because that's what you are, Taylor: a hero. You sacrificed yourself for the mission. You got the job done," said Mike.

"I sacrificed myself for her," I said, weakly.

"If you're looking to beat her up emotionally for what she did, you're doing a good job of it so far. I know Madison pretty well, and I can tell just how horrible she feels about what she did to you. I think it'll take her even longer to forgive herself than it'll take you. She's got a really good heart. She made an impossible decision and hoped for the best. Just make sure that you think about how she's feeling, how she's handling everything before you beat her up any more. For all her strength, she has a fragile heart. Don't do to her what you think she's done to you."

I let his words sink in. Rolled them around in my mind. I loved her. I love her. Even after what happened, I still loved her. Still wanted to be with her. And I knew that if I tortured her, I would end up losing her. Then what would have been the point of everything I'd done? Dantalion would win. Sure, he might not be around to enjoy his victory, but he would win.

Maybe with a little time I could find a way to truly forgive her for what she'd done. But tonight wasn't that night. Tonight was a night for rest, maybe a little celebration, and some grilled cheese sandwiches with soup.

51

Growing up, sometimes my Mom would be away and my Dad would have to cook for us. He didn't know how to make many things, but one thing he made really well was grilled cheese sandwiches. White bread with slices of American cheese. The kind that come in plastic sleeves. He'd butter the bread and the pan, flip them just once through the process. And he made tomato soup with milk, or sometimes Lipton's noodle soup, which I also loved.

What Mike made up was the gourmet version of that. He used baguette bread, aged Swiss cheese, garlic butter, and he made up a noodle soup from scratch that was off the hook. In some ways it was the best thing I'd ever eaten. You know how I mentioned that after a hard day's work food tastes better? It tastes even better than that after you've saved the world.

I finally allowed myself to celebrate a little. I smiled and looked up at Madison, who'd been sitting across from me at the kitchen table during dinner. She looked up, met my eyes, saw me smiling and smiled back. Then she turned her head quickly, and started tearing up. Instinctively, I reached a hand out and held hers across the table. This made her really start to cry, and she had to excuse herself for a few minutes. Angela looked over at me, confused. She gave me a smile, but I could see she was worried about her sister. She got up and walked to the bathroom to check on Madison.

I was finally alone with Mike and Calandre. Mike was a nice guy, and spared me having to tell Calandre what had happened. He told her everything that had gone on during the fight, including Madison killing me. She couldn't contain her emotions either. She felt so bad for me. So bad for Madison. It took a few minutes for her to stop the tears flowing. It was nice to know that someone else cared about us.

Calandre did make a point of telling me that she could tell Madison truly loved me, that she would do anything for me. I just kept quiet, didn't argue the point. She was probably right. Madison would do anything for me. If I were in trouble, she'd do her best to save my life. Believe me, I know that in the battle it was a matter of trying to protect Angela, that she made the right choice, did the right thing. But sometimes the right thing is the hardest thing. The thing that guts you, tears you apart. Unmakes you. That's how I felt: not whole.

After a few minutes of sitting in silence, Madison and Angela finally came back to the table. We finished our delicious meal, but I could tell everyone was having a hard time processing what they had found out. It seemed obvious to me from the look on Angela's face that Madison had just told her what had happened.

What I saw now instead of thanks on Angela's face was a mix of shock, pity, sadness, and horror. I turned to catch her eye and smile and let her know it was okay, but she broke eye contact as soon as I made it. It was her turn to cry now, and she excused herself for a few minutes. She eventually came back.

I couldn't stand the tension anymore; the pain and the heartache. I think everyone in the room was heartbroken over it. So I did something that I think was probably the bravest thing I'd ever done. Even braver than facing Dantalion alone. I told a knock-knock joke.

I turned to Angela.

"Knock-knock," I said.

It took her a few seconds to realize what I was doing.

"Um, who's there?" she said weakly.

"Europe."

"Europe who?"

"No, YOU'RE a poo!" I said.

Mike, Calandre, Madison and Angela sat in stunned silence for a second. I think it was Calandre who laughed first, but once she did we all giggled. We almost couldn't stop laughing. We laughed until tears filled our eyes.

After we calmed down, I reached across the table again and held Madison's hand. This time it wasn't out of concern. It was to show her that I still loved her, still cared, and I wanted to work on things. Get past it. Deal with what needed to be dealt with. That I wanted to be with her. I mouthed the words "it's okay" to her silently. A few more tears trickled down her beautiful cheeks and she nodded to me.

After taking showers, we went back to our rooms for the evening. Madison came into my room. I just kind of laid there, not knowing what to say or do. She leaned over, kissed me on the forehead. I made some room for her. She twisted her body away from me but still pressed up against mine, took my arm and pulled it over her, resting my hand against her chest, her fingers laced with mine. I held her like that all night.

52

Whem Madison and I woke up the next morning, we kissed. I finally let myself feel again, and not the feelings of pain and betrayal. I let myself feel love for her. I never stopped loving her, but I numbed myself to it to protect my heart. It's amazing how much we hold back from our loved ones. Seldom telling them or showing them just how much they mean to us. Sometimes we don't even realize how much they mean to us until they're gone.

If there was something my death experience taught me, it's that you tell the people you love that you love them. Every chance you get. Every day, at least once. Because you never, ever know when it might be the last time you talk to them. The last moment you get to tell them how much they mean to you. How happy and thankful you are to have them in your life. That you rely on them, care about them, and would do anything for them.

In the morning, after a long and delicious breakfast, we left the base. The drive to the airport didn't seem all that long. Mike and Calandre were just dropping us off, because their plan was to ride the train back to France. Mike was going to take some needed vacation time and get to know Calandre better.

Our goodbyes were filled with smiles and tears. I got a very warm hug from Calandre, and a very manly hug from Mike. I could tell I'd earned both his friendship and respect. To him I was a man now. Someone he trusted and cared about. My guess is that Mike didn't have too many people like that in his life. But he had two more, now that Calandre came into the picture. As he hugged me, he whispered something in my ear that kind of shocked me.

Calandre also kissed me on both cheeks. I guess it's a French thing. Anyway, it was sweet of her. I kind of awkwardly did the same thing back. She was so awesome for helping out, and I told her as much. Both Madison and Angela gave them even bigger hugs as thanks for rescuing them. Angela gave Mike a little kiss, although this one was on his cheek. He didn't blush, but he did grin like an idiot. Calandre backhanded his chest, more to be playful than anything. I can't say I blame him. Angela was every bit as beautiful as Madison, just in a different way.

"Take care of yourselves," I said to Mike and Calandre.

"We will," replied Calandre.

"And again, thank you."

"You're welcome," said Mike.

With that, we walked to the security station, headed for our terminal then up, into the air.

It wasn't until I got on the plane that I fully realized we would be flying again. Flights had never bothered me up until this one. I asked for an aisle seat, and when we started to taxi to the runway, I asked Angela, who had the window seat, if she could close her window. She was very sweet about it.

I held onto Madison's hand tightly as the plane started to shake a little. It jumped forward, which startled me, but holding onto Madison's hand helped. Not a lot, but some. I kept my eyes shut as we picked up speed, and started panicking a little as we lifted up into the air. But once we were airborne, and above the clouds, I was okay again. I knew that nothing would happen to the plane, and that I was safe. But it still scared me just the same.

It was a fairly long flight back home, mostly because the in-flight movies sucked, and I hadn't brought anything to read. I really didn't have much to say to Madison right then. It would take me some time to be fully comfortable around her again. I just needed time to heal and forgive. Not forget. I couldn't forget, even if I wanted to. It was a part of me now, those memories, and they still occasionally haunt me.

I tried reading Sky Mall, but even looking at pages and pages of things I really wanted but didn't need failed to help. So I rented a headset and listened to some music. I thankfully fell asleep.

When I woke up several hours later, we were given lunch. It was bland, and I can't really remember what it was. I think it was a turkey sandwich, but for all I know it was two pieces of cardboard with sawdust and mayo in between. I washed it down with a Sprite and tried to fall back asleep. I never really did fall back asleep though, as much as I wanted to. But I kept my eyes closed anyway and pretended to so I didn't have to talk.

The landing was just as hard as the takeoff, and I spent the time clenching my teeth, squeezing Madison's hand and freaking out on the inside. Or at least I did my best to keep it on the inside and not freak out the other passengers.

Once we gathered our things and left the plane, I held Madison's hand again. I even pulled it up to my mouth and gave it a little kiss. We only had a few small carry-ons, so we were able to skip baggage and head straight for the taxis. A nice man with a thick Russian accent helped us into his cab and we sped away.

It didn't take very long to get home. I had the cabbie stop in front of Madison's house and I gave him an extra-large tip. He seemed pleased and he sped off down the street, narrowly missing a parked car.

Madison had Angela go inside the house while she stayed outside with me. The day was sunny, but a bit chilly. The wind had started to pick up, which blew Madison's angelic hair around. Even after all we'd been through, I still thought she was beautiful. Still saw her as an angel.

Madison dropped her bags and I dropped mine. She reached out and held both of my hands, leaned into me and kissed me. Pulling back, she stared directly into my eyes.

"Taylor, I need you to know that I love you," she said.

"I know, baby, I know."

"No, you don't. You're smart, and rational, and realize that what I did was what I thought was best for Angela. That it was the right thing to do. And that was the whole point of what you did, to rescue us. You willingly sacrificed yourself for her. For me. Because of me. Because you love me that much. And rationally, you know that I love you more than anyone. That I would do anything for you. But your heart isn't sure. Your heart right now doesn't know how much I love you. It feels broken and lonely and frightened. And that's because of me; that's my fault. Well eff all of that, because I'm going to try to spend the rest of my life proving your heart wrong."

I let out a half-hearted chuckle. I did appreciate that she was trying.

"Madison, it's just going to take me some time to figure things out. I love you, I really do, but the only thing that will make things better is time. I don't need time away from you, I just need some time to work through things. I need you to help me with that," I said.

"Whatever you need. Just please, don't shut me out."

"I won't. I really won't."

We stood in silence for a moment.

"So I have to ask," started Madison. "What was it that Mike whispered to you?"

I just smiled.

"C'mon, you have to tell me!" she said.

"He told me his last name," I replied.

"No!"

"Yup."

"Well, what is it?" she asked.

"I don't think I should say. It's not my secret to share," I said.

"Please, I promise I'll do ANYTHING you want! Just tell me!"

"Anything I want? Anything at all?"

"Yes, ANYTHING!"

"As much as I want to, I can't. I'm really sorry baby."

"Not fair, not fair at all," said Madison, playfully smacking my chest. "But I guess it's good to know that if I told you a secret you'd keep it for me."

"I'd take it to my grave."

The thought of that actually kind of bothered me. It was a bit of a miracle I wasn't in one right now. But if I was going to give Madison a chance, I'd have to figure out a way to forgive her. Otherwise it would never work.

"Oh, and Taylor?" said Madison.

"Yeah, Madison?" I replied.

"Thank you. For everything. For saving us. For coming to my rescue. For being the amazing, perfect boyfriend you are. I really don't deserve you."

"I know," I said, smirking.

Madison laughed, wrapped her arms around me and held me tight, as I held her back.

In that moment, I wondered to myself just how much more danger life had in store for us. It wasn't long before we found out.

Thank you to everyone that helped make this book possible. Thank you to those people that read and enjoy it as much as I enjoyed writing it. And thank you to the big guy in the sky that gave me life. I am forever in each of your debts.

If you'd like to know more about me and my other books, check out www.tmbrenner.com. You can also find me on Twitter as @TimothyMBrenner, on Facebook as Author T. M. Brenner, and on GoodReads as T. M. Brenner.

This book, before some extensive editing, was originally published under two titles: *Madison* and *White Ops*.

An excerpt from the sequel - Clandestined: Dark Times

Dying is not an easy thing, and it hurt that she didn't trust me to have a plan. Even through all of that, I loved Madison. I would, and will do anything for her.

We stare into each other's eyes for a moment, when I realize that something is wrong. I can tell by her expression that she isn't in the moment, that she's distracted, maybe even worried by something.

"Taylor, you're glowing," said Madison.

"That's because I love you," I replied.

"No, seriously, you're glowing, and I'm not causing it."

I pulled back from Madison's warm embrace and looked down at my hands. The same white light that sometimes filled Madison's body was now coming from me. I took a step back, not sure what to make of it. Did I have angel powers like Madison now? Did some of her magic or whatever move into me? Was I going to become... a superhero?